Reverend Mother

Eron Henry

CreateSpace
Made in the USA
Charleston, SC

ISBN   978-0615445397

To All those who can, even if they haven't

Chapter one

This is the story of a woman who decides to have a child, though she has been told she should not *want* to have a child. We meet her first as a feisty, bumptious and scraggy twelve year old.

Nora's marble game is as good as the boys'. With her thumb expertly snuggled inside her second finger and the yellow-orange marble resting lightly yet firmly in between, she shoots. Two other marbles scatter on impact from inside the circle, drawn some five feet away in the dark brown patch of dirt.

"Lucky shot!" a few boys snicker as she takes another aim, this time missing the target. Her frown wrinkles into scorn.

"None o you can make the shot I make."

Her challenge goes unanswered as the heavy June showers descend. Everyone scatters in a race to beat the heaviest onslaught. This is the most enjoyable part of it for Nora, playing cat and mouse with the rain, allowing it to catch her, yet delighting in reaching her house before it grabs her in its tight blanket.

he shudders as she goes through the backdoor into the room she shares with her three brothers and grabs a tattered towel to dry her arms, head, face, and legs, choosing to keep on the damp clothes. The others chatter over supper, their excited giggles competing with the din of rain on the zinc metal roof.

The Campbells are frightened by the rain, and overcome the fear with conjured excitement. Occasionally someone casts a wary glance out the back window at the stream that threatens to invade the house during each heavy downpour. Nora's first recollection of the stream's violence was of her hands slung around her mother's neck from a piggy back ride while Junior, the youngest, cuddled in mama's arms as they negotiated the threatening watercourse. Papa was home from his seasonal job on a farm in the United States. He helped to guide the bigger boys through the water as they carried

1

bundles of clothing on their heads through the rising torrent. It is a ritual repeated twice since then. She fears the next heavy downpour. She dreads the rainy months.

It isn't that the family is dirt poor. Roy Campbell refuses to leave the family property, the half-acre perched precariously close to Irish Spring, a tributary for Rio Chico, and the main water source for the community of Danvers. Twelve year old Nora is perplexed as to why they live so close to the river when so many others don't.

Roy Campbell's vision for his four children differs much from others in the village. The house remains small because he intends on sending his children through college. No one in Danvers has ever attended college, and Roy is determined that his children would be the first. He is happy that the Jamaican government of the 1970s has instituted free college tuition.

Most folk in Danvers do not even know what inside of a high school looks like. James Redding's boy went to an agricultural school in Hanover but later left for England. And Joyce Simpson's girl was in high school up to two years ago, but at sixteen and in tenth grade, dropped out because she gave birth to a boy for Simon Gleason's son.

Nora knows the priority papa places on education. He preaches unremittingly that the day will come when no decent job can be had with anything less than a college diploma or degree. Her excitement builds as she prepares to start high school in September. Results for the High School Common Entrance Examinations are out and the community is in awe that she, a girl, passed. She is following in the footsteps of her two older brothers who will be going into the ninth and eleventh grades. Joyce Simpson's daughter was the first girl from the community to pass the highly competitive exam, and many thought it was luck, or because Joyce works in the school's canteen. Never mind that the exam papers are marked in far away Kingston, the capital city for Jamaica.

Danvers lies in the middle of a valley, some two miles down from the climb from up Orange Hill. It is cut off from the rest of civilization, except for the narrow dirt and rocky road that winds its way down. Getting to school is hard work. Nora and the two older boys get up before dawn to fetch water from the stream and to tether the goats. Tying the goats requires special skill, as the goats do get away and stray, sometimes into the plot of ground planted by George Taylor, or into the river, where they go missing. The deepest part of the stream, the blue hole, is reputed to be inhabited by a spirit that requires blood sacrifice ever so often. The villagers swear the water-spirit pulls the goats in its direction, hypnotizing them into a watery death. Everyone knows never to swim or wade near the blue hole.

Of all she has to do, Nora hates feeding the rabbits the most. The Campbells have no Spanish needle on their plot of ground, and getting the wild parsley requires walking up stream for a half a mile or more. The discomfort of the early morning dew on the wild grass leaves her skin itchy for the first half of the day, and the fog throws a thick blanket in her path.

By 6:30 all set out for school. Nora and Junior need to arrive by 9:00 a.m., the older boys, Jason and Paul, at Ipswich High by 8:30. The walk to Beckwith Primary School is only four miles, though Junior, a cranky eight year old, complains much about it when he is in no mood for school. Nora and Junior are usually there by 8:00. As Nora is so early, she helps to open the classrooms and even has the pleasure of helping the principal open up her office. This allows her to see Mrs. Logan up close more than most students have, and often wonders what it would be like to take a pair of scissors and clip off a rather dark and large mole under Mrs. Logans arm, which is exposed whenever she reaches up to unloose the latch at the top of the doorframe.

Jason and Paul, meanwhile, hitch a ride on whatever comes along first, but they try to catch the Northern Star bus that reaches Beckwith Square at 7:45. By the time it arrives at the gate of Ipswich High School, it is just in time for them to make a dash to catch roll call.

Not so for Nora. She has time, as both Jason and Paul had a few years earlier, to become an able assistant to her principal and class teachers. She, like her brothers did, receives much attention from teachers who reward her for her helpfulness and cooperation.

She hardly minds being teased by other students. The proverbial teachers' pet, she puts the teasing down to jealousy and bad mindedness. Besides, the teachers make her feel important and special. Which other student could knock on the principal's door and ask for a pencil when hers was done? How many other students are asked to help Mrs. Logan carry her bag and books over to the principal's cottage? And how many students are asked by the class teacher to sit at the desk and watch the rest of the class whenever the teacher takes a bathroom break?

There is much rejoicing now that the Common Entrance Exam results are out. Nora is the first student from Beckwith Primary School in three years to pass the exams, the first since her brother Paul. The celebration goes way beyond the small confines of Danvers and into the much larger Beckwith community. Walking the two miles from Beckwith down to Orange Hill each day is an expression of pride for Nora. Those who never noticed her before try to pick her out from the pack of two dozen school children that descend the long slope to Orange Hill, then she becomes the true leader of the smaller pack that descends the valley into Danvers.

Nora decides to join the others for supper. Daisy Campbell gives her daughter a stern look as she sits on one of the wooden stools in the corner of the small space that serves as both living and dining room. Nora knows she is late and agrees that it is only the excitement of the torrential rains that delays the obligatory tongue-lashing. There is simply too much noise coming from the rain pounding the zinc roof. The boys, Jason and Paul, a little manlier now, look at her with the same quizzed look their father would.

Roy Campbell rarely speaks, and the boys are adopting his characteristics and mannerisms. They, like their father, favor body language. Jason, almost seventeen years old, takes on the mantle of surrogate head whenever papa goes off to work on a farm in western New York, along Lake Erie, to harvest apples. Nora hates this. The idea of her brother trying to mete out discipline galls her.

4

She wants desperately to go to a high school other than where Jason and Paul go. She hears much of Windwood High School, the boarding school for girls; of the school's cute uniform of blue denim and straw hat and took an immediate liking to it, the first time she saw it. Most of the girls there go on to university and a lot are now doctors, lawyers, nurses and some are school principals. Her one dream is to be a principal like Mrs. Logan, only at a bigger school.

Roy and Daisy Campbell want to keep the children together, so off to Ipswich High School she goes in September. She hates the idea of traveling with her brothers on one of the rickety buses, or even worse, on the back of a truck that happens along, but comforts herself with the thought that Jason has only one more year of high school to go. She can bear having Paul around for a little bit longer.

The relationship with Jason deteriorated the day she defied his order to remove the pimento seeds that were placed outside to dry in the sun. Nora, instead, did what she has always loved, catching fish in the stream. The mid-afternoon precipitation drenched everything, ruining the entire pimento harvest that the family had been carefully preserving.

Daisy Campbell flew into a rage, first at the two older boys, then, after Jason desperately explained Nora's fault, redirected her fury at her scrawny daughter. It is still the worst beating that Nora has ever received. Mama fetched the whip she keeps handy, made of a branch from the pimento tree. The mauling created wheals on her back that stung for more than a week.

She now regards Jason with a mixture of fear and hatred, furious at the injustice she feels was dealt out to her at his bidding. The beating she received has emboldened her eldest brother, and he loses no opportunity to order her to do things she regards as work that should properly be done by one of the boys.

Nora is more comfortable around her father than with any other member in the family, and uses the opportunities when he is home to be with him as much as possible. Roy Campbell has never beaten his daughter. Stern yet quiet, he has never had to lift a hand, or raise his voice. A simple look or a piercing stare is sufficient to get her in line.

She enjoys watching him as he engages in his weekend routine, especially when he shaves, usually on a Saturday afternoon. Taking out his razor, he first pours coconut oil on an old broken black slate and slowly, carefully, massages the razor in the oil, gently caressing the surface of the slate while whistling one of the old spirituals they sometimes sing in church. He then takes out his old leather belt, which he no longer wears, instructs Nora to hold one end while he holds the other, and rubs the razor in an up and down motion, smiling and whistling.

He crafts the razor across his chin and face, expertly flicking hair and shaving cream as his whistle turns into a hum, the rhythmic movements of the razor moving in tandem with the rhythmic notes from his throat.

Nora wishes he were home.

Her supper is covered up in the middle of the table on a small plastic plate. Nudging herself, she reaches over and starts having her dumpling and yams with salted codfish. She peers through the window and sees the water rising, but decides that it is not yet a threat. The chatter of the others dims into the distance as her mind wanders into high school.

Chapter two

It is not that she is the brightest or cutest girl in school, but Nora is headgirl nevertheless. Now seventeen and in her final year at high school, she is ready to take on the world.

Nora Campbell feels vindicated. She was at the forefront among the students who, in tenth and eleventh grade, demanded that student leaders – headboy, headgirl, and prefects – be directly elected by students, not chosen by faculty, as has been the practice in the sixty-two year old institution. Now she stands as the first headgirl to be elected by students, along with headboy Trevor Weir and the fifteen prefects.

All this occurred even as she became increasingly absorbed by the politics of the times. Most of the faculty in her school, which has the largest per capita membership in the left-leaning National Union of Teachers, strongly supported the students' actions. The principal and vice principal, isolated and pressured, yielded to the demands of the students who were quietly yet powerfully backed by faculty.

It is no accident that Nora was among the leading protestors. Way back in eighth grade she convinced her parents, Roy and Daisy Campbell, to allow her to board with history teacher Jean Kellier, going home only on weekends. The journey, she said, is much too far for her to travel alone as both Jason and Paul have moved on to teacher training colleges. Besides, the long distance and late hours on the road would not allow her to take extra lessons, or to participate in extracurricular activities.

There is another reason she has not verbalized. Junior is still very much on her mind. His loss eats at her, and she needs to get away.

It happened on what was to be a normal day of grocery shopping in Hyattsville, the main shopping area for people in Beckwith, Orange Hill, and Danvers. Daisy was ill, Nora was home for the weekend, and it fell on her to go to the market, with Junior as her companion and helper. He never made it home. The truck coming down the narrow street into Hyattsville Town Square swerved for Junior as it attempted to elude the motorcycle in its path. She had crossed the street, thinking he was close behind her, only to look with horror at the screeching sounds, with Junior buried under the right front wheel.

Jean Kellier gave strong support, and both Daisy and Roy felt helpless to help themselves and their children through the grief. Nora boarding with a stranger was not an attractive thought, but circumstances forced the idea. They felt abandoned by their children – Jason and Paul at college in Kingston; Junior died; and now Nora is boarding out.

A divorcee with no children, Jean Kellier is the most left leaning of the leftist teachers at Ipswich High School. A member of the Workers Congress Party, she walks through the small town of Ipswich and distributes *Congress Report*, the quarterly propaganda paper of the communist party. Kellier never invites Nora to read the newspaper, or to be involved in its distribution, but enough copies are left hanging around the small teacher's flat for Nora to take notice and read. Books on Fidel Castro, Lenin and Marx are neatly stacked on a small shelf. A huge poster of Castro hangs in the living room.

Other than the support given through the tragedy, Kellier is her favorite teacher. History, particularly Caribbean History, is her favorite subject. Kellier is faculty adviser for the debating team, of which Nora is a member. Nora is one of only two female members on the Schools Challenge Quiz squad, which Kellier trains and manages.

Nora knows the names of all the major left leaning politicians and activists in Jamaica. Peter Barrett, Jamaica's Prime Minister, is a hero, but not a hero enough. His radicalism has not gone far enough. He is on his way there but is not reaching there fast enough. He needs to become like Maurice Bishop, the leftist Prime Minister for the Eastern Caribbean island of Grenada.

Nora remembers an incident that occurred while she was in the ninth grade. General Science teacher John Thompson struck male student "Peko" in the head with a chalkboard duster in a fit of rage. As Student Council class rep, she brought the matter to the attention of the Students Council Executive, only to be told that making an issue of the matter would create unnecessary trouble. In any case, the boy is a known deviant who tests the patience of teachers and students alike. Let the matter drop, they said. Fuming, Nora accused them of capitulating in fear of the principal, telling them in caustic language, "All o you dumb an fraid o her." Her fellow students missed the point. The teacher's action was not punishment or discipline but arbitrary violence designed to cause injury. She vowed that such an action by a teacher or other staff, if she ever becomes student leader, would never go unchallenged.

Nora now has her chance. The principal had caned a boy the previous week for scrawling graffiti on the wall of a corridor.

Headboy and headgirl are peerless. Most students hold them in awe. In the new dispensation of activism, they wield almost as much influence as teachers, except for principal Eileen Reid who, though she caved in to the students' demands during the previous school year, yielded only as much as was necessary in the circumstance. Stately and dignified, her personal authority is beyond question. Matronly, she carries a hard nose that sticks in front when she walks the corridors. Outwardly, she appears unperturbed by the new spirit of activism that has arisen in the school she has run for a dozen years. But she bristles inside, and has occasionally given vent to her feelings, mostly in private. It is all part of the madness taking over Jamaica, she reasons. No one knows his or her place anymore. Even those who should know better have caught the fad. She hisses under her breath whenever her senior teachers speak inanely about students' rights. Rights to what? They should be grateful they are getting a first rate education. How many have such privilege?

Ironically, Nora is one of her favorite students. She admires her strength in the loss of her brother. Principal Reid was chief cheerleader in getting two busloads of students to attend Junior's funeral, though he was not a student at her school. Even then, the little wisp of a girl distinguished herself. Few students have the courage to walk up to her and greet her as Nora did early in her first year at Ipswich. By the eighth grade, Nora suggested that the school form a Helping Hands Club to assist a boy in her class who lost all his books on a bus and whose parents could not replace them. The club has gone on to assist other students in need. Nora became its first secretary while Mrs. Reid named herself patron.

But Jean Kellier is spoiling Nora, Reid fumes. It is a mistake to have Nora living with her. The woman is turning the child into a communist even before she knows how to wash her briefs properly. The faculty too, is being swayed. Long loyal members of the National Teachers Council are abandoning this major teachers union for the socialist union, the NUT. NUT claims no political association, but Eileen Reid knows better.

Mrs. Reid is extremely bitter at the students' protest, the first in the school's history. She is embarrassed that heads in the Ministry of Education in Kingston came down to quell the disturbance. More galling than anything else, they instructed her to accept the demands of the students, and not to take action against the ringleaders, a decision that was backed by the school board. Left with no choice, Eileen Reid backed down.

She scorns Everald Wilson, her spineless vice principal. He is of no help, merely a wimp who stands up for nothing. She stood in the rearguard alone and, depressed, decides that saving the school from the radicals lies solely in her care. Knowing her time is running out as she nears retirement, she sees the need to rescue the venerable institution of Ipswich High from those who wish to destroy it. The children need to be saved from all these socialists and communists who are taking over.

Everything is going bad. Too many of the boys are using the lingo of the Rastafarians. They come to school wanting to dress like the Rastas and often adopt Rastafarian behavior. Three boys were suspended for marijuana smoking. Too many come with their hair uncombed. Many wristbands and tams bearing the Rastafarian colors of red, gold and green have been confiscated. She is not sure who is worse, the socialists or the Rastas.

Nora has mixed feelings toward Principal Reid. In many ways, Mrs. Reid is much like her mother: Stuck in her ways, hopelessly beyond change, but with a warm and gentle heart. She has seen that heart at work in the Helping Hands Club. Not many other students have seen that side of Mrs. Reid. But like her mother, Mrs. Reid needs to be resisted. She represents the old defenders of colonialism that desperately try to hold on. They believe it was a mistake for Jamaica to have sought independence from Britain. Britain, for them, represents the highest in class and standards. The old ways were better.

Nora identifies more with her father. Roy Campbell sees the changes in government policies as opening up opportunities for his children. Holding merely an elementary school education like most others his age, he realizes his own children will reach heights he never dreamed of achieving. His years of travel to the United States on Jamaica's Overseas Farm Workers Program opened his eyes to possibilities beyond what Danvers or Beckwith or Orange Hill has to offer. Daisy, on the other hand, believes the old ways are best as they teach children to know their place, passing on those principles that make a girl a good wife and mother and a man a good husband and father. It is enough for her to know that her children are properly trained to raise a good family.

Mrs Reid, Nora suspects, takes the same attitude as her mother's. Students are to be taught to be good citizens, and those who leave school should join the government service or the teaching profession. That was how she did it in her day. That was the only choice for advancement people had in her time. The civil service or the classroom is the best training ground for bright young men and women. That is where the British influence remains powerful and strong. That is where girls like Nora need to go. She needs to follow her brothers' footsteps.

Nora smiles when she remembers the rantings of Principal Reid. They both agree, but for different reasons. Nora has not given up her dream of being a teacher, but Mrs. Kellier has opened her mind to wider horizons. She now wants to become a teacher and help free Jamaicans from the imperialistic tendencies of the old colonial era. Peter Barrett has done much to challenge the old colonial ways. The Workers Congress Party promises to do more. She has firmed her mind to join the youth arm of the WCP. *Congress Report* details how young members of the party are involved in the exciting changes taking place on university and college campuses across the island.

Nora has her special agenda item with Principal Reid on this particular day. Headboy Trevor Weir reluctantly agrees to go along. She senses he has a crush on her, but is too shy and gentlemanly to make it known. He became headboy because of his brilliance, the deep voice he carries, and the fact that he is a decent quarter miler. He has lost a race on sports day just once in all his years at Ipswich. Girls like him, though she suspects he is scared of them. Despite his brilliance, Trevor lacks confidence in his abilities.

Nora believes Trevor to be too nice a guy to stand up to anyone, least of all Mrs. Reid. But she knows he will do whatever she asks, and his presence sends the message that the entire student body is giving her its full support. She knows this is not exactly correct as she only discussed the matter informally with some prefects. It is largely her own doing as she fears those who would encourage her to back down or who may throw cold water on the mission.

Mrs. Kellier had long told Nora that physically hitting a child constitutes an assault by the teacher. Nora was one of the debaters on the school team that addressed the subject of corporal punishment in schools, a common topic being discussed in Jamaica, and feels well armed and prepared after such a debate. She is now convinced that corporal punishment opens the door for further abuse by teachers. Moreover, she senses that Mrs. Reid is vulnerable

12

as the principal does not enjoy widespread support from faculty, a knowledge that comes from being close to a teacher like Mrs. Kellier.

The secretary ushers them into the principal's office. Going to Mrs. Reid's office is always an event. This is Nora's third trip. The first was when she boldly asserted she wanted to see the principal and made her suggestion for the Helping Hands Club. The second visit was last school year after the students' protest. Then, she and four other suspected ringleaders were hauled into the office. Mrs. Reid was shocked that the five students determinedly stood their ground and insisted on their demands that they choose their own student leaders rather than the faculty doing so. Shuffling of feet outside her window alerted her to several hundred students standing guard. Nora felt it was brilliant organizing.

The cramped office has certificates and diplomas from schools in England hanging on the walls. The biggest display is a degree from the University of London. Two photographs sit on her desk, which Nora assumes to be a husband and children. A few trophies won by the school stand on a small corner desk. Nora looks proudly at the newest among them – won last year in the regional debating competition for schools. She was the second speaker on that debating team and was voted best speaker. A small bookshelf stands to the side. She notes, with a smile, and not a little surprise, that George Beckford's "Persistent Poverty" is among them. She can't help being impressed.

Eileen Reid wonders what Jean Kellier has put Nora up to this time. She makes a mental note to revisit Kellier's file. She blames her for all the new fuss and trouble going on among the students. It is disingenuous of the woman to be using the students to further her own personal and political agenda. But Principal Reid cannot find a way to have her fired. Kellier has never acted directly outside school policy. She is a brilliant teacher who gets results. History has the third highest percentage pass among all subjects, not bad for a subject most students loathe.

"What can I do for you sir and madam?" The sarcasm annoys Nora. Trevor shuffles nervously.

"We have a request from the student body," Nora declares, trying to hide the fact she is not spot on with the truth.

"What? Did you conduct an opinion poll?"

"We are requesting the end of all forms of corporal punishment," Nora went on, ignoring the jibe.

Nora notices a flinch and a twitching of the upper lip.

"And the basis of your request is?"

"Corporal punishment is an act that does not achieve its desired results." She pauses. "Besides, it is a form of abuse." She immediately chastises herself. That other point came in too quickly. She is much too anxious to make her case.

Mrs. Reid latches onto her blunder. "Abuse! Abuse! Are you saying that all the many great men and women in history suffered abuse simply because they received a little bit of spanking?"

Nora tries to get the argument back on track.

"We want to suggest a better way to enforce discipline."

The twitching of the upper lip turns into a curl. "I'm listening."

"A number of the schools we checked out are now using a demerit system. It works like this–"

"I know all about the demerit system. Do not presume to lecture me."

Nora looks at Trevor for help. She sees that none is forthcoming. "Then why can't it be implemented here, instead of flogging?"

"You seem to be doing all the talking. What do you think about all this Mr. Weir?" Principal Reid is no fool.

Trevor shuffles, Nora groans inside.

"Well, I… we believe it is time we move on to more enlightened ways of helping students in school. Flogging is not as helpful as it used to be." He flashes a nervous look at Nora. She looks at him with awe. The boy actually has some gumption after all.

"The students in our day do not respond the same way that students in the past did. This is the 1970s. What worked twenty years ago won't work today," Nora says, feeling out of breath. It seems the longest statement she has ever made. Both she and Trevor look at each other, then their gaze lock on Mrs. Reid. Her countenance softens. She stares out her window.

"I don't understand you children nowadays."

Her thought drifts into the distance.

"You're probably more right than you realize." She throws up her hands. "I'm from the old school. I need not tell you that. Things are so... different now. There's a mentality taking over this nation that worries me. I don't think it's good. Look at the violence, it was never like this. It's the lapse in discipline that has led to all this. Not a day passes that you don't hear of some gun crime or some demonstration or something."

A long pause follows. "Let me think about it."

Both students remain transfixed while Mrs Reid stares off. This is too good, too easy. Moments later Mrs. Reid shows surprise that they are still there. She recaptures her principal's persona, "See yourselves out."

Chapter three

Nora stands watch as tires burn. The mess throws ash and black confetti into the brooding sky. Rumblings reverberate in the distance as policemen try to clear debris, M-16 rifles held at the ready, one front-end loader offering assistance. Two army jeeps ride the sidewalk to get around the chaos.

The guilty mingle among the curious while Nora stands as defender. A comrade beside her says to no one in particular, "The reactionary forces are striking back." She looks up at him, takes his hand and heads up the road. He follows her, not unwillingly.

The spine along Prince Consort Road is choked. Fear has gripped the city's nerve center. Nora walks with purpose while Stephen struggles to keep pace with her. He is slightly overweight with a minor limp, but she needs to get to Independence Square, more than a mile ahead, and where the majority of comrades are gathered. The walkie-talkie command is that they gather at South Avenue. She does not know why, but figures that attempts will be made to do something for the television cameras. Perhaps an interview is scheduled with CBC TV.

Several rounds of gunfire burst off an adjoining lane and they both dash through the gate of a private home and stoop behind the wall. Excited chatter erupts, followed by hastening footsteps along the roadway. They figure others are also taking cover. She looks around to see that no one appears to be at home. Nora tells herself that these folks are stuck elsewhere, perhaps at school or at work, and are too fearful to try and venture home.

The excitement subsides and both resume their journey.

Things have been simmering for sometime. Socialism has gained ascendancy in government, segments of the media, at some of the island's colleges and at the sole university, but strong resistance remains in business and among the middle and upper classes. The political opposition refuses to yield ground against what it calls the "Cursed communist incursion."

Radicals such as Nora get more hopeful that the full blast of socialist ideology will take over Jamaica. It is the only way to liberate our people, she reasons. Now in her second year at the University of Jamaica, she decides to do political science because the major socialist thinkers are in the Department of Government. She has no idea what the degree will be used for, but is certain she could play some part in a socialist government.

Her three years at St. Helens Teachers College were mixed. A student with good, if not spectacular grades, she nevertheless felt out of place: The atmosphere was too tame, the lines too neatly drawn, the traditions too rigidly enforced. Questioning and inquiry were not widely practiced, though there was a small band of students who pushed the envelope and were not afraid to express their views. Most students viewed them as strange, a few considered them dangerous. The all-female campus was much too engrossed in traditional female "thinking" for Nora's liking.

She felt liberated the first day she set foot on the UJ campus, not minding the harsh initiation that all freshmen endure at the hands of returning students, and resisted every attempt to have her live on Pringle Hall. A Lalor Hall girl she must be. So she switched halls with another girl she knew from her St. Helens days, moving to Lalor Hall. Lalor Hall, the champions! She listened eagerly to tales of legendary rivalries between Lalor and Patterson Halls that go back to the beginning of the university, from the days when it was established as a symbol of the coming of age of the Jamaican people and as a precursor to Caribbean regionalism.

The excitement is heady. Many of the strategies to plot Jamaica's future take place at the university. Students are convinced they will eventually take over as leaders of the country and plan for this with fervor. UJ lecturers and professors form the intellectual nerve center for the island, with socialist ideology as the under girding philosophy. Other Caribbean countries send their brightest and best.

Even those who are not socialists hold a strong Jamaican nationalist ideology. Disagreements between the socialists and nationalists are not infrequent, but they share a common goal to break the stranglehold of colonial-era politics and economics that hold sway in Jamaica. Both groups are upset that foreigners, or locals tied to former colonial elites, control the major industries. The wealth of the bauxite does not remain in the country, but is sent to other countries and overseas companies; workers' rights are trampled; and no serious attempt is made to change the lot of the poor – not until Peter Barrett came to power and espoused his socialist philosophy.

But the forces are gathering. News runs wild that CIA agents roam the capital. KGB and Cuban agents allegedly walk the corridors of power and are out in the field. Some weeks earlier a senior lecturer told a small group of students of his brief encounter with a KGB agent on Columbus Street in the heart of downtown Kingston. The KGB agent alleged that the Silver Street Massacre that killed seven youth and the burning of the National Home for the Aged where one hundred and fifteen elderly and destitute people perished, were the work of the CIA to make the government look bad.

"Too many truths to tell," Nora declared then.

The rhetoric of the opposition party, which promises to bring down the government before the year is out, also leads Nora to believe the tales.

Then there is the story Jason told her just before he packed his bags and shipped himself off to Florida in the United States. After spending just one year in the classroom, Jason worked as manager in one of the island's larger private companies. Well liked by the owner, he was appointed executive assistant in the office of the Managing Director. He had no specific assignment except to do the boss' bidding, which could be anything from ensuring his coffee was properly fixed to arranging meetings with high profile managers from other companies to negotiating with union delegates. One particular day he was sent on an errand with a brown paper bag containing a pouch. The delivery was to a prominent music producer at the Colonial Hotel. Though not told of its contents, he was warned to exercise great care.

It was six weeks later that Jason became aware of the purpose of the mission. After a brief staff meeting one Monday morning, the Managing Director, George Massad, called Jason into his office. Although he had been in Massad's office many times, Jason often felt intimidated by its expansiveness with its huge blue mahoe desk. Tall, with a podgy face, Massad's Arabic features stand out more prominently than most of his other relatives who work for the company.

"Jason, there's something that puzzles me about you." Jason knits his brow. *What have I done now?*

"I know the politics of most of my staff. I don't know yours."

"I don't understand."

"What are you, Democrat, socialists, or the other one... the... uh... the communists?"

Jason feels uneasy. "My policy is not to bring politics into the workplace, sir."

"Good answer. But that is not the answer I want. I pay you to be truthful at all times, diplomatic when necessary.

"I have no strong political leanings, sir."

Massad looks at him suspiciously. "Everybody does."

Jason knows the politics of not only the managers, but of many of the five hundred workers as well. He has no doubt as to George Massad's politics.

"We want some bright young men to be involved in our political program."

Jason pretends not to know. "Whose program, sir?"

"The National Democratic Party needs young vibrant people like you."

Massad hesitates, then resumes. "Don't you see what's happening to our country? In a short time from now companies like this will no longer exist! These commies will nationalize everything. My business is on the line. Your job is on the line!"

Massad pauses, as if for dramatic effect. "I have made my own contribution to the cause. I want you to make yours."

"Mr. Massad, with all due respect, I have no interest in politics."

"You're more involved than you know."

Jason's puzzlement grows.

"Remember that pouch I asked you to deliver some weeks ago?"

Jason hesitates. He has done several deliveries.

"The one at the Colonial, to Hugh Chen."

Memory dawns on Jason's face.

"That pouch contained one hundred thousand dollars in United States currency."

Jason stares incredulously at him.

"Do you remember a shooting incident at Railway Corner that same evening?" Jason gets more uneasy as his curiosity deepens. "You were being followed by persons from the other side. Our men, who were sent to ensure that everything went well, had to deal with them."

Jason eases back in the chair and stares at Massad with a clouded expression twisted in shock.

Massad waves a dramatic hand. "So whether you like it or not, you're involved."

Jason's life flashes before him. He imagines being caught in a corner with guns blazing. "Mr. Massad, it appears that, based on your own account, I've already made my contribution. Now sir, if you don't mind, I have some assignments to complete."

It was the first time he ever spoke that boldly to his boss, but he knew what he had to do.

Nora recalls Jason telling her he drove the more than eighty miles straight home to Danvers that evening, down the rocky, narrow slope from Orange Hill, told Mama and Papa goodbye, found Nora the next day, and stated he would be joining Paul who is on an exchange program in Florida.

Jason's story convinced Nora that imperialistic forces are determined to derail the march toward freedom of the Jamaican people. The latest eruption is the clearest evidence.

Short of money and under pressure to resign and call new elections, the government announced an increase in the price of gasoline, just one of many commodities over which the government exercises price control. The price hike has had cataclysmic results, catching the government off guard, and leaving the Workers Congress Party flat-footed.

Nora and her cohorts reel at the reality playing out before them: Looting and burning in all major towns across the island; students terrorized; the shooting death of two young girls and a high school boy heading home from school; the killing of a junior minister of government as he drove in his private car; and an attack on Police Headquarters.

The WCP finds itself unprepared to respond.

Independence Square is chaotic. The streets are deserted of motor vehicles except for those belonging to security personnel and burnt out cars strewn on the sidewalks. Heavy-duty equipment push burnt-out cars out of the way to clear passage on the roadways. Curious crowds hang around, scattering occasionally at the outbreak of gunfire, only to gather shortly after. Jamaicans are drawn to the latest danger.

Nora and Stephen hurry through the center of Independence Square toward South Avenue, picking their way through the crowd and security personnel and old cars and debris. The smell of burning rubber hangs heavily in the air. Soft, silky smoke curls through a gaping hole upstairs a building blackened by smoke, suggesting that whatever is in the building has burned itself out, mercifully sparing other property close by. Several store windows are bashed in. A number of shutters show signs of tampering. Stephen suggests that attempts were made to use chainsaw to get through the shutters. Nora says that is impossible. Not in Independence Square.

Camera crews wend their way through human traffic. Stephen expresses his suspicion: Jamaica has only one television station, and most of the crews do not look Jamaican. "They started this war and are filming it to show to the world," he hisses under his breath.

Stephen is about the only young comrade Nora knows to be as diehard as she is. He is from a solid middle class family in St. Andrew, not of a poor, rural background as she is. His father is a lawyer in private practice, his mother a senior administrator in the Central Bank. Nora hangs with him because they share similar views and his greater experience in the party. He is one of the chief recruiters for the WCP, knows where all the political hotspots are, and is skillful in getting things organized on the ground. He has been a good teacher so far.

Nora remembers the first student protest he organized at the UJ campus. They agitated for the removal of the deputy warden for female students over at Johnson Hall. Word got out that the deputy warden was attempting to keep suspected left-leaning students from living on hall. Stephen put together a damning list of allegations before the Guild, the student government. None of the allegations related to the real reason why they wanted her removed. Some allegations implied an abuse of position, others suggested financial impropriety, one mentioned "inappropriate behavior unbecoming of an administrator in the conduct of her personal life." Although the administration of the university backed her as there was lack of sufficient proof, she left the job out of frustration and embarrassment. Nora does not know for sure if the accusations were real or fabricated. She never asked.

Mild confusion reigns on South Avenue. Groups jockey for position as a CBC camera crew moves around to get comments from persons gathered near its gates. An editor looks at a note handed to him through the metal fence by James Parchment, chief organizer for the WCP. They exchange nods and the guard is instructed to allow him in. Stephen, Nora, and two others, one she knows only as Peart, the other, Jimmy Hines, squeeze through the gate closely behind James.

James wants to organize a televised broadcast from party headquarters by the party leader on happenings around the country. The editor indicates that only one camera crew is at the station. All the other crews are currently with the Prime Minister, the Leader of the Opposition or getting footage in other parts of the city. The leader has to get to the station. James tells him that police advised the leader it is unsafe for him to travel throughout Kingston. They have good reason to suspect a plot on his life. Could they not go to him? "No," the editor responds, "This crew is standing by for any late breaking story that may arise." Nora suggests that James be interviewed. After all, he is a senior party operative. The mention of the threat on the party leader's life increases the editor's interest. He agrees with Nora's suggestion. "No," James says, he cannot do so without specific instructions from the very top. Walkie-talkies crackle. A quick consultation between James and the leader leads to James nodding his head. They turn to enter the building.

The studio is cold. For Nora, the lights are much too bright. A minor fuss is made as they prepare for the interview. James sits and makes himself ready. The editor suggests that Nora, the only female, and one other person join James. The group exchanges puzzled glances. "Why?" James asks. He would like to hear from more than one voice, the editor suggests. James shakes his head. "No, that is not the understanding." The editor mocks exasperation. "Do you want the interview yes or no?" He looks at his watch to suggest he is out of time. "Take it or leave it."

Nora is not prepared to be on national television. For the first time, she feels conscious of her appearance. She wonders about her hair. The Afro is cropped fairly low, but she wishes she could at least run a comb through it. She looks down at the loose cotton blouse she wears, and notices too many wrinkles and a few black streaks on it. This is not good, she says to herself. A makeup artist quickly fumbles makeup on her face and gives a light brush to her hair. She feels slightly relieved, but wonders how it makes her look. Other than the odd lipstick, she is not much into makeup.

The news anchor steps into the room with purpose, as if late to catch a plane, yet without undue fuss. Nora has seen her on television numerous times, but hadn't realized she is this skinny and tall. She quickly introduces herself and takes her place, making pretentious chitchat, all simultaneously.

The lights beam even brighter. The shock of their brilliance catches Nora off guard and she squints to see through the burning haze. She does not realize they are near to being on air until the floor manager begins his countdown. The studio becomes still.

The presenter's voice is smooth and melodious. Nora vaguely hears her asking them to make personal introductions. James does so first, then Peart. Nora's heart pounds as her turn comes around.

"I'm Nora Campbell, student at University of Jamaica." Her voice sounds surprisingly strong despite the toad deep in her throat

"Could you tell us what you think is the real reason behind the riots? Is it about gasoline price or are there other reasons? " Nora glances at James but he already knows it is his question. He explains evidence in the possession of the WCP that there are reactionary elements within the country creating instability, and that the violent reaction against the increased price in gasoline is a mere cover for what is a blatant move for political power. At the same time he castigates the government for not moving far and fast enough to effect changes that are necessary in the country. He promises that a government formed by the WCP will do much to dismantle many of the oppressive systems that are still abroad in Jamaican society.

"We have reports that there are threats against the life of your leader."

"Yes, the police have informed us that they have reason to believe there are plans to assassinate the General Secretary of our Party."

"And who do you think is behind these threats?"

"The same reactionary forces that are trying desperately to take over the government and hold on to economic power."

"Do they have a name?"

"We do not wish to identify any particular group at this time. But rest assured that it's a conspiracy between local and foreign groups."

"Foreign groups? What groups are we talking about?"

"It would not be wise for me to say," James retorts.

"Miss Campbell." Nora is startled. "As a member of the UJ community, is it true that the majority of the student body has signed over to the radical WCP?"

Nora tries to find Stephen in the small studio audience to read his face. She takes a sideways glance at James.

"Well, we wish that were true. But the truth is that our movement is growing and it's getting stronger on campus."

"What would lead bright, inquiring minds to join a group such as the WCP?" The scorn is heavy in her voice.

"You asking me?" Nora asks, hoping to get out of answering the question.

"Yes, I'm asking you," the melodious voice insists. Nora feels foolish.

"Well, the question is why not? This country has lived long under a system that is not geared for the liberation of our people. It was designed to subject and oppress us. People like me were not meant to be at a place like UJ. Like our fore parents, we were meant to be hewers of wood and drawers of water."

Nora looks sideways to see that James is giving her a look that shows he is impressed. She is surprised as to how easily the words come to her lips.

The questions move to the role the WCP itself has played in creating instability in the country by preaching radicalism and what some Jamaicans interpret as change by violent means. Peart denies that this is so, that it is propaganda spread by opponents to discredit the party. The presenter makes reference to abuses of power by communist governments in other countries. James insists these are fabricated reports in western media that have a vested interest in maintaining the imperialistic capitalist system.

The interview lasts fifteen minutes and ends with James declaring that the WCP will eventually come to power and make a big difference in the life of every Jamaican.

Ten minutes later, James crushes the half-smoked cigarette with his boot in Independence Square. Incessant rat-a-tat gunfire sounds in the distance. Nora breathes a slight sigh of relief. She is happy the gunfire is in the opposite direction to where she and Stephen are headed. The group of fifteen communists mutters goodbyes and sets off in smaller groups in different directions. Stephen, Nora, and two other UJ students head up Stanley Road.

Die the long day. Welcome the long night.

Chapter four

The telephone call is a surprise. Jean Kellier's voice is just as commanding, but there is greater respect this time, akin to speaking to a peer. Nora finds it difficult to call her "Jean," but Kellier insists on it. Would she be willing to speak at the school's upcoming graduation ceremony?

It is now 1989, and Nora has not been to Ipswich High for more than eight years. She is out of touch with the institution, except for the odd former student she bumps into from time to time. Jean has long ceased being an active member of the Workers Congress Party. The party's reach outside Kingston is almost nonexistent, and Jean is preoccupied with issues of her own.

Remarried, she has tried settling into a routine that includes three stepchildren. The stiffer battle is with the Ministry of Education. With the retirement of Eileen Reid, Jean was appointed vice principal while Everald Wilson was bumped into the principal's office. Everyone knew Wilson would not last long. The removal of the firmer hand of Mrs. Reid led to further instability within the institution. The pressure became too much and Wilson resigned to become an education officer within the education ministry. Appointed to act as principal, Jean had to contend with a hostile administration from Kingston.

The National Democrat government has expunged most anything that looks or smells of socialism. Its overwhelming victory in the 1980 General Elections led to a national purge. When the question of Jean's permanent appointment as principal came up, the Ministry of Education balked. When the ministry moved to appoint someone of its own choosing, Jean filed a lawsuit. The matter dragged on before the courts for two years until the ministry, on advice from its attorneys, settled, and Jean's appointment was made permanent. Jean Kellier remains an oddity: An avowed communist running one of Jamaica's premier high schools in the midst of exuberant capitalist expectations.

Pre-election opinion polls showed the Workers Congress Party would not have been a factor in the 1980 election. Yet for Nora, the election loss was devastating. The near total control of parliament by the National Democratic Party gives legitimacy and total control to reactionary forces and undermines the liberation movement. This will set back the progress of the Jamaican people several decades, Nora reasons. The Peoples Movement party, which swung violently left-of-center during its years in government in the 1970s, went into a period of soul searching after its election loss. What emerges from its introspection sinks Nora's heart. The party now embraces capitalist ideals and ideology. The leftists in the party are sidelined, and the so-called moderates took over.

The WCP sticks stubbornly to its communist ideals, but the ranks thinned since the election. Partly because of a vacuum created by the exodus as well as her own abilities, Nora is now Deputy General Secretary with responsibility for administration, finance, and recruitment, reporting directly to the General Secretary. Purely voluntary, it is a position that consumes much of her time.

Yet it places her in a position to liaise with communist operatives in other countries. Travels to Cuba, Hungary, Czechoslovakia and other socialist countries are regular and extensive. Her most memorable trip was to Moscow. For her, it was a pilgrimage, going into the communist heartland and visiting the major shrines of socialism. Nora and participants from more than fifty countries walked past the seven Kremlin Towers and all the major landmarks of the city. Nothing however, was as breath taking as Lenin's Mausoleum. Seemingly asleep, Nora imagines that the great leader's right clenched fist would rise up at any moment to give the salute.

Back home, Nora turns to her former stomping ground to recruit new talent, the University of Jamaica. But Jamaica is in the grip of Americanism. The country inhaled after its flirtation with socialism and released its breath with fury. Students have little patience with an ideology that is now passé in Jamaica. Consumerism and materialism are the mantra of the new era.

Nora plugs on. She took on the role of editor for the party newspaper when no one else would. Formerly published monthly, now quarterly, it teeters on an edge, often rescued just before it folds. She is writer, editor, paginator, and circulation manager, often standing in Independence Square and Railway Corner, two of Kingston's busiest intersections, to hand out copies to passers-by, most times on a Friday afternoon. The paper is produced cheaply as funding dried up with the exodus of party members.

In time, Nora becomes the only person working out of the office as the secretary was released because the WCP can no longer afford her salary. Nora goes by the office three evenings per week to work the phones, write letters, plan appeals, and arrange meetings and forums.

Nora does her best to plan this evening's forum in a lecture hall at the university. Four hundred letters were sent to present and former party members and leading intellectuals. Heavy promotion is done through distribution of fliers at University of Jamaica and other colleges. The forum focuses on "Critiquing Caribbean society: Marxism and the new direction."

Nora sweats. At 6:30, no one has turned up, and she is convinced that the 7 p.m. start will be delayed. She looks at the lonely desk with its small center floral arrangement and wonders at the awkwardness of the angle it is turned, but decides against adjusting it. She looks around at the cascading seats in the theater and recalls her days as a student reveling in the exchange of ideas between some of the most erudite minds of the university, many of whom were communists or socialist sympathizers. Few still maintain membership in the Congress party, but have for the most part become inactive. Nora misses the intellectual fervor of those former days and hopes she can rekindle participation and interest in the party and its ideals.

Professor Anderson Dunahue, the main forum speaker, arrives at 6:50 and Nora's heart sinks. He was one of her favorite teachers at UJ and held in godlike regard. Now he is here, with two companions, surveying the empty theater as if trying to determine if he has the right place or time. Nora quickly emerges from the corner seat she occupies and, hiding her embarrassment, welcomes Dunahue and his guests with the widest smile. He continues the survey of the room even after Nora's assurances and apologies. Just then the doors burst open and a group that Nora recognizes walks in. The twelve persons are all young radicals that banded as a group to refuse to "sell out" to "imperialistic, capitalist hegemony." Nora is their leader, and she is relieved that they have arrived. Most are teachers in high schools in Kingston, and, like Nora, had cut their political teeth in the flamboyant communist movement of the 1970s. They meet regularly, once per month, and are about the only ones that Nora can rely on for volunteer work, often assisting her in producing and distributing the fliers and newspaper. The greetings, warm and friendly, are accompanied by hugs and slaps on the back.

The General Secretary for the party arrives at precisely 7 p.m. and everyone immediately scampers to take a seat. Nora escorts the professor and the General Secretary to their places at the desk. Both are colleagues at the university and know each other well. The pleasantries are quickly dispensed with and the forum starts at 7:10.

The General Secretary starts by trying to shore up the flagging morale of the sparse crowd. "A lot of persons are asking if our party have a future. I'm here to say it does. The cause is not over. We have much more to do. The reactionary forces make it appear as if they've already won the war. Their control of the government does not mean the fight is over. In fact I'm here to say that the war has just begun.

"We always knew it would not be easy, for the forces lined up against us have gathered all the resources and kept it all for themselves. Through their selfishness and greed, they've left most of the people desolate. The twenty one families who control the wealth of this country will do everything in their power to ensure the majority of our poor black brothers and sisters will remain poor.

"If nothing else, this is clear reason why we should not give up the struggle. It depends on us. If we fail, the poor and destitute and dispossessed will have no one else to turn to. Every other major institution, from government to business to the church is a reactionary force that forms an oligopoly to ensure that they keep an iron-fisted control over all materials and resources. The struggle is not over until the war is won. It is we who will have to set the oppressed free."

The loud applause echoes around the hollow room, made to seat one hundred and fifty students, but barely thirty bodies now struggle to fill the void.

Professor Dunahue, a Grenadian, shaped and influenced that country's political leaders before taking up a teaching position at UJ, eventually becoming a tenured professor. His books and other writings are the gospel of the socialist movement for the Caribbean. His thick, guttural accent strains the eardrum, but those who seek audience with him listen as if in the presence of a saintly sage. He stands at the lectern and surveys the room.

"I get the sense there's some level of resignation among our comrades. This is not just the case in Jamaica, but throughout the Caribbean. The rise of rightwing leaders in America and England, as well as in this country, has formed an unholy alliance aimed at suppressing the struggle for equal rights and justice for all. They want to repeal the achievements we've made to free our people and turn the clock back to when we were all slaves. In fact, if you were to visit our sugar plantations, you will discover that the conditions under which these people work and live are not very different than they were during the time of slavery and colonial rule. This is one reason why the trade union movement which forms part of the struggle is so important. We need to get into these companies and seek worker representation so that we, at the very least, can better the conditions of these workers. But our goal, of course, is much more than that. We aim to change a system that dehumanizes people and makes them chattels, no better or different from animals.

"Marx was insistent on these points. 'Capital is dead labor, which, vampire-like, lives only by sucking living labor, and lives the more, the more labor it sucks.' Those words from Marx are an indication that the only way to stop the sucking of the blood of the worker, is to change the system. Capitalism is a vampire, and therefore one has to kill it, be rid of it. That is the only way change will come, the only way change will take place. The system cannot be reformed, it cannot be changed. It has to be eradicated. This makes revolution necessary. This makes revolution normative.

"Those who engage the struggle are always the few, never the many. Strength is not found in numbers, but in commitment to the cause. The cause itself is the goal, the focus, the aim, the direction. It's a principle that is sustained by the power of that selfsame principle. The principle of the idea is its strength, its ethos, its core, its very being. But it is expressed rationally and experienced practically. This is no abstract science. 'The philosophers have only interpreted the world in various ways; the point, however, is to change it.' That is what Marx said, and how can it be otherwise? The point of all philosophy is to change the world. Otherwise, what is the point of philosophy? In that case, what is the point of anything? This is why religion is pointless, for religion reinforces the status quo rather than seeks to change it. Religion is the means by which the oppressed are co-opted to support the cause of the oppressor. This is done by duping the people into believing that their physical state, that their physical condition do not matter. Their salvation is postponed into an afterlife rather than in the present. In that way, they can be robbed and exploited and used without protest, without resistance. How can any rational person countenance this? How can any person who has any sympathy for the cause of the oppressed embrace this?

"Those who oppress the people always have religion as the ideological underpinning for their agenda. It is the same everywhere – in Asia, in Africa, in Latin America, here in the

Caribbean. Religion is the opiate of the people because it lulls them into accepting their fate as a given, as pre-ordained, as divinely ordered, as that which is their lot in life. 'Religion is the impotence of the human mind to deal with occurrences it cannot understand,' Marx said again. The people are kept from understanding and they are fed religion instead, religion that numbs the mind by making it dumb. 'The social principles of Christianity preach cowardice, self-contempt, abasement, submission, humility, in a word all the qualities of the canaille.' This is why 'The first requisite for the happiness of the people is the abolition of religion.'"

The speech is interrupted with hoots and applause.

"Like Marx, we need to rigorously critique our society and refuse to accept it as it is, for accepting it is death. It would, in other words, be feeding ourselves to the vampire. The vampire must be killed, or at worst chained. The day is truly yet to be born when all this is so in the whole Caribbean region, but it is not far off. Like our brothers and sisters in other parts of the world, we too will soon throw off the yoke."

The speech flirts with applause throughout.

Enthusiastic questions and exuberant answers follow. Nora pinches herself, happy that, despite the small gathering, the evening is not disastrous.

Chapter five

Nora's Ford Angler spits and sputters before it kicks itself into a start. Driving an unreliable vehicle, she travels down a day ahead of the graduation ceremony at Ipswich High School, using the opportunity to visit her parents. She has not been home in a little over a year, and is happy for the two-day break from her teaching job and the party office. At Jean Kellier's request, Nora arrives several hours early at the principal's cottage on the school's campus on graduation day.

Jean looks old and Nora does her best to conceal her surprise. The once rosy cheeks are slightly sunk and light bags rest neatly under each eye, defying attempts to undermine their appearance with makeup. Flecks of gray intermingle with the over processed hair. Jean nevertheless greets Nora cheerily and takes her immediately into the living room where Jean pours her favorite drink, Gold Jamaican Rum. She offers a glass to Nora, who accepts it. Nora remembers that her favorite teacher had a reputation as a "hard drinker" when she was a student at Ipswich High, but did not see much evidence of it while boarding with her. She knew that Jean hung out at one of the bars in the town on a Friday evening, but cannot recall seeing her drunk at any time. There were always several bottles of Gold in her cabinet however, and Jean would occasionally have a glass after dinner.

Nora notices that it is 1:30 p.m. and relaxes when Jean seems dismissive of the time.

"So tell me, how're things?" Nora expects the question and eagerly tells Jean of her work for the Congress party. Jean listens calmly without interruption and allows Nora to expel her excitement. She smiles occasionally when Nora recalls the group of young communists who have sworn not to "sell out to the imperialists," of their meetings, their general work for the party, and how they are the major writers of articles for the party newspaper.

"Reminds me of the Young Hegelians," Jean finally responds. Nora is baffled at the comment.

"The Young Hegelians were mainly students and young professors who were followers of the German philosopher Hegel. Marx was an original member of this group out of which leftist ideas were born." Nora forms her mouth into an O and nods her head with comprehension. Then Jean puts some weight on her words, "But Marx eventually broke with them," and stares Nora in the face while saying so. She takes a deep sip on her glass and places it on the coffee table.

"I know what's going on in the party. Everything is not always as they seem."

"I know that," Nora responds. "Lots of things happening in this country that the people don't know nothing about."

"You're right, but that's not what I'm talking about. Things are not always as they appear." Nora fixes Jean Kellier with a puzzled gaze and wonders why she repeats herself.

"You need to look closely around you. My advice! Keep your ears to the wall and your eyes on the trees."

"You speaking in riddles."

Jean Kellier smiles and flashes her head. "So tell me, how does it feel to be back on your ol stompin groun?" she drawls, as she sometimes does, when she gets impish. Nora takes the cue.

"It's been a while since I came back here."

"You're right about that. You been neglecting us." She pauses as if caught in midair. "Mrs. Reid would die if she knew you were main speaker at one of our graduation ceremonies," and both laugh.

"So how tings with you?" Nora finally has the courage to ask.

"Girl –" the term and tone adds an air of familiarity between them that Nora is still trying to get used to. "Life does take some very interesting turns. Whod have thought that I'd have ever remarried and become a mother? Certainly not me! Granted, they're not my children but I'm their mother." She shakes her head. "With all the challenges, it's mostly good though. He's a good man, and just to show my appreciation of him, I even go to Mass."

35

Nora's mouth slackens into astonishment.

"Yes, yes, I know I know. But it aint that bad. Did I not tell you I was Catholic? Yes, I was baptized as a baby girl, still have my baptismal picture." She laughs. "You know that once a Catholic you're always a Catholic, unless they excommunicate you. So far as I know, I've yet to be excommunicated." She grins and picks up her glass and swipes a sip. Nora is unsure how to respond.

"So this is accommodation to a new situation," Nora says, not sure if it is a question, a rebuke, or a statement. Jean Kellier shrugs.

"I just felt awkward being left here alone on a Sunday morning while they're all trooping off to church. He says since his first wife died, he made sure to take his children to church every Sunday. That's one way he's able to establish some kind of framework for the girls, some kind of foundation, some semblance of order. The ground fell away under him so this is one way he was able to find his footing. It was for him a way of getting involved in the life of his daughters with whom he was not particularly close before. He never attended Mass before. But he felt that, after she died, he at least owed this to her to continue the tradition. Now he's a serious Catholic."

Nora is not sure how to proceed, but she ventures forward. "So this is your way to fit in," again, hovering between a question and a statement.

"Could be," Jean answers noncommittally, and pours another drink, holding the bottle to ask Nora if she cares for more. Nora shakes her head and looks into her glass from which she has taken only three sips.

"That does not sound like you."

"Again I say, you never know how life turns."

Nora looks into her glass. "A number of the old guard has fallen away from the party." She looks up to square Jean in the face.

Jean shrugs. "People jus tired. They jus got tired," she trails off. Then she musters herself. "Of course, some were in it just for the ride. Many had not a clue what the struggle was about. They jus went along with a popular wave. Or they felt that this was a way to make a name for themselves. People were involved for all sorts of reason. When those reasons no longer hold, they jus stop."

"And what about you? You're no longer in the struggle."

Jean pauses to reflect and twirls her glass. Nora becomes conscious that Jean might just be drinking too much, but she shows no sign of intoxication.

"My heart is still in it, but I now know too much. I know too much." She looks at the clock on the wall. "Wow, time to get ready. I'm not young like you. I need a longer time to make myself beautiful, to hide these bags and old lines." She bounds up off the couch and shows Nora where she may freshen up and get dressed, then head for her own bedroom.

Chapter six

The call for an emergency meeting had Nora scurrying to reach every member of the Central Committee of the Workers Congress Party. The General Secretary gave her only one week to contact the leaders, and it is a relief to her when she sees the comrades, the majority from Kingston, gathering in the Senior Common Room at the University of Jamaica.

The General Secretary is flanked on the right by Norman Greaves, Deputy General Secretary in charge of international and political affairs, and Nora. The fifteen members sit in a wide semicircle in lounge chairs, most sipping beverage and nibbling light finger food made by Endora Smith, home economics teacher and long standing Central Committee member.

Nora knows the main subject of the evening. Pleasantries aside, the General Secretary begins with the matter at hand. "Comrades, this meeting is called to address new developments that will have a bearing on our future.

"Our membership has suffered a massive decline since the election in 1980 and we became almost completely dependent on subventions we received from overseas. But you all know that our comrades in other countries, especially in Europe, have had some challenges in recent times. We were informed just this past week that all our overseas funding will be cut off within the next three months. By then, if we cannot find alternative means of funding our activities, then many of the things we do, and perhaps even the existence of the party itself, is under threat. We call this meeting not only to inform you, but to hear from you any solution you may have."

A long silence follows. James Parchment, who now works as an insurance sales agent, and who has not had much involvement in the party in recent months, is the first to speak. "It would help us if we were to see financial statements."

The General Secretary shuffles in his chair and clears an uneasy throat. "The urgency of this meeting is such that we had not had time to put together the kind of report that this meeting would deem acceptable."

"But even an outline of the financial situation would aid us in our discussion," Parchment insists.

Nora whispers something in the General Secretary's ear and, after he nods his head, reaches into a bag she has next to her chair. Nora reads a rudimentary statement of accounts that shows the expenses of running the party office, how much was given to the office of administration, how much spent on stationery, printing, transportation, and other items. It shows a balance of less than two thousand dollars in the bank account opened exclusively for running the office.

"I'm happy that the Deputy General Secretary has kept what appears to be impeccable records of her own stewardship, but we still have not heard the full story of the total monies received and spent by the party," says Wendell Stephens, who Nora succeeded, and who lectures accounting at a college. "We all know there are monies set aside for various activities of the party, through its different organs, and all we hear are the expenses of the administrative functions."

The youth leader, still a student at University of Jamaica, reports that the Youth League has its own core executive and operates a small fund with its own bank account. The amounts received, spent and in the account are insubstantial, and come mainly from the youth themselves. The president of the Women's Movement reports essentially the same, except that it has an account with four thousand dollars.

"Mr. General Secretary, part of the problem is that everyone is operating his own little show. We need to centralize all the activities and all the accounts of the organization. Operating in these splinter groups and in this scatter shot way is a recipe for disaster. No wonder we're in the bind we are," offers Harold Peart, who recently returned from pursuing a medical degree in Cuba.

"Even if we were to do that, it would not solve the long term problem of financing the party," another member joins in.

"But we're all speaking in a vacuum here, for we have nothing before us to show the true state of affairs of the party," James Parchment insists.

"What of the trade union? That seems to be doing well. The union has gained representation in several companies over the years, and has a growing membership."

The General Secretary, who doubles as President of the Workers Compensation Union, jumps in. "The union is a completely different entity from the party and the two organizations are completely autonomous from each other. Each has its own structure and own executive and the union is related to us only as an affiliate."

"But one is not sure where the party ends and the union begins. It's not all very clear to me. There's a symbiotic relationship between the two. This party gave birth to the union. Certainly we have a right to know what's going on there and to have some say in the union's operation. And one should expect that the union would make its own contribution to the party."

"I repeat. Both the union and the party are two separate entities. Both share a close and cordial relationship, but legally, both are separate and we need to be careful that we do not allow the one to intrude on the other," the General Secretary advises.

"What I can tell you," the General Secretary says, trying to steer the discussion, "is that our comrades are doing tremendous work with the little resources we have. Comrade Campbell has performed remarkably running the office over the past two years, doing promotion work, recruiting, and publishing the party paper. She does this as a volunteer with a very enthusiastic group of other young comrades helping her. She accomplishes a lot with very little. Sadly, these are the kinds of activities that will have to be curtailed due to the shortage of funding."

"And if we stop doing those things may as well we cease being a party," the women's president intervenes. "I'm willing to offer the little we have, but as to how far that can go, I don't know."

"We need to expand our reach outside of Kingston. Other than few pockets in other parts of the island, we have little or no presence beyond the capital. We're not a national party, that is part of the problem," another member observes.

"But how can we do that if we don't have funds in the first place? Our recruiters on the ground need financial support for travel, for accommodation, etc.," another voice chips in.

The Women's Movement President stands up to speak. "We need to start with ourselves. A number of us here tonight have fallen down on our own involvement and are members of the party in name only. We're the leaders, and yet too few of us make ourselves available. We're beginning to pay attention only to our own affairs and are neglecting the struggle. I have an extremely hard time getting people to come out to meetings, much less take part in any of our activities. I was at the party's forum the other day, and so few of us were there. How many of us as Central Committee members turned up at the forum where our General Secretary and Professor Dunahue gave such brilliant presentations? The only thing that heartened me was the presence of the youth. Though the numbers in no way measure up to what we had in the past, their enthusiasm puts the rest of us to shame."

Silence weighs on the room.

"We cannot solve the money problem in a big meeting like this. A special committee or group of persons need to get together to study the problem and report back to us. At the very least, I have to see some numbers before I am able to make any meaningful contribution on the matter," Parchment finally breaks the guilty mood.

With most persons declining to serve due to "personal reasons," "other commitments" or "I will be traveling," three persons are named with Nora, who is elected chair, to conduct a study on the present state and future of the party.

Chapter seven

The group of young comrades huddles in the dark inside Nora's small studio flat. A single candle casts ghoulish shadows on the wall as they pore over a map, the electrical blackout haunting half the city.

Terrence speaks rapidly and excitedly as he whispers in the group of four. "We can do it, it'll be easy," he tries to convince them. Nora sits uneasily and shakes an unconvinced head. She places a forlorn palm on her cheek and looks with trepidation at the others.

"You can't possibly believe we can go through with this?"

"Why not?" Terrence asks, as if Nora just asked the silliest question.

"I'm not into anything like this," she says. "This is going way too far."

"What other choice do we have? You said yourself that we're out of options."

Terrence is one among the group of twelve young comrades that meets every month to discuss revolutionary ideas and political philosophy. Ardent and from one of the depressed areas of the capital city, he did well enough academically to be now enrolled at one of the technology colleges in Kingston. While in high school, he became an ardent leader in the students' council, serving as a second vice president. He transferred that political ardor into his college and personal life, and is consumed by the thought of overthrowing the system that keeps the majority of Jamaicans locked in economic and social bondage.

The other two members are recent graduates from the University of Jamaica and, like Terrence, are under Nora's tutelage. They admire her for her knowledge and history of being at the very heart of the struggle, hearing of her reputation while they were students at UJ. Duane and Milton, both of solid middleclass background, are unsure of how to respond to Terrence's idea. Both are disaffected by their parents' bourgeois lifestyles and joined the WCP in rebellion. The group of young comrades spoke glibly in the past of doing something revolutionary and even talked of taking up arms on the behalf of the struggle. But neither Duane nor Milton, or Nora, has actually thought of going through with it.

"None of our elders would approve of this," Nora tries to dissuade Terrence.

"Who says? Do you really know that?"

"Breaking the law is not exactly part of our agenda."

"What kind o statement is that? How many times you break the law by protesting and demonstrating?"

"But we've never actually done anything violent, or deliberately committed a crime, certainly not anything like this."

"You sure bout that? How you tink I got involved in the party in the firs place? The party needed enforcers in my community and I helped the party there, even while I was still in grade nine. I had to do a ting or two on behalf o the party. It look like you don't understan how tings run. Or you jus playin innocent?"

The retort stings Nora. She escapes by opening a window to ease the stifling air. Stickiness clings to her blouse as sweat drips from her face. She wishes the electrical power would return so that the ceiling fan may run. She notices that the others disapprove of the opened window, and she closes the louvers. Secrecy trumps comfort.

Duane is thoughtful in his response. "One great revolutionary says 'you cannot make a revolution in white gloves.' Every revolution involves getting one's hands dirty. This is just part of the reality."

Nora turns around and surveys the others in the dimness. She shakes her head and sits down. "'There are no morals in politics; there is only expedience,'" Milton chimes in.

"There must be some other way to get money to run the party."

"If there is, then tell us," Terrence challenges her.

"Why not let us fan out across the island to sign up people? Let's make the dues for membership minimal. If we sign up one thousand people at one hundred dollars a pop, that alone is one hundred thousand dollars."

"How long is that goin to take us huh?" Can the few of us do that? How many people can we really count on to join? That's not feasible. By the time we're done, the party would've already been out of existence," Terrence counters.

"I'm not prepared to see the party die," says Milton.

"I'm prepared to do whatever it takes," agrees Duane.

All three stare at Nora in the gloom, awaiting a response. She tries to shake herself from the stifling scene, dying for the power to return and the meeting to be over.

She sighs the deepest sigh. "Let's do this carefully."

Chapter eight

The rain has pelted all day, and it is only through the sheer determination of Terrence why they travel the sixty five miles from Kingston to the small town on Jamaica's northeast coast. Nora, and even Milton and Duane, suggest halfway along the journey that they change the plan to another day, but Terrence insists the conditions make it even better for the operation. The Junction Road poses its own challenge as they maneuver the tight, steep, and sharp corners before finally easing themselves onto a slightly more commodious road along the coast.

The four remain silent, each absorbed by the gravity of the moment. None is willing to verbalize unsettled thoughts, and each does a mental run of the plan. The rain eases without making conditions better as the sloppiness settles determinedly in the roadway. The tension rises when the car turns off Main Street unto the narrower, messier road that leads in the direction of the Peoples National Bank. Terrence jumps out of the car with purpose after turning the car around at an intersection, and parked on the opposite side, one chain away from the bank, facing Main Street from which they came. He quickly surveys the area and sighs with relief when he sees the empty street. Nora takes her place behind the car wheel, the engine running. Milton and Duane get out of the car and take their position behind Terrence, each donning gloves with cut off stockings held ready in hand. The three head in the direction of the bank as the rain lulls into a slight drizzle.

Business ends half day on a Thursday in the small town and, except for the banks, most other businesses close at 1:00 p.m. The Peoples National Bank, like most banks across the country, closes to the public at 2:30 p.m. It is precisely 2:20 p.m. when all three alight from the car that Terrence borrowed from a friend who lives in the same community he does in Kingston.

Nora sits with the engine running and taps the steering wheel, every few seconds snapping a look through the rear-view mirror, the side mirrors, and in front. Her palms are oily with sweat and she wipes her nose, brushing a hand across her eyes as if to clear a mist.

A sound comes from the left side of the car and Nora's heart leaps, careening her neck to see. She inhales a deep sigh and places a damp palm on her breast when she notices a dog foraging in a small pile of soaked garbage, its tail clung between its short spiny legs covered with gray-dirty hair. The dog sniffs and, dissatisfied with its lack of find, moves on. Nora returns her gaze in front and lightly revs the car engine to satisfy herself that it still runs.

The minutes seem hours.

Soft plopping sounds give her another start, and she looks with trepidation as a Rastafarian walks hastily past the car from behind, and chastises herself for not seeing him coming. The man hesitates slightly as he looks curiously at her and, unhappy with the conditions of the slight drizzle and the puddles he has to maneuver, moves on in the direction of Main Street. She watches him round the intersection and returns to her tapping of the steering wheel.

The minutes drag.

Blam! Blam!

The two explosions freeze Nora in the car seat.

Blam! Blam!

Nora's mind goes blank as she considers what to do. She puts the car in gear and instinctively moves off then screeches to a stop. She sees Terrence and Duane through the rearview mirror struggling with Milton as both push and shove him in the direction of the car, stocking masks turning their faces into grimaces. She slams the car into reverse and erratically speeds toward them. The car lurches as it stops. The boys fumble with the doorknobs before finally getting them open and bundle themselves into the backseat, as Milton cries out in agonal pain.

"Go, go, go!" Terrence bawls out. Nora, fumbling with the gear stick, finally gets it stuck in first gear, and lurches the car forward.

She does not stop even at the intersection and wrests the wheel to its extremity as the car zigzags onto Main Street. The sharp right turn splashes puddles of water in every direction. After a split second of thinking, Nora decides against braking when she sees an elderly woman crossing the street, and in a skill that surprises even her, rounds the woman who stands frozen in the middle of the road. She darts a look in the rearview mirror and returns focus on the road.

"What happened?" She finally manages to ask, and casts an anxious glance at Milton through the mirror. He writhes in pain and she sees blood.

"Jus drive!" Terrence shuts her up, pulling off his mask before removing Milton's.

The drizzle turns into driving rain as they head from the coast into the hills, every now and again glancing nervously behind them. After 30 minutes of erratic driving, Terrence protests when Nora turns off into a pasture.

"What you doin?"

She gives him a look that shuts him up. "You want him to die on us? We have to get him help." She reaches around and over the seat toward Milton at the back. "You come drive," she commands Terrence. "Duane you come to the front."

The two boys get out of the car to go to the front while Nora slips between the two front seats onto the backseat. She lifts Milton's shirt to see blood oozing from the top of his arm, near to the shoulder. She removes his belt and quickly tightens it atop the wound, slipping it under the armpit, wrapping the belt several times until she makes a crude knot. She looks with concern at Milton and uses the three stockings left on the backseat by all three to sop the draining blood.

"We can't drive to Kingston with him like this. We have to stop somewhere."

"Hospital? We can't go to no hospital!" Terrence retorts.

"You want him dead?"

Duane looks around at Milton. "Mi bredren, she right, we can't drive with him like this."

All sit silent for several moments.

"Drive," Nora commands.

Terrence looks around at her. "Drive? Drive where?"

"Jus drive," she says firmly.

Dark silence hangs in the car. For the very first time, Nora pays attention to the wet bag on the seat between her and Milton. She opens it and sees stacks of cash. She half shoves the bag as she closes it and looks contemplatively out the window, and idly watches the rain beat against the glass. A light groan from Milton draws her attention back to the present and she looks at him with a heart sunken with despair. She fights off a sense of disbelief at their predicament.

"Tell me what happened," she says in a hardened voice. No one volunteers a response. "Tell me what happened!" her voice drips with steel. Terrence's eyes form a square with hers in the rearview mirror.

Duane stutters a response. "We didn't know that there was a plainclothes guard. We hol up the 'Blue Bag' and take him gun but the plainclothes one start fire shot when we leaving. Terrence pump two in him."

"Jeez, it mean say you kill smaddy!" Nora's heart slumps deep into her chest and then heaves into her throat. She sits speechless. Terrence's eyes meet hers again.

"Wha we to do? Make him shoot an kill we?" His eyes blaze through the mirror.

"We not sure if him dead," Duane tries to ease Nora's fear.

"Turn here so," Nora instructs quickly, and the car makes a sudden right onto another road in the pelting rain. They are driving through an old bauxite mine, and eventually enter Reynolds Road, which is all too familiar to Nora.

"Who have the gun?" she suddenly blurts out. No one answers. "Where's the gun that belong to the Blue Bag?" Duane eases up to take something from his waist, and holds the gun up so that Nora sees it.

"We can't keep it."

"So what we mus do wit it?" Duane asks.

"I will keep it," Terrence offers.

Nora looks with eyes transfixed in the back of Terrence's head.

"What?" he asks, glancing at her in the car mirror. "Me know nuff man who would do well with this piece o iron."

Nora's regret and despondence deepens and she fights back tears.

"When I go back I not only goin return three guns but I goin bring back four. The men who len me the guns goin glad," Terrence says haughtily.

"Stop here so," Nora interrupts him and Terrence pulls to the side of the road, close to an abandoned shop that has half its roof caved in. Its extended roof at the front offers slight shelter as Nora gets out of the car. She pulls an umbrella out of the bag she has and disappears onto the side road next to the abandoned shop. They have been driving for almost ninety minutes, and the heavy clouds and rain makes it look later than the time of 4:15 p.m.

Nora climbs the steep incline before arriving at her destination. She raps on the door and waits with bated breath, looking hopefully at the car in the driveway, surmising that he is home.

Jean Kellier opens the door and stands uncertain at what she sees. Seconds pass before she catches herself and ushers Nora into the house, who tries to be careful not to drip water all over the tiled floor. Jean's surprise remains unabated while Nora looks around suspiciously and tries to speak in hushed tones. She quickly guides Nora into the study and closes the door. Nora is out of breath from the walk and nervousness.

It takes Nora twelve minutes to explain her ordeal and Jean another seven minutes to let it sink in. She shakes an incomprehensible head and turns to stare at the wall, her back turned halfway to Nora.

"Wait here," she says, and gets up with a stiff face and back.

Jean returns five minutes later with her husband, Dr. Nathaniel Carpenter, the family physician for the community and Ipswich High School. Nora remembers him only fleetingly as she never had reason to see him while she was a student, but knows of his medical practice, the oldest in the area. Back then, he was married to his first wife and had no direct link to the school except in cases of emergency for students who required urgent medical attention.

He frowns a disapproving look at Nora and listens while she explains, in less detail this time, the reason for her visit. Both Dr. Carpenter and Jean walk out of the study and she could hear the two arguing in the living room. Nora feels helpless and the urge to run away sweeps over her. "This is a police matter," she could hear Dr. Carpenter saying. "No, no, no," she hears Jean pleading. "I want to have nothing to do with this," she hears his response. "Do this for me," she responds. "This was one of my favorite students. Remember she spoke at our last graduation." "I can't," he says. "Please," she pleads.

Dr. Carpenter looks at his wife with steel in his gaze and she looks up at his tall, gaunt face beseechingly. "Where's the boy," Nora hears him finally ask. "Out in the car," she hears Jean says. "I can't do it here; they have to go to my surgery. Tell her to meet me at the back entrance." "I'll go with her," Jean says. "You're not going anywhere!" Dr. Carpenter almost screams through his whispers. Jean does not argue, "I'll meet you down there," she says, and walks into the study. She gathers herself and an umbrella and follows Nora down the road toward the car. A light tap on the car window wakes the startled boys as Nora and Jean bundle themselves into the car.

Dr. Carpenter shows his displeasure with a scolding face, but he dutifully sets to the task of mending Milton's wound. He scowls as he conducts the various tests, and mutters that "He may need blood and should be in a hospital." Jean pulls Nora into a private room while Terrence and Duane sit uncomfortably in the waiting room.

Jean fixes Nora with piercing eyes. "This is beneath you," she finally says, and sits back glumly in the chair. Nora twists a nervous lock of hair that droops loosely to the side of her face, defiant of her effort to set it back in place.

"Do you really think the party deserves you doing this?" Jean clicks her tongue at the end of the question. "You really don't know what's goin on do you?" She resumes the piercing look. "Why do you think the party has no money?"

Nora's brain sputters for a response, trying to loosen the tautness of her mind and to steer Jean away from the subject of the party or the bank robbery. "Comrades both in Jamaica and overseas are facing challenges and persons are not able to give to the struggle as they used to."

"That's only part of the story my dear," Jean says in a condescending, motherly tone. "As usual, there's always more to it than what meets the eye." She shakes a head and offers an ironic smile. "Tell me, where does your beloved General Secretary live?"

"On the university campus," Nora replies, incredulous at the question.

"That's what you and most others think. Indeed, he does have a flat on campus, but his real dwelling, which is bought in his wife's name, is in Cherry Gardens." Jean looks at Nora with a triumphant stare as if she just revealed the greatest secret. "Yes, salubrious Cherry Gardens, the place where all the money-grubbing capitalists and bloodsuckers live." Jean smiles and looks askance at Nora.

"Remember when all those business people were selling out their businesses and houses and leaving Jamaica out of fear that communism was coming to the country? Who do you think helped to buy up some of those businesses and properties?"

Nora stares at Jean as she speaks and is afraid of the answer that she is sure is coming.

"Ah, you're getting it, aren't you?" Jean says mockingly. "And where do you think all that money came from to buy these houses and businesses? Banks? No. Banks aren't willing to lend money to people they're not sure would pay them back. A few get their money through the ganja trade. Yes, ganja, that great Jamaican capitalist money supply machine. Big and small, high and low benefit from it. Some so-called comrades, those connected with the party, and the trade union, know where to get their money."

Nora feels herself wanting to cry, and her best effort not to only results in her bursting out and, without quite realizing it, throws herself into Jean's arms.

"Never mind my dear. Never mind," Jean pats Nora's back who, finally realizing the scene she has created, eases up herself and sheepishly wipes her eyes. Jean looks understandingly at her and continues her story as if there was no interruption.

"I'm a good friend of the former treasurer, who, incidentally is not in Jamaica for obvious reasons. She told me what happened to all that money the party and the union had. She was told to sign blank checks and hand them over, only to find out afterwards that the accounts were all cleaned out. What did she do? She promptly resigned, packed her bags, and left the country incognito. My house was her last stop before she took her flight from Montego Bay. She dared not try flying from Kingston. The deputy treasurer, who had not the presence of mind to make similar arrangements, was found in a gully somewhere in Western Kingston, shot in the head. It was made to look as if it was a hit from the other side. But I suspected what really happened."

Jean pauses with drama hanging in the air. "That, my dear, is the party for which, and the people for whom, you just made the most costly sacrifice."

Chapter nine

It's been two weeks since Nora is holed up in her apartment, except for the odd evening adventure out to the store. She feels safer under the cover of darkness and night.

She returned to school on Monday following the dramatic weekend, trying to behave normal, but quickly found that her pretense became burdensome. The news – the first bank robbery in Jamaica in more than a decade – dominated headlines on the weekend and was a major talking point at work Monday and Tuesday. Discussions of the incident in the faculty staffroom had her sitting on pins. Each conversation sank a new needle deep into her heart, piercing further than the previous one.

She left work early Tuesday and promptly went to the doctor. Diagnosed as suffering from stress and exhaustion, Nora put in for the maximum ten sick days allowable plus an additional week of "departmental leave."

With eyes glued to the television and ears to the radio, Nora keeps touch with every report on the investigation. She obsesses with the newspapers and traces every word in every report, heart leaping at any suggestion of a new lead. The telephone goes unanswered, the answering machine replayed at the end of each call. Two colleagues called to see how she is, and she returned the call to assure them she is making good recovery, but that the doctor ordered her to rest. The only telephone call she initiated was to Jean Kellier, and it is the only call she returned other than to the two colleagues.

Last night was the worst. For the umpteenth time, she jumped at the sound of something at her window, listening for footsteps and other signs of human presence. She waited with dread, fearing the worst, hoping it's her imagination. The nightmares were more intense last night as she woke twice, the last with the sensation that she was falling into a watery abyss and drowning, but death would not come. The drowning sensation lagged and dragged until she was out of her mind with breathlessness and desperation. She was dying but death refused her. The agony was prolonged until she lunged to a sitting position, gasping and heaving for air. She sat transfixed in bed for long moments until the reality of her bedroom came back to her.

Determined to keep sleep away tonight, Nora dresses and decides to walk. There is no intention or purpose other than to ward off sulfurous thoughts. Her mood runs opposite to the balmy November evening. Low pressure systems pelted the island for more than a week before the sun started playing hide and seek with the clouds. Today sees a definitive break in the weather. Nora was happy for the rains, as it warded off both friend and potential foe. It was the only comfort she had, cocooning her in her apartment.

Nora runs through her mind what she and the boys did as she walks at a fast clip past the middleclass houses and apartments on her street, down its intersection with Meadow Drive, heading toward Hilton Road.

Terrence replaced the fake license plates he had put on the car. With Milton's gunshot wound mended, they stuffed the moneybag in the trunk, under the spare, and headed for Kingston, driving within the speed limit, hoping that the rains would keep the police off the road. They figured the cops were less likely to be out conducting spot checks and forming speed traps during the showers.

Nora insisted they rehearse their story. They went to the south coast with friends, they would say. This tale puts them at the opposite end of the island, far from the scene of the bank heist. Milton's injury was the result of a bad fall while jumping off a ledge into the water, they would say. They were to stay away from specifics and relate only generalities to anyone who asks, including family or friends.

It was Terrence's job to dispose of the four guns, the three he "rented" from friends, and which were used by the three boys during the robbery, as well as the gun taken from the uniformed Special Constable, the Blue Bag.

Nora was to take and secure the money. This proved harder than she anticipated. She feared having it in the apartment, and she felt unsafe depositing it in the bank. She had no idea where to put it without inviting suspicion or danger, so she called Jean Kellier. Jean sent Nora to an old friend who owed her a favor. "Just tell him Jean sent you. And don't worry my dear, I didn't tell him anything. I just told him that I gave you something to put up safely for me, and that when I'm ready for it, you'll pick it back up."

Nora was skeptical. Jean deadpans over the line, "Do you think you are the first person for whom I've kept secrets and confidence? Just remember that some people, though they've committed crimes worse than robbery, are still out there because of those who could turn them in but didn't. Leland will do whatever I ask." Jean pauses at the other end of the line. "It's silly of me to say it, but you know you can't tell anybody bout this. Not even those other guys, no matter what or how much they ask you. You can't afford to sheg me up on this. I'm placing myself on the line here." Nora's assurance was greeted with a mild 'hmph' from Jean who promptly said a quick goodbye.

So with that, Nora called Leland and met him at Railway Corner, identifying him by the make and color of his car. They drove in his car to a house off Old Tyre Road which seemed unoccupied but not abandoned. Upon entering, he took her to a room, opened a safe behind a wall painting, had her put the bag in it, and gave her a key with the admonition, "Make sure you don't lose it. It's the only key we ave for this safe. Miss Jean ave the other one, an you know ow far she live – way in the country." He said it while laughing, as if amused by the thought of Nora having to drive deep into rural Jamaica just to get a key for a safe.

On the way back to Railway Corner where Nora left her car, the heavyset fellow with wide-gapped teeth and a long scar on the right cheek kept saying. "So you is Miss Jean frien? Good woman, good woman. Like a mother to me," all along not giving her much chance to respond. It is like he knew to talk without asking, without prying, respecting the confidence, but wanting to make an impression.

Back in Railway Corner, the drive not much more than five minutes, he squinted at her in the late afternoon sun that squeezed itself between several rain clouds as she alighted from the backseat. "You can go by the ouse by yourself when you ready, you know where the key is, or if you want you can call me." He noticed her uncertainty. "Jus call me when you ready or if you need anyting. Miss Jean frien is my frien."

He sped off in the direction of Downtown.

Nora's trek has her crossing several streets until she hits Hilton Road, and walks with purpose but discontent in the direction of Hilton Mall. She feels slightly exhilarated with the flow of her sweat and begins to concentrate on the walk itself, blocking out the sound of voices and traffic. The smell of jerk chicken distracts her, and she notices the familiar row of white-robed young men near the sidewalk with their "drum pans." Hating the breast quarter, she buys leg and thigh and a large slice of hard dough white bread, wrapped in foil. She feasts on it and, hearing music playing on Pugh Lane, turns into the small community. A Friday night street dance is going on and kids, many not older than seven, are performing various dance moves, some on the top of their head with their little bottoms up in the air "wining" to the beat. She shakes a head despite herself, and sits down at a thatched bar with stationary wooden stools to take in the scene. She is surprised to see some middleclass looking young men and women among the crowd, clearly distinguished from residents of the inner city community nudged between, and close to, more affluent areas. This is the paradox of uptown Kingston. Inner city and affluence existing side by side, each in a world of its own, but occasionally invaded by others from the other side, mainly for work or entertainment.

Nora's thoughts drift to the deepest hurt. A sense of betrayal and deception is on the rise, commingled with anger and bitterness.

She tries to disbelieve Jean, but her words gnaw, "This is the party and the people for whom you've made the most costly sacrifice." She remembers the death of Maximilian Grey, deputy treasurer, and its impact on the party. Everyone was convinced the reactionary forces were out to exterminate the leadership. The General Secretary immediately took a sabbatical to Eastern Europe and stayed away for six months. The sudden departure of Treasurer Imogene Frank was seen as an attempt to avoid becoming a casualty. That was when Nora, in final year as a university student, became more than a foot soldier for the Workers Congress Party and started to volunteer her evenings at the party office. The absence of the General Secretary, the departure of the treasurer, and the death of the deputy treasurer all left a gaping hole in the party administration and leadership. Over the past several years, she has given unbroken service in the office and to the party. She bristles at the thought of being used, having slaved so long and hard for the party, often using her own money to help print fliers and buying supplies when the money ran out. She finds it hard to believe that, in the midst of all that, money would be used by party bigwigs to enrich themselves.

Nora scowls at the beer she just bought, taking a swig and then pondering the red banner running diagonally across the stubby, ugly brown bottle. She runs her hand along the banner as if trying to make sense of the design. The "selector's" voice intrudes as he introduces a twelve year old whom he claims to be a future dancehall star. The spiny young boy starts toasting and launches into sexually explicit lyrics to the delight of the crowd of adults and children. Nora picks up her beer bottle and heads out, leaving the foil with chicken bones and half of the slice of bread on the counter.

At the intersection of Pugh Lane and Hilton Road, she ponders her next move. She does not want to head home, but does not want to drift too far. Nora turns left in the direction of the Hilton Mall and walks at a brisk pace, as if heading somewhere definite. Sounds and sites of traffic recede as the stab of Jean's words sinks deeper into her heart. Nora grows more morose at what now seems her impossible plight. Not for the first time, she feels guilt about the robbery. Each time guilt appears, she argues with herself. *No need to feel guilty. I did it for the right cause. It's the party leaders who failed. Comrades right across the country placed their faith in these leaders, and they let them down. I've worked hard for the party. I gave it my all. I did all I could do.*

She recalls the letter she penned to the General Secretary three days ago. "I regret to inform you that, due to personal reasons, I am no longer able to serve the party as Deputy General Secretary or in any other position. I therefore resign with immediate effect. The WCP has helped to shape who I am, and I leave with a debt of gratitude. I wish you, the party and all affiliates the best for the future." She thought long and hard about the last two sentences, the hypocrisy of the paragraph weighing on her, then decided it was more politically astute to include some platitudes, even if it means being a little dishonest.

It was a huge wrestle to write the letter. She wondered if the letter itself would raise suspicions, but then decided it shouldn't. She grappled with the thought of staying and leading her own internal reforms, but felt herself inadequate. Imogene Frank left without even trying, and Maximilian Grey got killed. Jean Kellier, long devoted to the cause and to the party itself, exited the party in a manner to suggest she simply floated away.

The bitterness of gall spilled into her mouth as she wrote the letter, and was just about to set it alight with a match stick when she decided to call Jean. Jean listened on the phone as Nora read the letter, and agreed with the move to resign. It was then that Jean asked what Nora plans to do with the money. "I don't know," Nora said, surprised that she had not given it much thought.

"You just can't leave it where it is indefinitely, I will want it out of there at some point. I allowed you to put it there until you're able to sort your mind out. You need not worry as to whether it's safe, but at some point, I want it out of there. That's my parents' original home and it's now mine. I definitely don't want it to be there forever."

Nora frowns as she ponders what to do with the cash. The thought of keeping it for herself has never entered her mind. She thinks of discussing it with Milton and Duane, but immediately dismisses the thought. The agreement is that they sever all contact, at least for now.

A horn blears and she finds herself in the middle of a lonely but well lit road. Startled, she jumps out of the way onto the sidewalk as a car slows down as it passes her from behind. "You mad!" a male voice shouts at her, and both men in the front erupt in laughter. "You should be in Bellevue!" she hears the voice again as the car picks up dust and speeds away.

Nora stops and wonders where she is, not recognizing the street she is on. She becomes aware of the beer bottle in her hand and disdainfully throws it onto the grassed curb in front of a house. She turns to go back, stops as she realizes she has no idea of the route she took, turns around, and resumes her walk. She has no idea where the road leads or ends, but concludes she is in a quiet, decent neighborhood. Like most homes in Kingston, all the houses are heavily grilled with steel bars. She feels lonely yet unafraid, and quickens her step.

Long moments later, she sees a busy intersection where cars zoom by. Quickening her pace, Nora's heart lifts a degree as she recognizes the intersection. She stands and watches the cars zip by on Lyons Road, surprised at the distance she has walked. The thought of the distance brings exhaustion, and she sits on the piazza at a haberdashery, holding her head in her hand.

Nora sits a good half an hour in that posture, then raises her head and, embarrassed, wipes her eyes, squinting to see through the haze of tears in the glaring street lights. She looks furtively to see if anyone notices her and is relieved that she is ignored by the few passersby. She stands on reluctant legs and ponders her next move. Her watch shows 8:35. Wincing at the thought of going home, she heads purposelessly up the road, not caring where it takes her. She glumly ponders the foolishness of leaving her car at home and wandering the streets of Kingston at night, but the regret is short lived. Soon she concentrates on her strides, watching her feet stretching in front, increasing her pace, as if to give meaning to her walking.

The sound hits her suddenly, so that she lifts her head in apparent puzzlement, trying to make sense of what she hears. She grates at the intrusion on her thoughts and looks to see where the noise comes from. The street lights are fewer and spread farther apart from each other. Her heart shudders when she recognizes that she has walked into a less busy, less intense location, with only the occasional car passing by.

She rounds a corner and sees the source of the disturbance, slightly relieved to see cars parked along the curb and signs of activity to the left of the road. The voice she hears is an aberration in the otherwise tranquil setting. She continues her walk, but is distractedly curious at the activities and stops to observe. A few hundred people are under a tent offering verbal response as the lights burn in tandem with the intensity of the speaker. "Amen" resounds as the congregation agrees with the speaker's imperatives. Nora listens fitfully and grows tired of standing, drawing closer as the commanding voice hits a high note before receding. The congregation claps and "Halleluiah" echoes around. She sits on a vacant chair at the back.

"Christianity is a religion of progression. Christianity does not stand still, it is dynamic, it has energy and direction. This is why even the conversion experience, the very beginning of the walk for the Christian, has several phases." Nora shuffles on the chair and ponders if she wants to listen to this, but her feet ache.

"Conversion consists of at least four distinct features – confession, repentance, reconciliation and restitution. In confession, the person admits he is a sinner and declares her misdeeds.

"Repentance is also critical to the conversion experience. Repentance is the first recorded message preached by Jesus. St. Mark tells us that Jesus went throughout Galilee preaching, 'The time has come, the kingdom of God is near. Repent and believe the Good News.' Repentance involves a deep sense of remorse or guilt for some wrong the person did. The individual blames himself for what he did. But repentance does not end there. Repentance involves a changing of the mind and heart. It is changing course or direction. Repentance is recognizing that the direction in which one is headed is wrong, or the road on which one is traveling is incorrect, and deciding instead to turn to the opposite direction or to move over to the right road. Repentance is a radical experience that leads to a radical change of life.

"But while confession and repentance are important to conversion, not many persons move to the other two phases of the conversion experience. Not many recognize the importance of reconciliation. Reconciliation is the repairing of a relationship that has gone sour, a relationship that has broken down. The person who becomes Christian is reconciled to God. But it is not the person who makes the move to be reconciled to God; it is God who makes the first move to be reconciled with the person. St. Paul tells us that God 'reconciled us to himself through Christ.'

"Reconciliation extends to relationships between persons – between Christian and Christian, and between Christians and others. Jesus once told his audience that if they brought a gift to the altar and remember that there is someone who has something against them, they were to 'First go and be reconciled to your brother; then come and offer your gift.' Sadly, we tend to forget that being reconciled with the person we hate and the person who hates us is important. The gift to the church is meaningless if we are not reconciled to each other, for reconciliation is important to being Christian."

The speaker's face gleams in the cool November night, his eyes burning with intensity.

"And the fourth stage of conversion is perhaps the one most neglected – that of restitution. Restitution is the payment of money as compensation for some loss or injury. It is what the courts order the guilty to pay as a fine. But restitution is also restoring something to its original state, back to what it was before. It is to give back that which has been taken, to return that which has been robbed and to restore to the person that which was lost.

"The biblical story that speaks most powerfully to this is the story of Zacchaeus. After having an encounter with Christ, Zacchaeus made the promise, 'Here and now I give half of my possessions to the poor, and if I have cheated anybody out of anything, I will pay back four times the amount.' Jesus said in response 'Today salvation has come to this house, because this man, too, is a son of Abraham. For the Son of Man came to seek and to save what was lost.'

"Restitution is part of the conversion experience, but it is often overlooked. How many persons, after having come to Christ, seek to repair the damage they did in their former life? How many persons seek to undo the bad or the evil they did before they came to Christ? Worse, how many Christians try as best they can to undo the wrong that they have done, even while a Christian? We often do and say the most terrible things that cause the deepest pain, and we fail to do the right thing by repairing the damage, by restoring that which has been lost. Zacchaeus stands as an example to us that restoring that which we have taken or repairing that which we have damaged or replacing that which we have destroyed is part of the conversion experience."

For the first time in two weeks, Nora is able to concentrate on only one thing at a time. The pathos of the speaker, and words that she has heard for the first time in her life, has her spellbound. She sits confused and ridicules herself for allowing a Christian to have this kind of effect on her. Angry at herself, she gets up and walks away, but stops at the sidewalk, unsure of what to do. Since leaving home several hours earlier, where she goes next suddenly matters and she thinks hard whether to retrace her steps or to continue walking up the road.

"Confession, repentance, restitution." The words echo in her ear. Confession? Jean Kellier agreed with her that this is the last thing she should do. "Neither to God nor man," she says to herself. Again she castigates herself. *God? That outmoded concept! Which intelligent person believes such crap*? Nora hisses her teeth in that peculiarly Jamaican way and heads up the road to continue her pointless journey.

"Some of you have been running away from God all your life," she hears the preacher say over the sound of a bustling car as it screeches past. She chuckles mockingly and continues her walk. She turns another corner with no streetlight to illumine the way and suddenly feels herself having no energy to go on. She stops, looks up at the dark sky, and as abruptly as the next set of screeching tires passing her, Nora bellows her lungs.

The eerie screech rings until her ears shudder and, gripping her stomach, she collapses on the sidewalk, her body convulsing with heaving sobs. She caves in on herself on the hard concrete, knees burrowing into the pavement. Curled in a fetal position, she retches unspoken words that come out only as wails.

She does not hear the hurried steps and only becomes aware of company when she overhears urgent whispering. Lifting her head, she glimpses shadowy shapes around her and is gripped with terror. She tries to get up and run, but is paralyzed. Then she hears a tentative voice, "Are you alright?" Someone with a flashlight turns it into her face. Mingled embarrassment, fear and terror have her burying her face to the pavement. The whispers grow more urgent and uncertain. Finally, after brief silence, she feels several pairs of hands lifting her.

"I'm fine, I'm fine," she tries to struggle against the firm grips but find herself only limp. She is led, she realizes, between two males, with a third trudging ahead with the flashlight. She notices the tent coming back into view and, her dazed ears adjusting to the sounds, hears the voice of the preacher trumpeting. Curious stares are cast her way as the three men lead her backstage. Offered a chair, she plods down and immediately curls herself into the fetal position with face in lap, resting in her palms. Her convulsing subsides to mild epileptic-type spasms.

Shuffling feet hurrying through the shaved grass underneath the tent arouses her. A gentle hand rests on her back, between the shoulders, and a female voice asks, "I'm a nurse. Are you alright?" Nora does not respond and the voice continues. "You were screaming. What happened?"

Nora raises her head to look into a plump round face partially camouflaged by a round hat pressed down too low over the eyes. "I – I'm fine. Nothing happened, I – I just thought I saw something moving in the dark." The eyes look at her searchingly before producing a glass of water. "Drink this, it should help to calm you down." Nora takes the glass reluctantly and is surprised at how thirsty she is. She finishes it and is offered another, which she quickly drinks until the glass is almost empty.

"You look tired."

"I'm fine really."

The plump nurse makes to say something then hesitates. "Do you want to come around to the front and sit with me?" She finally asks.

"No, no, I'm fine. I should really be going anyway."

"Not in this condition. Where do you live?" Nora hesitates, and does not answer. "Stay here. I'll check on you after the service" she says and, after looking with sympathy at Nora, insists, "Remember, don't leave," and then shuffles away.

Nora returns to the fetal position, and in her stupor, hears the preacher's voice.

"The Christian walk does not end with conversion. Conversion is merely the beginning, the starting point, the place where Christianity makes its beginning. There is a trek, a road on which each person travels, and that road heads in a particular direction and has a particular end. The walk of each is different but the terminus, the end is at a particular place at a particular point in time. That place and that time is judgment. If conversion is the beginning of the journey, then judgment is its end. Each person, including each Christian, faces judgment. Paul says 'We will all stand before God's judgment seat. Each of us will give an account of himself to God.' Peter said judgment begins with those who are part of the household of God.

"Judgment is no more, and no less than each person being asked to give an account of his life's journey. Revelation describes it as an opening of the books. 'And I saw the dead, great and small, standing before the throne, and books were opened. Another book was opened, which is the Book of Life. The dead were judged according to what they had done as recorded in the books... each person was judged according to what he had done.'

"Accountants and auditors should understand this language very well. The books of every major business are audited. Shareholders, those who own the business, as well as the government, expect to get a report as to how well the business did. But more importantly, shareholders and the government want to know if the managers and leaders fulfilled their obligations and did what they were supposed to do. It is all part of giving an account of how the business performed and how the managers did their job. Each time an audit is done, the business is being judged as to how well it did and if it did the right things.

"The same is required of each person. Our individual lives will be audited, and this is what judgment represents. Judgment is inescapable. Not even the grave, not even death is a barrier to this judgment. Jesus made this plain. 'A time is coming when all who are in their graves will hear his voice and come out – those who have done good will rise to live, and those who have done evil will rise to be condemned.'

"Judgment has as much to do with heaven as it is to do with hell, for judgment is calling us to give an account of our lives. The unbeliever will be judged for his rejection of Christ, and the believer will be judged as to how he lived his life in Christ."

Nora's daze takes shape as she feels herself sinking once more into a watery abyss. Her throat constricts and the urge to scream blankets her, but the tightness of her throat stifles her rather than gives her release.

"So each person has a journey to take, a journey that begins with conversion and ends in judgment. All persons, regardless of who we are, will, in the end, face judgment. The kind of judgment depends not only on the beginning of the journey, whether or not we are converted, but also on the walk itself.

"In the end, all the books will be opened, and we will be judged according to what are written in the books. When the auditor opens the pages to see what we have done, he will determine the verdict that is to be passed on our life's journey. Have we done well, or have we failed?

"Every one of us here tonight needs to examine ourselves. If you know that you are yet to be converted, it is time to come. You know deep in your heart that you have something to confess, you need to declare the wrong you did before God. You know you need to repent, you need to change the direction of your life from where you are going to the one Christ offers. You know you are alienated from God and man, and you need to be brought close to God. And you know you did some bad things, some really bad things in your life and you need to make restitution."

Nora grows uneasy under the onslaught of the preacher's words.

"Don't just sit there, come to Christ. Remember that at the end of all this there is judgment. This judgment is not so much a punishment for your misdeeds, but the consequence of life's choices and the kind of journey you take. The judgment is the result of the auditing of your life, or putting to the test what you did in your life.

"We are waiting for you. Come to Christ now."

The congregation erupts and Nora listens to what seems like an eternal round of clapping, singing, and shouting. Her mind wavers between the world of the tent and another world that tries to trap her in its numbness. She seethes between reverie and unrest. Her heart swells and contracts like a vice. She is vaguely aware of a deep pain that thumps in her chest and sharpens the closer it gets to the surface. She is near explosion when the boisterousness of the tent subsides.

The preacher's voice breaks in and she is surprised at how much closer he seems. She looks up, and her knees buckle two degrees when she realizes she is standing in front, facing the platform, surrounded by a dozen or so other persons. Nora's heart leaps higher in her chest and the urge to escape seizes her. Her mind moves but her feet remain planted. She lifts a leg but there is no motion. Fastened to the spot, she is dismayed that the preacher, tall, slightly angular with a straight, handsome face, is piercing her as he appeals to those in front to fully "surrender their life to Christ." She shifts her gaze to the right and becomes aware that the plump nurse with the round hat is standing next to her, nodding a smile at Nora while placing an arm around her.

Chapter ten

It is three weeks since Nora's life changed under the tent. Her heart skips a beat from joy, her happiness soaring to match the fresh brightness in her apartment. Colleagues comment how she glows, how the rest at home did her well. Some ask if she met someone, and a few times she almost said "Yes, Jesus," but stops her tongue from blurting it out.

On this late Tuesday evening, she lifts and replaces the phone twice before having the courage to dial Jean Kellier's number. She reads the tone in Jean's voice before asking.

"Remember you said that you now go to church? Tell me what that's been like for you."

Jean hesitates. "Where this question come from?"

"Jus curious. You were never a church person, so I wanted to know."

"I don't know," Nora is disappointed to hear what sounds like a flippant response. Jean hesitates once more. "I guess – I think – it's just a new phase of my life that fits." Nora's disappointment deepens. She decides to pry.

"But what was the experience like when you first decide to be a Christian?"

"Christian? I'm not sure I ever consciously decided to be a Christian. It jus sort of happens. In fact, I never really consider myself a Christian. I mean, I go to church and I guess that would mean that I'm a Christian in the eyes of most, but I never really thought of myself as a Christian really." The long pause at the other end increases the curiosity in Jean's mind. "Why are you asking all of this?"

Nora hesitates before venturing forth. "I had an experience a few weeks ago."

Jean is hesitant before exhaling "Oh?"

"I met Jesus!" Nora finally blurts out.

She is almost sure she hears a gasp over the line.

"Interesting," Jean tries hard to gauge her response.

"Yes, and it's the most wonderful experience I've had in my entire life."

"H – How did this happen?"

Nora's recount of the events takes several minutes, and Jean is silent at the end of the tale. She finally realizes she has to give some kind of response. "That's – that's great, I'm – I'm – happy for you," Jean tries to clear her throat as she speaks.

"Yes, yes, this is so amazing. All the burdens and all the weight just drained away."

"Good, good for you, I'm glad you're happy."

"I'm to be baptized this coming Sunday."

"You are?"

"Yes, I can't wait. It's like it can't come soon enough."

"Nice, nice," Jean offers and sinks into awkward silence.

"I wish you could come," Nora saves Jean from inarticulate quietness.

"It would be nice if I could."

"You sure you can't?"

"Tough weekend. Dr. Carpenter's girls are expected home for the weekend from boarding school."

"Oh."

"But it would've been nice to share in this wonderful experience." Jean clears her throat. "So, what – what do you plan to do about that other matter?"

For a moment Nora sits perplexed and Jean senses her confusion.

"You know – that other little thing that's at my house?"

"Oh, that." Nora sounds almost childish. "That's one of the things I wanted to talk to you about."

"OK."

"I've prayed long and hard about that."

"You did."

"I know I have to do something about it."

"Of course you do."

"After I'm baptized, I'm going to turn myself in with the money. In that way, I'll wipe the slate clean."

Jean catches her breath. "Is that so?"

"Yes, it's the only right thing to do."

"Really? So – what of the others who were involved? Are you going to turn them in too?"

Nora draws silent.

"I've thought about that too but I decided I shouldn't. I was the leader of the group. I'll take the full blame for it."

"How're you going to do that? They know that more than one person did it. They'll not stop until they get it out of you. They don't even know that a female was involved. They believe it was four men, three holdup men plus the driver."

"True, but, conscience wise, I can't just go on pretending I didn't do it."

"While you have an attack of conscience, remember that other peoples' lives and livelihood are at stake here. My name could certainly come up, may be even Dr. Carpenter's. You don't want to run the risk of messing up other peoples' lives." Jean takes on the strident voice of the principal as she speaks.

Nora goes dumb on the line.

"I'm not sure I can trust you to handle this matter properly. This is the very thing I've been afraid of. It becomes even more urgent for you to get the money out of my house as soon as possible."

A long pause ensues.

"Tell you what. I'm going to call Leland and tell him to get in touch with you. I'm simply going to tell him that I'm ready for the bag. I'm going to have him contact you and get the money out of there. Whatever you do with it after that is up to you. Just make sure my name or Dr. Carpenter's are not mentioned anywhere or anytime."

"I'm going to pray about it," Nora offers meekly.

"You do that. In the meantime, I've got to do what I've got to do." Jean hangs up without allowing Nora to respond.

Nora bites her fingernail and shakes her legs, causing the bag on her lap to vibrate slightly under her tight embrace. She flashes furtive glances at every sound, and is startled by the light patter, patter walk of the caretaker as he walks past her into Rev. Sydney Gooden's office. She hears the sounds of the Friday afternoon traffic as it builds toward the 4 p.m. peak hour.

Leland arrived at her apartment on Wednesday morning before she left for work, got the key for the safe from her, and was sitting in his car, waiting for her as she arrived from work that same afternoon. He got out of his car, brusquely gave her the bag with the money, and with a mere nod of the head, returned to his car and sped away. She stood at her gate and held onto the concrete column for balance. Overloaded with handbag, a chart and another small bag, the weight of the money bag cast her off balance. She tried to clear her head from the suddenness of what just happened and, catching herself, struggled to hurry into the apartment.

The money was a menace the entire night. She woke twice, the first from a sense that someone was in the room and grabbing the bag from under the bed, and the second time by a dream that she was being held up by two gunmen. The grimace of the one holding the gun to her head softened into Terrence's evil smile. His raucous laughter as he pulled the trigger snapped her out of sleep as she bolted up in bed, her heart thundering.

Nora operated in panic mode the entire day. Stuffing the bag in the closet, she imagined the police raiding her apartment to discover her crime. She kept a constant lookout, expecting at any time to see a police car driving to the school and asking for her. Returning home on Thursday, she drove past her house twice, trying to ascertain if any unfamiliar car or faces were around. She called Rev. Gooden as soon as she went in and told him she desperately needed to see him. "This evening is difficult," he said, "as I have two meetings running back to back before I go to a late night worship service. Is it something that can wait until tomorrow?"

Despite her manic state, Nora said, "Yes, sir, tomorrow will be fine."

"Good, you want to meet in the morning or in the afternoon?"

Calculating quickly that a morning meeting would disrupt her day, she said, "Afternoon is fine."

"Good, is four o'clock OK?"

Nora left school as soon as the bell sounded at 2:35 in the afternoon, headed straight home, stuffed the bag in the car trunk, covered it with a mat, and headed for the Boulevard Reformed Church.

Rev. Gooden arrives late, offers quick apologies and asks her to "Give me 15 minutes." When he summons her at 4:25, Nora walks with the bag clutched to her chest and sits on the wooden, padded chair to which he directed her. She smiles at him as he asks about her "New life in Christ" and how she has been doing.

As host pastor for the tent meetings, Rev. Gooden sat on the platform that night and noticed the distraught looking young woman who stood at the front. Her disheveled hair swirled around what appeared to be an intelligent face. Having long abandoned her afro, Nora's processed hair hung loosely around the sides of her face and Gooden wondered if the young woman was mentally ill. He was mildly surprised to discover, after she started baptismal classes, that she is a schoolteacher at one of Kingston's prominent high schools. Her eloquence, quick wit, and sharp mind left no doubt that she is highly intelligent. He began to regard her as one of the fine catches for the church.

An inadvertent glance at his watch thumps Nora's heart faster as she realizes that the moment has come. Without speaking, she rises from her chair and places the bag on his desk. A perplexed look crosses Rev. Gooden's face as Nora sits and says nothing. She holds down her head and averts her eyes.

Curious, the pastor gets up and, tentatively, as if expecting it to explode, he zips the bag open. His heart stops a beat when he looks in and, eyes wild with astonishment, drops involuntarily into his chair.

"W – What's this?"

"Remember the bank robbery some weeks ago?"

The pastor looks at her with alarm as his jaw slackens.

"That's the money."

He searches her face as she lifts her head to look directly at him. "How – how did you come by it?"

Nora smiles ruefully and looks up to the ceiling. "I – I – I was one of the bank robbers."

The pastor leans back in his chair so hard and suddenly that it goes off balance, and is kept from tipping over only because the chair's back braces against the wall. Rev. Gooden gathers himself and, with blustering lips, makes as if to speak but nothing comes out. He stares at her for long moments without speaking.

Nora breaks down.

Gooden sits confusedly before getting up and, looking suspiciously out the door of his office, bolts it before sitting in the chair next to Nora's. He places a tentative hand around her in an attempt to offer comfort, fighting his own discomfiture.

In her convulsed sobbing, Nora tries to relate the robbery and the events that led to it. Stammering and stuttering and slobbering, her words come out in sniffles and snuffles. Gooden tries to make sense of it, putting together the different pieces along with those he does not understand or what he may have missed.

When she is finally done, he waits for his mind to take shape before venturing to speak. Just when he is about to say something, Nora, in a surprisingly calm but trembling voice, relates the night of her appearance at the tent. Gooden listens with knitted brow, all the while looking at the floor in front of him and nodding his head.

Having absorbed her story, he leans back in his chair and stretches himself out before carrying his legs back under and in an upright position, his thighs parallel to the floor. He sits with a straight back and hangs his hands loosely between his legs. He sucks in a deep sigh.

He asks about the young men. Nora tells him she has had no contact with them since. Gooden furrows his brow. He asks who else knows. She tells him that, other than Jean Kellier, she has told no one. He wants to know how she is sure the others have not told anyone. She says she cannot say for sure, but she doubts they would. He wonders if she would want him to contact the boys, she looks at him in fear and says no.

"What do you want to do with the money?"

She hesitates, then says resolutely, "Give it back."

"How?"

"I don't know."

A long pause lingers as Gooden thinks while tapping his fingers. "How much money is it?"

"I haven't counted it through but the news reports say it's over seven hundred and fifty thousand."

Gooden peeks in the bag and sits back in his chair, swinging himself and the chair from side to side, deep fissures crossing his face.

"Leave it to me," he finally says. "I'll take care of it."

The baptism is held Sunday night, on a cool December evening. The fourteen baptismal candidates are lined up by age and gender; males followed by females, each beginning with the youngest till the eldest. There are five males, the youngest nine years old, the eldest a gentleman in his late sixties.

Of the nine females, Nora is fifth in line. Sister Harriot, the nurse with the round face who assisted her the night at the tent, stands nearby the baptismal pool, a wide smile on her face. She now calls Nora "my daughter" and constantly dotes over her. Sister Harriot's interest in Nora grew when she discovered that Nora has no close family in Kingston.

Nora shivers with the eleven year old who emerges from the pool as the little girl's hands shake and her teeth chatter. The female deacon, assisted by Sister Harriot, wraps a white sheet around the child and dispatches her quickly into the changing room.

At Nora's turn, she goes nervously down the steps into the water that reaches her just below the waist. Rev. Gooden grasps her clasped hands and recites the words, "Nora Campbell, on the profession of your faith in the Lord Jesus Christ, and your repentance toward God, I now baptize you into the name of the Father, the Son, and the Holy Spirit."

Nora holds her breath and waits for what seems a very long second. The sensation of being brought backwards into airlessness is quickly arrested by the buoyancy of the water. Soon, she is submerged. Fighting the urge to struggle against the firm grip of the pastor, she is brought up and is relieved that she is finally able to gasp for air. Weightlessness descends on her as she ascends the steps, and, even in her wet clothes, receives a huge hug from Sister Harriot who then proceeds to fussily place the white sheet around her. Nora shivers her way into the changing room.

Rev. Gooden gestures Nora into his office, pulling her away from the group that chatters among itself at the conclusion of the baptismal service. He locks the door securely behind them as each takes a seat, he at his desk, she in the very chair she sat just two days earlier. Without hesitation, yet speaking in hushed tones, Rev. Gooden hastily dispatches the subject at hand.

"Just to let you know what I did."

Nora's happiness is broken by anxiety and eagerness.

"I made an anonymous call to the bank late Friday, after you left, and told them where to find the money."

Nora looks at Gooden with eyes growing wider and rounder.

"Don't worry, I left it somewhere safe, and I called from a public phone box."

"Where did you leave it?" Nora cannot stifle her curiosity.

"You sure you want to know that?" He looks at her with grave, clenched lips pressed back against his teeth.

Nora stands. "Thank you."

"Don't mention it."

As she turns to leave, he interrupts her stride.

"You know, after our talk on Friday, I struggled as to whether I should turn you in."

Nora whips around and catches her breath.

"This may seem silly but the one thing that made the difference is that the security guard did not die. I'm not sure I could've done this if it was a case of murder. You may have wrecked his life but at least he's alive. He at least has a chance to make the best of what's left of it."

Nora bows her head and, with the dismissive tone of Rev. Gooden, walks sheepishly out the door.

Chapter eleven

More than one hundred young people travel from Kingston to the north coast the last Friday of April 1997 for their annual weekend retreat. As at previous retreats, the energy level remains at fever pitch throughout. The highly charged worship sessions are complemented with late night pranks of "soaping" and "polishing" hapless victims and an over exuberant "sports day" mid-Saturday afternoon.

Most of the group, who are in their mid and late teens, keeps the few twenty-somethings, and the even fewer thirty-somethings, such as Nora, breathless from the moment the two buses pull out of the churchyard late Friday evening. As one of the senior members of the group, and one of the leaders, Nora is exhausted by Sunday afternoon, and she worries slightly as to how much rest she will get before facing other teenagers the next day at school.

It's been seven years since Nora became a member at the Boulevard Reformed Church, and her life revolves around the church's youth ministry. When encouraged to join the Women's Guild, Nora frowns and gives the excuse that it's for "old ladies," a remark that puts her at odds with older church members.

Her advocacy on the behalf of the youth does not help either. Her efforts at urging the church to appoint at least one youth deacon no older than thirty is greeted with outrage each time she proposes the idea, which is every year during the annual members meeting.

The three years she served as youth fellowship president saw attendance moving from an average of fifteen at their Friday evening meetings to more than sixty. Boulevard quickly became the most well known and best organized youth group among Reformed churches in Kingston.

The church's youth gospel group "Angelic Voices" performs at barbecues, harvest festivals and concerts at other churches, most times accompanied by the "Angelic Dancers." In time, the youth ministry took full charge of the church's Christmas Cantata, lesser in importance only to the Easter Cantata and annual Church Barbecue.

Nora is already contemplating her bedtime several hours and almost one hundred miles hence when the last session at the retreat begins at 2 p.m. She slept only fitfully the past two nights, going to bed after midnight and rising before 5 a.m.

The band whips the energetic group into a frenzy for more than half an hour before Alexander Thompson, guest speaker for the weekend, winds up for his final charge. Nora wills herself to listen.

"The Bible has several examples of persons who, having come face to face with God's call on their life, try desperately to get out of it. This was the case with Moses. Hear him as he makes one excuse after another: 'Who am I that I should go to Pharaoh, and bring the Israelites out of Egypt? I have never been eloquent, neither in the past nor since you have spoken to your servant. I am slow of speech and tongue.'

"When God called Jeremiah, his response was, 'Ah, Sovereign Lord, I do not know how to speak; I am only a child.'

"But the most extreme case of someone refusing God's call is Jonah. It is at once humorous and fascinating. The Scriptures tell us that God said to Jonah, 'Go to the great city of Nineveh and preach against it, because its wickedness has come up before me.'

"Jonah's response was to run. 'Jonah ran away from the Lord and headed for Tarshish. He went down to Joppa, where he found a ship bound for that port. After paying the fare, he went aboard and sailed for Tarshish to flee from the Lord.'

"The call was too much for Jonah to bear, so he ran away. If we were to get a sense of the geography of the place, then we would understand Jonah's desperation. Jonah lived in Israel. He was told to go to Nineveh, which was seven hundred miles to the east of Israel. What did Jonah do? Jonah, instead of traveling east, decided to go to the farthest place west, two thousand miles away to

Tarshish. Jonah was prepared to travel two thousand miles over rough seas and treacherous territory in the opposite direction, than to travel seven hundred miles, a far less distance to Nineveh.

"You know what it's like? It's like God calling anyone of you here who lives in Jamaica to go to Cuba, ninety miles to the north of us, but you decide instead to go to Buenos Aires in Argentina, the southernmost country in South America, more than three thousand eight hundred miles away.

"Why would Jonah not want to go to Nineveh? It could be that Jonah was aware of the terrible reputation of the city. The prophet Nahum delivered a list of vitriolic tirade against the city: 'Woe to the city of blood, full of lies, full of plunder, never without victims! The crack of whips, the clatter of wheels, galloping horses and jolting chariots! Charging cavalry, flashing swords and glittering spears! Many casualties, piles of dead, bodies without number, people stumbling over the corpses – all because of the wanton lust of a harlot, alluring, the mistress of sorceries, who enslaved nations by her prostitution and peoples by her witchcraft.'

"Nineveh had a reputation for cruelty, corruption and evil. Perhaps Jonah was so much aware of its reputation he was scared to go there.

"Whatever the reason, Jonah did not want to go to Nineveh, so he ran. But as Jonah later discovered, you can run, but you can't hide. Jonah did not know the words of Psalm 139, or he did not take these words to heart, 'Where can I go from your Spirit? Where can I flee from your presence? If I go up to the heavens, you are there; if I make my bed in the depths, you are there. If I say, surely the darkness will hide me and the light become night around me, even the darkness will not be dark to you; the night will shine like the day, for darkness is as light to you.'"

Nora sits upright and listens more keenly. Thompson's face glistens with intensity, passion and perspiration.

"When God called Jonah, he was on top of the mountain, but in running from God, he ended up in the valley. Then in trying desperately to get further away from God, he ended up at the seaport, then on a ship, then finally, at the bottom of the sea. So long as Jonah kept running away from God, his life went downhill until he hit rock bottom. His life never started going back up again until he answered the call of God."

Nora looks around at someone who yelps a wail, and sees faces that are set spellbound. She struggles with her own tears.

"Some people have been running from God all their life. From they were young men or women they have been running away from God. Some have run from God so fast they're running straight into hell. They have no intention or desire to follow God. They have no intention or desire to do what God wants. I wonder if such a person is here, running from God to your own destruction."

Thompson pauses and surveys the audience, purposely walking up close to each person who sits in front, moving from one row to the next, impaling faces with his eyes.

"These persons know that God has been calling them. These individuals know that God has been speaking to them, but still they will not listen, still they will not heed."

He stands directly before Nora's row, to the left side, and, rolling his eyes and lifting his head, proclaims in the manner of an ecstatic prophet. "There's someone here whom the Lord has been calling to full time ministry, but you've been resisting the voice of God." He pauses, closes his eyes, inhales a deep breath, then Nora feels his eyes burning her when he looks at her with inflamed wildness.

"It's time you stop fighting God and come. If you don't accept God's call, your life will be like Jonah's. You'll keep on going downhill until you hit rock bottom."

An incongruous smile crosses the speaker's lips.

"You're worried as to whether you'll make it. You need not be scared, just be like Peter. Step out of the boat and walk by faith to Jesus. So long as you keep your eyes on Jesus, he'll keep you walking. You'll not sink, you'll not falter."

Seriousness snaps back on Thompson's lips and he speaks barely above a whisper. "It's time to stop running. It's time to stop hiding. It's time to answer 'yes.'"

Nora's quiet tears wash her resistance away.

Chapter twelve

"What is your name?" Nora fidgets from one leg to the next, trying to hide her annoyance at the silliness of the question.

"I say, what's your name?" Despite her best effort not to respond, Nora answers sarcastically. "Nora Campbell."

"Nora Campbell! What kind of a name is that?"

Nora ponders her next answer, trying to get the initiation leader, whom they are all told to address as High Priest, off her back. "It's the name my daddy gave me," and immediately pinches herself for giving such a lame answer.

"So you're a daddy's girl! You sure you ready for this? This is big people tings you come to deal with."

"Nora. What a name!" one voice shouts out.

"Give her another name!" a female voice shouts from the gawking audience.

"I know!" says the High Priest. "You're none other than the wicked Nero come back to life." Raucous laughter and applause greet the ridiculous pronouncement.

"Yes Nero," the female voice that suggests the name change joins in.

"This is wicked Nero who persecute and kill the Christians come back to life. You come to persecute us?" The High Priest gestures to the crowd of students. "Worse, he come back as a woman!" Loud cackles erupt and hoots go up.

"Yes, Nero!" the silly banter goes on around the hall.

Despite herself, Nora is annoyed and flustered. She promised herself to take charge of the situation but now finds herself swallowing hard and hoping she can maintain her composure.

"From now on you shall be known as Nero the persecutor. You know what happened to Nero?" asks the hooded High Priest, his eyes and nose peering through holes in the black cloth mask.

A silly, expectant silence wafts the room. "He committed suicide!" Laughter pierces the hall that doubles as cafeteria for students and faculty.

The group of robed students (the High Priest is the only one with a hood), draws menacingly close to Nora and the other new students, encircling them. The "grubs," or new students, instinctively pull closer to each other for support and protection.

Nora thought this "orientation" would be a cinch compared to the one she went through at the University of Jamaica, but the images of several horror flicks now play across her mind.

The rest of that first week at Jamaica School of Theology is a recurring ritual. Roused at 4:30 in the morning, huddled together for the three mile run to and from slave castle, and taken to the school's pig or chicken farm for "devotions." At the end of classes, round after round of "interviewing" and bantering until past midnight.

The first morning with the pigs was the most eventful and frightening. The stench hung heavily in the dense morning atmosphere and the disturbed pigs grunted disconsolately. Clement Fisher of the Turks and Caicos Islands was placed upfront. "You claim your name is Clement. That is too worthy a name for you. Clement was one of the great Fathers of the Church. How dare you claim to be Clement!" The High Priest shrills, this time dressed in military fatigues and with a broad floppy hat covering part of the hood. "If you're Clement, then preach. Preach to these hogs."

The frightened young man looked at the pigs and back at the group behind him, and attempted to run, but the pigpen in front, the large cotton tree to the right, and the crowd blocked his path.

"This is evil. You're all evil!" he started to wail, looking with desperation from the High Priest to the students to the pigs. "How could you? And you all say you're people of God!" Snorting from the group only deepened his desperation.

"I'm leaving! I cannot stay in this place. I'm going to pack my bags."

"Seems like this boy can't take the pressure," the High Priest counsels. "This place is for men and grown women, not for boys or little girls. You're right to want to leave if you can't take the pressure. Give him space everyone, let him go."

A path was opened for Clement, and he, holding back and halting, started to walk away slowly. Just when he seemed unsure as to what to do, with his head bowed in the opening dawn, the High Priest rescued him. "If you know how to get back without falling into Deadman's Sinkhole, you can go. The last person who fell in it got lost for a week. He almost got washed away by a heavy shower of rain."

Clement stopped in his tracks.

"Who else is brave enough to take on these hogs?" The High Priest asked. With no one volunteering, the group was herded back to the dorms on campus.

On this the last morning of that first week, Nora is told to preach the "final sermon of the week to the hogs." She, with great acumen begins:

"When Jesus cast the devils out of the mad demoniac, the devils sought permission to be embodied inside a herd of hogs nearby. Jesus granted the wish and all the pigs ran madly over a precipice, fell, and drowned in the lake."

Nora then turns to look squarely at the High Priest. "Ever since then, all mad demoniacs have been fascinated by hogs, and each morning gather at their pens, hoping the hogs would relieve them of the devils within them."

Chapter thirteen

Turbulence, uncertainty, doubt, and faith mark Nora's first two years at Jamaica School of Theology. In her first year, she struggled to conform to rules stricter than those she encountered at the University of Jamaica, and wrestled with the overtly male-dominated campus.

In the middle of her second year, Nora found solace in Womanist Theology. Her experience as the first female pastor for the Reformed Church, and one among only a few women at JST, closely aligns with the experiences of many black women in America. She gobbled Karen Baker-Fletcher and engaged in several heated exchanges with the librarian "For the poor quality and paucity of books on women and female issues on the shelves." She harangued her Contemporary Theology lecturer, Selvan Ranger, for "The course's deficiencies by excluding issues that affect women in general and women of color in particular."

Now in the middle of her third year, Nora is convinced, after her initial doubts and struggles, that she is doing the right thing. Becoming a pastor is the right decision.

But someone else has also captured her heart. She started to fall for Jason Peddy in her first year.

His Trinidadian accent keeps ringing in her ear. His singsong intonations and hearty laughter sweeps her away in waves of gentle emotions. For more than a year, she kept her admiration quiet. She grew ravenously jealous when he showed interest in a girl who occasionally visited campus to visit her brother, a Methodist trainee and Peddy's closest friend. When, after several months of not seeing her, and discreetly inquiring, she was relieved when told the young woman is on scholarship at a school in England.

Nora shared her desires with Janet Ffrench, one of only a few persons at JST she feels close kinship with.

"You sure you want to go there girl?"

"I can't help miself."

Janet gave her a cockeyed look. "You don't want to do this."

"I can't go on being dishones with myself. I like the guy. What am I to do about that? Continue to ignore it? That sure hasn't helped. I know. I been strugglin with this ting for nearly two years."

Janet allowed air to purse through her lips as she contemplated a response. She drew closer to Nora on the dimly lit corridor as they both sat on the concrete in the cool February breeze. She began in a voice barely above a whisper.

"You never heard the story of what happened to Angela Moulton?" Nora, in the semi-dark, shook an unknowing head.

"Well, Angela has become the paradigm for all women in this place."

"Who was Angela Moulton?" Nora began losing her patience.

"Angela was a student here about eight years ago, the first for the Episcopalians. She fell for this guy who is also Jamaican, but a Baptist." Janet hesitated and the inexplicably long pause caused Nora irritation, who involuntarily nudged a gentle elbow in Janet's side.

"Well, the church would have none of it."

"Which church, hers or his?"

"Both, but mostly hers."

"So what happened?" Nora asked the obvious.

"Simple. It is either they break up or be thrown out."

"You can't be serious."

"Think I'm not?"

"Damn," Nora involuntarily blurted out. A long silence followed.

"So what happened?" Nora asked again.

"They got married."

"They got married?"

"Uh-huh."

Nora was flabbergasted and waited for Janet to clarify. No clarification seemed to be forthcoming. This is one thing Nora hates about Janet; she turns everything into a mystery.

"So?" she insisted.

"Everyone eventually tried to compromise but it didn't work. The Episcopalians desperately tried to save face with their first female minister 'doing that to them.' It proved too complicated in the end, so she resigned before she was ordained."

"So where is she now?"

"Last I heard she was working with the national Adoption Agency."

"And he?"

"Still a pastor."

"That is so unfair! Why is it the woman who has to always pay the price?"

"Stupid question Nora. You know how it goes."

"The question is not stupid. It's this whole... thing that's stupid," Nora hovered before finding the right word.

"What thing?"

"How do you mean what thing? This! The whole 'stupidness' of us having to be at the mercy of what men say and men do and... and... and the whole setup. It's all so wrong."

Janet remained in knowing silence before breaking it. "You want to fight the system, you gotta be prepared to pay the price."

Nora offered a chuckle and a sigh. "Oh boy, got to take serious ting make joke." Another long silence followed. Then, as if drifted far off in thought, Nora confessed, "This still doesn't change how I feel bout Jason though." Glimpsing Janet looking at her through the corner of her eye, she continued, "If we could just do without feeling anything for anybody it would make life oh so much easier and simpler."

"So what are *you* going to do about it?" Janet deadened the weight in her voice.

Nora chuckled once more. "Do what we always say. Continue to take cold showers." Both ladies laugh at the familiar joke.

"Seriously though, I don't even know if there's anything sexual in this. It's just – it's just a connection. I feel a connection with him I've felt with nobody else. It's not the first guy I like. I've been involved with guys before. But this one – this what I feel is different."

"Your mind telling you it different."

Nora felt anger rising in her at Janet's retort. "Look, I never tell myself to like or love or whatever it is I feel for this guy. It jus happened. It jus did. It was the las ting on my mind. How could you suggest that I would contrive someting like this? I wouldn't."

"OK take it easy, take it easy. I never mean anyting by it." Janet looked a long look at her. "I jus don't want you to get hurt, or to set up yourself for some big heartache. Trus me, that's a whole big mess to clean up."

"I've cleaned up a few good messes in my time," Nora joined in absentmindedly.

"Anyting you want to tell me?" Janet grew inquisitive.

"Not anyting that would interest you," Nora cut her off.

"Oh, I hear you," came the sarcastic response.

That one year old conversation plays itself in Nora's mind as she sits beside Jason.

"Did I ever tell you that you have my brother's name?"

"I do? You never tell me that."

"There are some secrets I should keep to myself."

"There's nothing secret about that."

"Hello, you could have begun to think I'm some weirdo who wants to live with her brother by finding a substitute."

"That is a weird thought to have. Where did that come from?" And both laugh at each other.

The inevitability of the night's conversation weighs on both but neither seems anxious to begin talking about it. Nora penetrates one of the few visible stars with her gaze and hugs herself into Jason's arm, resting her chin on his shoulder. A slight shudder runs through her and she buries her face into his shoulder. He looks straight ahead, as if not noticing her desire to draw close to him, seeming to want to get into him. He barely flinches a look when she unburies her face and looks at him. She cannot see fully into his eyes so she stretches her neck to look into them. Failing to hold his long gaze in front, he looks down into her face. He is disappointed to see her eyes glisten with tears. He remains determined not to let feelings overpower him, hers or his. Rocking herself against him, Nora musters herself.

"We need to talk about this." Jason does not answer, but reverts to gazing in front, focusing on a fountain in the Kingston Park as light plays with the flowing water. The late Wednesday evening crowd is sparse with a few walkers and joggers passing their bench occasionally.

"How're we going to work this out?" She finally asks.

Jason hesitates to say what needs to be said. "What is there to work out? We always knew that this relationship has no future."

"Jason don't say that." The stab in her heart creases her face.

Jason refocuses on the fountain and wonders how the light changes from bright orange to red to green so effortlessly. He flings his head back and shakes it as if clearing it of fire. He eases up and in the process pushes Nora away from him.

"No one is to be blamed here, for I too came into this relationship with my eyes closed."

Anger mixes with Nora's hurt. "Don't patronize me Jason. What are you implying? That I deceived you into this?"

"That is precisely what I am not saying," he retorts exasperatedly, his Trinidadian accent deepening with his emotions, which he tries to keep in check.

"So what're you saying?"

"That we both made a mistake and we both knew it to be a mistake. From the get go we knew it wouldn't work."

"So what's this? You merely wanting a girl on your arm while you spend your time in Jamaica?"

"Nora, you're being totally unfair to me. Don't do this."

"Don't do what?"

He jumps to his feet and makes as if he is about to walk off, then turns and faces her. "What do you want me to say, huh? What do you really want me to say?"

"That you love me and that we're going to do our best to work this out."

"How? Please tell me how we're going to work this one out?"

"I don't know but we need to try. We must try," she starts to plead. She looks at him with fear and abandonment etched in her eyes.

Jason looks away and then walks up to her. "Are you going to come to Trinidad with me?"

"You know I can't do that."

"So, I am to stay in Jamaica just to be with you."

"What do you mean 'just to be with you?' What kind of a statement is that? Am I not worth you staying here?"

"And am I not worth you coming with me?"

Nora desperately seeks a retort. "But you're already here. You don't have to go."

Jason pauses, then, taking her hand, begins speaking as if to a child. "Nora, the same way you cannot just up and leave your church and your country, it is the same way I cannot just get up and leave *my* church and *my* country."

"But what of love, *my* love? Doesn't my love matter?"

"And what of commitment and loyalty? I've been committed to the church all my life. It's all I know. Unlike you."

"And what does that mean?"

"Nora, when did you join the church, eh? When? Just how many years? You had a life before church, you had a life outside of church. I never had a life outside the church. I know no other life but the church. This, the church, is my life."

"It can still be your life here."

"You just don't swap one family for another Nora. Gosh, you don't understand."

A drawn silence lingers.

"I have absolutely no intention of putting any kind of pressure on you."

"Well you are. You are Nora, and it is pressure I could do without."

"So I'm being selfish."

"You said it."

Jason is reluctant to sit beside Nora, and turning sideways from her, pushes his hands into his pockets. His eyes follow an imaginary beeline to both statues at the end of the park.

"So is this it?" Nora interrupts his wandering thoughts.

The low flowing sound of the fountain eats up the depressing silence.

"I guess it is," he gathers himself to finally say.

Chapter fourteen

Nora decides to run for president of the student body at the Jamaica School of Theology. It is now the year 2000.

A coalition of mainly final year students opposes "The wannabe High Priestess." Normally held by a male, there has been only one female president and high priest in the seminary's 84-year history, an occurrence that many see as an aberration.

Nora's campaign team consists of Janet Ffrench of the United Evangelical Church and Basil Newton, final year student and the only one of her fellow Reformed Church students to give her open, overt support. Three nights before the election is held the presidential candidates face each other in a debate.

Congregationalist and Guyanese Inshan Persaud is the first up to give his opening statement.

"Fellow students of this noble institution, we are part of a long tradition. We follow the footsteps of great leaders of the church who passed through these hallowed halls. We have an obligation to continue the tradition. I stand squarely in that tradition, and I'm proud to declare that I will continue to uphold the values and principles that govern the Jamaica School of Theology.

"I will continue to foster close relationships with faculty and the surrounding community. I intend to foster a stronger sense of community and close cooperation. This is the only way that this institution will continue to survive. A house divided against itself cannot stand. I live by that motto, and my prayer is that all of us live by it. If you vote for Inshan Persaud, you are voting for someone who knows the heart and soul of this place and pledge to keep it alive."

Persaud's supporters, about one-third of the gathering, whoop and yell. The other students sit or stand stone-faced.

Jeremy Flanders stands with his imposing tall frame, a six footer built like a football player. The Barbadian Methodist's sonorous voice resounds to the farthest corners of the spacious hall.

"My fellow students; my friends and colleagues; those with whom I've walked across the lawns and spent hours sharing fellowship over the past three years. Those of you who were here before, my seniors who leave this place in a matter of weeks, and those who came after; the friendship and collegiality we have is among the most precious things I cherish the most.

"I speak to you tonight as a friend. Not one who comes with grandiose plans, but one who, as your friend, knows what your needs and concerns are. I know your concerns, of your concern that the services delivered on this campus need to be improved.

"All of us, the ladies in particular, are concerned about security. The break-in two months ago is still fresh in our minds. We need to prevent that from happening again. I will insist that the administration improves security. The lone guard, or 'watchman' as they call him, who is largely untrained in matters of security, is far from sufficient. I will agitate for an electronic security system for the entire campus, but especially for the students' quarters.

"The cafeteria leaves much to be desired. You know how terrible the food is -." Flanders is interrupted by loud applause and banging on the cafeteria tables. He acknowledges the applause by pausing for effect.

"The concession agreement leaves much to be desired. We were not consulted, and the agreement did not bear our wishes and concerns in mind. We need better food." Less intense, but more erratic applause ensues.

"And what of the conditions of the classrooms? We need fans, better yet, we need air-conditioning. The desks are old and need to be replaced. In what era do we live? The computers in the lab are from a far gone era. Are we living in modern times? All these things need to be addressed.

"Vote for me, and you are sure to have a president who knows and understands your concerns and will make them known. I will do my best to ensure that your concerns are all properly addressed."

Loud applause and whistles echo from the walls as Flanders returns to his chair.

Expectant silence greets Nora as she approaches the podium. She reaches up to adjust the microphone down to her height. Having trouble with the adjustment, one male student rushes up to assist. The delay leads to awkward throat-clearing from the audience and an uneasy hush. She steadies herself and surveys the room, takes the slightest of deep breaths, and begins.

"I'm not here tonight to tell you that I'll change the world. I'm not here promising that I'll make things different or better. What I'm here to tell you however, is that I will try. I believe in trying to make things better, not leaving them the way they were.

"So yes, I'm proud of the history and tradition of our school. I'm proud of the great people who walked these halls and have been outstanding leaders within the Christian Church. This institution is as great as it is unique, drawing so many future leaders from almost every Caribbean country in almost all the major Christian denominations. I too am proud to be part of that legacy.

"But legacies are not immutable. We believe in and talk about an unchanging God. But what do we mean by that? Is it that God remains static? No, none of us believe that. When we say that God does not change, we mean that God is constant in love and compassion, that there is nothing we can do to let God stop loving us. We mean that the nature of God does not change.

"But such love and compassion is displayed and applied differently in different situations, and it is in that context that God does change. God dealt differently with Jonah as he dealt differently with Jeremiah. It's the same loving and compassionate God who acts differently in different contexts.

"What's more, our understanding of God and what God does change with time. There're things that were embraced in the past that many Christians and churches would not dare to embrace today, because our understanding of the nature and being of God has changed.

"It is within this context that I'd like for us to ponder the things about us that need to be challenged, and ultimately, change. We need to ponder the very nature of this institution, and what contribution we can make to bring change.

"I agree. The food is horrible. The facilities are not what they should be. And like all students, I too am concerned as to the poor security arrangements for the campus. But for me, we need to look beyond those things, as important as they are. Those have to do with our comfort, and while I for one moment do not suggest that our comfort is unimportant, there are other things, perhaps even more important that we need to put on the table.

"What of course content in our curriculum? What of failing to keep pace with developments in the various fields of theology, Christian Education, Pastoral Counseling and the like? What of the need to incorporate other courses into our program that better prepare us for ministry? What of outdated methodologies of teaching and instruction? What of what it means to be a pastor in today's world? What of the activities that we engage in, or do not engage in, that affect our formation as pastors?"

Nora pauses as she seeks eye contact with a few. "What of our long held prejudices that are perpetuated by the structures themselves? How can we include those in this place who have long felt excluded, those who belong to minority groups or who are of a minority persuasion? Is it too far beyond us to reach beyond ourselves, or rather, reach deep inside ourselves to recognize those things that need changing, and to make every attempt to change them?

"I'm simply asking you to join me so that we can at least make an attempt to make things different and to make things better, and not simply to leave things as they are."

A grudging applause follows Nora as she returns to take her place at the table beside the other two presidential candidates. Oral

Gifford, outgoing president and high priest, and the lone US Virgin Islander on campus, opens the floor for questions.

Tyrone Beecher of the Outreach Mission Church: "Miss Campbell. You listed a long menu of concerns, but what is missing is how to address them. It is good to know what you want, but how to get what you want is another matter entirely, and this is always more difficult than articulating the needs and concerns themselves. Could you suggest how you expect to address these concerns of yours?"

"First of all, they're not just my concerns, or rather, they should not only be my concerns. They should concern all of us, because each of these affects who we are as ministers of the Gospel much more than the menu in the kitchen or the temperature in our classrooms."

Nora is surprised at the applause that emanates from the right corner of the room and a few snickers directed at Flanders.

"I'm from a background that teaches me that each person has a role to play in both articulating and executing a vision. I prefer participatory democracy over representative democracy. Everyone is on an equal level, and each person has a stake in not only the outcome, but in being actively involved in the process that leads to the outcome. My hope is that we'll find a way to include all of us in determining the way forward rather than it being left up to just one or two or a few of us."

"But you still have not told us how you plan on ensuring that this participatory democracy work," Phil Pennington, a Pentecostal out of the Bahamas, asks.

"There are different ways. There are the usual: polls, surveys, feedback and so on. But for me the main thing is that we act together. Not just for us to use some means to find out what you think and how you feel, but for us to go beyond that and find ways so that we all may participate in achieving what we all agree on."

"This sounds like a lot of fluff to me. I hear air, what I want to hear is some substance. I want to hear concrete goals and definite means by which you want us to achieve those goals," Pennington counters.

"I'm surprised that those of us who regard dreams as fluff are even here. What is life if we cannot dream what should be and how things should be different? Aren't we all here because of that dream and that we can help to make the world and this life very different? My proposal is essentially a dream, because it will hardly be a reality for those of us who are here now; at the very least, those leaving at the end of this school year and who return for their final year next year will hardly benefit. But we need to do it for the benefit of those coming after us, those following in our footsteps. This is an important legacy that we would be leaving behind."

"I believe in a definite God who gives very clear and definite promises," Pennington retorts.

"True, but such definite promises are worked out in very definite lives in very definite situations through some very *definite* thinking." The right corner of the room again surprises Nora as it erupts in laughter and applause.

"I believe that this kind of exchange is best done in another forum. We want to stick to the issues of this election and I'm hoping that the questions and answers will bring further clarity to help those of us who will be voting," Gifford interrupts.

An unexpectedly long pause ensues after this. Gifford coaxes the group of students. "Don't we have questions for our other two candidates?"

Andrene Fairmount of the Holiness denomination and one of the quieter students among the 147 enrolled at JST, raises a hand.

"Miss Campbell –" Fairmount starts. Gifford makes a face and the audience bursts out laughing. Fairmount stands bemused at the laughter.

"It's not about you Miss Fairmount, it's that I was hoping that some question would be asked of our other two candidates."

"Well, my question is for Miss Campbell."

"Continue."

"Miss Campbell, you referred earlier to your background. Our information is that you've had a very colorful personal history. Am I to suppose that such personal history is what informs your own participation in these elections? You have such an interesting political past."

A long pause ensues while Nora sits perplexed.

"Was there a question in what you just said?" Nora finally asks.

"Yes," Fairmount shouts from where she had returned to her seat.

"I'm sorry but I didn't get the question."

"Perhaps you need to elaborate some more on the question Miss Fairmount," Gifford intervenes.

Andrene Fairmount returns to the microphone in the middle of the room, her slight figure lost in the ballooning oversized dress.

"Perhaps I should state the concern of my question. We're a Christian institution guided by Christian principles. I'm not sure I want to be led by someone who's primarily a politician, who has politics steeped in her blood. To me, this election is about you being who you are, a politician, and nothing else. This is an election, and being the politician you are – what you have always been – is just another opportunity to be part of the political hustings. In other words, you cannot help yourself because you're a politician pure and simple. The only difference here is that you're using the language of the church rather than the other language you're used to using. But it's all to the same end, no different. I'm not sure I'll be comfortable being led by someone such as you. I'm sorry, but I cannot vote for you."

A noticeable gasp, like a hiccup, precedes stunned silence.

Nora finds her hands trembling slightly as she takes the microphone. She looks up at the ceiling before breathing a response.

"Have I made mistakes in the past? Yes. Do I regret these mistakes? Certainly. Have I paid the price? I have. But which of us haven't? Isn't that what the whole story of redemption is all about? All of us who are imperfect are loved by a perfect God regardless?

That *was* my past. By raising those questions, you're seeking to make my past my present. My past is no longer my present.

"I will not say that I've not been shaped, or affected in some way by past experiences. Again I ask. Which of us have not been so affected or touched by our past? I'll never excuse the things I did that were wrong. But you want to know the truth? I've learned some good things from my past as well, and while I regret the mistakes of the past, I cannot say that I regret the past. God came into my life at a time when I needed God the most, and God changed me. That's all part of the experience that has made me who I am, and I thank God for that. I cannot, and will not explain my past away. But one thing I know, I experienced a change that is real and almost tangible to the touch, and this is why I'm here, this is why I'm at JST, and this is why I'm in this election."

A long pause follows, and then a lone hand clap starts to ring from the left corner of the room. It is Jason Peddy. He lifts himself from his chair. Others start to join him, until the entire room rises to its feet, clapping with gusto and emotion.

A trickle pours down Janet's face.

Chapter fifteen

Nora is disappointed with the character of the church. The building is dilapidated and seems to hang to one side. The ceiling has several holes, made of long worn-out lumber many generations old. Pews hang on for dear life, standing in place only from a force of habit, only because they are glued stubbornly to the spot, with no relief.

There is no organ, or rather, only the shell and few skeletal pieces of an old "pump" organ. Her inquiry is answered with, "From Sister Simpson died more than fifteen years ago we don't have nobody to play. So it jus lay there and we never bother to get another one." Her heart sinks and she wonders about the job at hand.

Things are only slightly better at the manse. The freshly painted walls mask cracks and lesions and the board floor creaks at the slightest movement, protesting at being disturbed. The two-burner gas stove stands idly to one side, unused to being used, and the kitchen counter and cupboards beg for proper alignment and straitening. Nora tests the water tap and has to be assisted by Deacon Francis who apologetically assists her, eventually taking out a small pair of pliers to get the tap turned.

She is the first pastor of the Mason Hill Reformed church in 13 years, the last pastor having spent only three, and he took over after the church was vacant for nine years. She guesses why nobody wants to come, or stay here. Deeply remote, high up in the hills, roads similar to tracks, crisscrossed several places by streams. It reminds her of home, except that whereas Danvers lies in a valley, Mason Hill lies perched on top of a mountain three thousand feet up, with nowhere else to go, but down. Nora is convinced that condemning her to here is an attempt to hasten her failure.

The community shares its weekend between the newer Seventh Day Adventist church, the Reformed church, and the equally melancholy-looking Prophecy church. She is the only pastor to live in the community as the other two churches are visited occasionally by others who have other, larger charges, in far larger, more developed communities.

Deacon Francis is polite but uneasy. As Senior Deacon, he raised mild objection to a woman pastor. While having strong reservations on having a woman as his pastor, he is more worried the embarrassment it causes other church members, whom he regards as much less enlightened than he is.

After the debacle of her first Sunday morning worship service, Deacon Francis tries tactically to steer Nora. "The people in this place don't always keep up wit the latest tings happening. We watch TV like everybody else, and we listen the news, but is not everyting all o we understan or accep." He takes the chance to look her in the eye as he speaks. "You might want to consider wearin a hat when you conduc worship."

"Hat? Deacon, I don't look good in those things. I never like how hat look on me and I don't like how it feel."

"Sometimes we have to forget good looks and do the tings that are right." He looks at her with a hint of anger. "You mus know that the whole community wonderin how you could ever be conductin worship and not cover your head. You don't see the amount o people who refuse to take the cup from you?"

"Deacon, I don't know. I don't know whether all these people are communicants or what."

"Well, I tellin you that them vex. Some decide aready that dem not takin no communion from no woman, an you not wearing a hat jus make everyting worse. You see any other woman in church witout a hat?"

Nora squinches her face and admits to herself that all she saw was a sea of white and black round and boxy hats, perched to the side or at the center of each head. She now wonders about everything that happened that morning. There was what now seems to be an unwillingness for the deacons to join her at the communion table; and what now looks to her to be an

101

unwillingness to sing the songs, though she had put it down to good old time country singing of "dragging" the hymns. Though the church was full, she now wonders at the level of participation and involvement by the congregation.

Since that talk with Deacon Francis, Sunday services are gradually becoming a drear, but the number of young people who turn out is a surprise. Apparently devoid of many social opportunities and activities, church is the one major outlet. Nora is relieved to discover an energized group of young people, several of whom attend high school twenty five miles away. To reach school on time, they leave at 4:30 in the morning, crossing the rivers bare feet before drying and replacing their shoes. The lucky ones who leave this early catch the "Grand Duke" bus in Craig River three miles away at 5:30 in the morning.

For Nora, Saturday evenings provide the greatest relief when, having done all their chores, the young people, sometimes as many as 30, gather in the small church for games and discussions and debates. Once she convinced a health aid worker, who lives halfway between Mason Hill and Craig River to speak on health topics relevant to young peoples' interest, and she once had the principal of the Craig River Primary School come give a talk on "Present and future opportunities for young people." But for the most part, she gives most of the "expert" talks and tries to lead the youth in a process of self-discovery of their needs, talents and gifts. A youth singing group is formed, as well as a drama club. An attempt at forming a dance group fails after older members of the congregation protest and with the unwillingness of the young people to offend their elders.

The community regards Nora as an oddity and curiosity. Despite the fact she does not particularly like Sunday mornings, the church is packed during the first several weeks of her arrival, with even some Seventh Day Adventists among the lot. They all "Want to hear how a woman preach, and to see her give Holy Communion."

When several of the young people, now heavily influenced by and in awe of Nora decide to get baptized, it becomes the biggest talk in the village. As baptism by immersion is the lone choice, and as none of the three churches have a baptistery, everyone waits with bated breath "To see the little woman-pastor baptize them big young people in the river." For now, before the baptism, Nora becomes the center of attraction and curiosity. None have ever seen, or heard, a female like her.

The sense of excitement generated among the youth is countered by the antagonism of others in the church. She is "Curry favoring up to the young people them" and "Doin tings in the church that is ungodly." Discussions on dating and relationships lead to sneers. "What kin o topic she discussin in God's house? Those tings not right." She comes here with her "Airy fairy ideas and causing pure problems in the church."

But there is another group to which Nora endears herself – the shut-ins, mainly the elderly who are too aged or infirm to attend worship. With little to do during the first several weeks, she does house calls. These visits last hours at a time. Sister DaCosta, her favorite, always has a ready tale.

"Mi dear chil it is so good to see you," the octogenarian, almost paralyzed by arthritis, often says. The last visit was the most moving.

"Tings an times change. I never tink I would live to see they make woman into pastor, but everyting happen in its own good time." She squints a look at Nora. "Dem givin you a hard time no true?" She chuckles when Nora gives her that look of acknowledgment. "Mi ol but mi no fool. I know what goin on.

"In my day, woman could not even say prayer in church much less preach. All woman could do in church was sing and teach the children them in Sunday School. You live in better times."

"I not sure bout that Sister DaCosta. From what I can see, tings not so different up here now from in your days."

"Some people still hol on to the pas. You can't afford to let them hol you back. They goin, you comin. They don't have much else to achieve or offer. Them always lookin back, you mus always look forward."

Nora looks with admiration at the shriveled eye lines set behind glasses that appear to be crumbling and pats her on the hand with a smile. The old woman draws a slight breath and, as Nora knows by now, gets herself ready to tell her tale.

"I remember when we use to have harves when I was a little girl." She gives a little girl's laugh as her mind gets transported back many decades. "My mother used to make a special frock for me and mi bigger sister and dress us up nice, nice. Mi father used to bring all o the provision them from the field – yam, chocho, cassava, dasheen, you name it. We would dress up the church on Friday or Satday with the tall banana trees and cane. The top o the cane would all touch the top o the ceiling.

"On Harves Sunday we always have a visitin preacher. Sunday evenin was the nices time." Sister DaCosta attempts a whoop and shakes her head as if she is standing in church as a seven year old. "We would all process with we little baskets singin 'Bringin in the sheaves.' Some carry cake that them mother bake, while some carry drops and grater cake and gizzada. Mos o we bring we provision from in the fiel. After the program done, we would all gather outside and sell the tings to the people in the village."

Sister DaCosta pauses. "Dis one time, we wait an wait an wait till dusk start to fall, an the visitin preacher would never come. It was supposed to be Deacon Hibbert from the Craig River Baptist Church. When we never see him, we decide to start the program. When the time come for the message, everybody sit down and look on them one another, even the big, big senior deacon. Then Miss Smellie – God bless her soul – a lady with the sweetes spirit you can ever fin, decide to give a little talk. That is what she call it, 'a little talk.' That is one of the bes sermon I ever hear preach inside Mason Hill Reformed church. I never forget it."

She nods her head, takes Nora's hand, and caresses it. "Don't mind mi dear. Don't mind. God know what him doin."

The baptismal procession to the river begins 5:30 in the morning from the church grounds. The nine youth are led upfront by Nora who wears a flowing white robe that hangs elegantly on her. The seven females are dressed in white, mainly white T shirt and white skirt, with white scarf covering their heads. The two young men are also in white T shirt and black pants.

The festive atmosphere gathers as others join the procession. It is the first baptism for Mason Hill Reformed Church in more than five years, and the most candidates at any given baptism in living memory. The singing and loud chatter attracts curious onlookers who peer through windows and doors from their dwellings, some hurriedly getting dressed to join the growing throng. By the time they arrive at the river, more than two hundred gawking pairs of eyes wait with unabated enthusiasm. Members of the church who are censorious of Nora are among the chief cheerleaders, each competing for the best vantage point at the river's edge. The villagers get in the way, wanting to have the best spot themselves. The cramped space on the damp, slippery surface causes a few to lose their footing and to hold unsteadily unto each other.

The singing is joyful.

At the cross at the cross where I first saw the light
And the burden of my heart rolled away
It was there by faith I received my sight
And now I am happy all the day

Nora, shorter than all the baptismal candidates except for one 12 year old girl, reads from the minister's manual, standing on the river bank, steadied by a foothold in a cleft between two rocks, her robe hanging at an angle. Her voice sounds above the descending hush as the expectant crowd waits with breaths held in check. Calling each by name, she asks for an affirmation of their faith:

"In presenting yourself for baptism, do you confess your faith in Jesus Christ as Savior and Lord?

"I do," they affirm.

"Do you promise to depend on God's grace to follow Christ and to serve him forever in the fellowship of his church?" Nora's voice echoes off the dim mid-December morning.

"I will," they promise.

Chatter erupts the moment she and Deacon Fray, the youngest deacon at age 56, descend into the water. Light pushing breaks out as those farthest back jostle closer to the front. The shuffling of feet leads to "plops" as some of the crowd decides the best view can be had from wading in the river. Nora looks around at the overeager mob with steely eyes and holds back an annoyed tongue. Pinched with nervous energy, she feels strangely energized. Not since August when she first began as pastor had she felt this light. The buzz subsides as she prepares to baptize the first candidate, a young man aged 17, slight of build with an elongated neck, and almost touching six feet in height.

"Jervis Gray, on your profession of faith in the Lord Jesus Christ, and your repentance toward God, I now baptize you in the name of the Father, and of the Son, and of the Holy Spirit."

A splash sounds in the water as one child, standing on the bank, is pushed over by an adult bystander at the same time that Nora and Deacon Fray immerse the youth. Struggling under their grip, they force Gray underneath the water's surface, eventually lifting and releasing him to gasp for air. The gasp of the crowd breaks out into singing.

> Goodbye world, I want to stay no longer with you
> Goodbye world, I want to stay no longer with you
> I've made up my mind to go God's way the rest of my life
> I've made up my mind to go God's way the rest of my life.

The eighth candidate, Joy Nesbeth, an ample young woman of 19, gingerly picks the spot on the bank to place her feet and unsteadily drifts into the gently running stream. She throws nervous glances and decides it is safer to stare into the brooding, uncertain sky, still midway between light and fresh dawn. Nora reaches up to grab her by the neck with her right hand while holding Nesbeth's trembling, clasping palms with her left hand.

Nora loses the sure footing she has and tries to steady herself. Deacon Fray takes his place on the other side, resting his hand on Nesbeth's shoulder.

"Joy Nesbeth, on the profession of your faith in the Lord Jesus Christ, and your repentance toward God, I now baptize you in the name of the Father, and of the Son and of the Holy Spirit." As both dunk the young woman, Nora loses her grip slightly and, with a deft move and strength that surprises even herself, catches Nesbeth while she is still half-submerged. Both Fray and Nora bring her up. Nesbeth's aunt, known to everyone as Miss Puncie, blurts out from the crowd, "Dip her again pastor." Laughter resounds as Nora and Deacon Fray submerge the frightened young woman once more.

Chapter sixteen

Nora has not taken vacation in two years. That mid-December baptism at the river turned her life into a constant stream of activities. Three other baptismal services are held in the two-year period, adding thirty new converts to the church, more than doubling its membership. It is unlike anything in living memory in any of Mason Hill's churches, except for the time, 25 years earlier, when the Seventh Day Adventists made a push into the community, poaching many of the families affiliated with the Prophecy and Reformed churches.

Nora finally gets her dance group going, doing it over the protests of conservatives in the congregation and skeptics throughout the village. The youth, who are the majority of the new converts, stage both Easter and Christmas pageants, the main social events in Mason Hill. The introduction of reggae Gospel into their performances outraged many, but Nora prevails. Some "pillars" of the church stop attending worship and other church activities. The youth, filled with new boldness and unfamiliar enthusiasm, do not care. They sing, dance, and stage skits.

She establishes an evening institute for those who did not attend, or fail to complete high school. Nora teaches three of the four subjects, history, English, and social studies. Mathematics is taught by Miss Brown, a teacher at the Craig River Primary School. The ostentatiously named Mason Hill Community Development Association, in addition to these classes, holds monthly town meetings in the church to discuss community concerns and plans to address them.

Repairing the church building has become a community effort. Deacon Francis, through donations from his children, who mostly live overseas, contributes most of the materials for the repairs. Church members and students of the institute work to restore the building and pews. In three months, the renovations are finished, complete with a fresh coat of paint.

The Rev. Basil Newton, who attended the Jamaica School of Theology with Nora, is invited to preach at the re-dedication service for the building. For modesty's sake, rather than staying at the manse, the usual courtesy extended to visiting pastors, he stays with Deacon Francis who, along with his wife and a mentally retarded daughter, lives in a four bedroom house.

A festive atmosphere pervades the Thursday evening worship service and concert. Most persons connected with the congregation take an early day off from school, work, or from their farms. Those who cook and serve and decorate take the entire day off. A hefty meal is prepared for all who attend, a makeshift kitchen constructed in the churchyard just for the occasion. Visitors from other churches outside of Mason Hill brave the journey up the hill to share in the celebration. The churchyard is cut and swept clean of all weeds, even some stones are removed. By 4 p.m., the half acre spread is filled to near capacity. A large tarpaulin hoisted onto a rectangular frame to catch the overflow swings easily in the gentle afternoon breeze.

The dedication ceremony begins with a gathering and the litany outside the front entrance:

As they enter the sanctuary, the prayer of dedication is offered by Basil Newton:

"Father, we thank you for the revelation of your love and mercy through our Lord Jesus Christ, and that you have made known to us the light of truth through your sacred Word. We thank you for all those whom you have called to join the remnant of the church in this community, and that your presence is made manifest in and through them. We are grateful that you have put it into the hearts of your people to erect this place of worship, and we thank you for those who were engaged in its refurbishing and repairs. But we also confess that we have not always been as faithful as we ought, or as loving as we should. Too often, we place our hands to the plow and, instead of looking forward, we look back. Like Lot's wife, we long for what we left behind rather than yearning for the things you have in store. We pray your forgiveness, and that you will also teach us to forgive one another. We now offer this building as our humble gift to you, not only that you may dwell here, for this is your house, but that this place will be an expression and a symbol of your love. We dedicate this building to you as a house of prayer for all who come here, and that it will be for many, a house of refuge. May it be a bright and shining light in this community and a faithful, authentic witness of our faith. We dedicate it as a place of worship, for the celebration of the sacraments, for the saving of our children and youth, and for the fellowship of your family here on earth. May your Spirit rest here among your people. May it welcome sinners to repentance, and may it be a gateway to heaven for many. May those here, as part of the church visible and invisible, take their place with the many hosts of heaven in your service. Amen."

The short ceremony is followed by festive choruses, hymn singing and hand clapping. Basil Newton stands at the new lectern and surveys the sea of mainly female hats.

"I have known your pastor over the past six years, and I can testify that she is a most remarkable woman. Rev. Campbell is a trailblazer in more ways than one. She is the first woman in our church to be trained for the ministry. Within a matter of a few weeks, she will become the first woman to be ordained as pastor within the Reformed Church in this country. She is blazing a path that other women will follow, and it is my hope that one or two of you young ladies here will follow in her footsteps.

"This event here today is testimony to the will, drive and determination of your pastor. She has proven that not only can she survive, but thrive. You are privileged to have someone such as her serving you."

Loud applause resounds from inside the building and from the outside. "Is good woman this!" a voice shouts through a window from outdoors. "We proud o her!" another declares. One man sitting at the front asserts, "Bes ting ever happn to Mason Hill!"

Most persons in the congregation join the applause.

After Newton's sermon, which lasts twenty five minutes, a concert is held, which includes performances from visiting churches, a number of which bring monetary gifts. The concert's fun is in "putting up" and "taking down" performers based on the audience's like or dislike of the item or performance.

Joy Nesbeth's first note is greeted with a shout from Brother Josephs, "One hundred dollars that she stop." Laughter breaks out. Miss Puncie, her aunt, gets up from her perch at the end of a pew. "My Joy can sing, two hundred dollars for her to sing again." Nesbeth smiles and starts straining at the opening notes. One young man gets up branding two one hundred dollar bills and one fifty dollar note. "Two hundred and fifty dollars for Miss Puncie to sing with Joy." The audience claps and laughs in delight.

The concert ends with a song from Peaches of the Living New Born Church of God in Greenfield, three miles down river. She gets the response all performers yearn for.

> Oh the blood that gives me strength, from day to day
> It will never lose its power
> For it reaches to the highest mountain
> And it flows to the lowest valley
> Oh the blood, that gives me strength
> From day to day
> It will never lose its power

Twenty and more members of the audience take out fifty dollar and one hundred dollar notes, move from among the pews, and proceed to surround Peaches, "fanning" the banknotes in a swaying motion in acknowledgment of her strong contralto that pierces the sanctuary. Each places the notes in the offering plate at the end of the performance.

The fifteen items on the program stretch into three hours of dancing, singing, and play acting. By the time the last person departs at 10:30 p.m., few are in the mood to make the long trek to work or school in the morning. Friday will be taken off as well.

Chapter seventeen

Ordination is a major event for the Reformed Church. Held at headquarters chapel in Kingston, it brings together church leaders, national dignitaries, members of the ordinands' congregations, their families, and friends.

Like all ordinands, Nora arrives in Kingston one week before the event, and stays with Janet Ffrench. Janet pastors a small United Evangelical Church congregation in Kingston's downtown area but lives uptown in a quiet, middleclass neighborhood. The very change of scenery makes Nora's breath come up short. Except for the time she attended Janet's ordination a year earlier, it's been two years since she has spent more than a day in Kingston. The bustling system whets her appetite as she remembers her days living in the Caribbean metropolis. She is reminded of how strong and driven the culture of the city is. Memory feeds her ardor for the place. She longs to see Jamaican plays at the Shack and just to stroll the business district that doubles as the main entertainment venue.

It is time to catch up with Janet. Without the benefit of telephone in Mason Hill, their contacts are largely through letters. Nora is relieved at last to have the time to talk with someone she feels close affinity with.

Tonight – the night before the ordination service – Nora, as she has done the previous nights of her stay, is hesitant to let Janet go to sleep. Both sit up in Janet's bed.

Nora breaks her contemplative silence.

"How was it during your ordination?"

"Nothing different. Jus like any other."

"You're fortunate you don't have the burden I have."

"That doesn't mean I have it any easier."

"I'm not saying you do, but you're fortunate not to be the first woman to be ordained in your church."

Janet thinks about it and shrugs. "I guess you're right."

"How many of you are there?"

"Jus twelve."

"Jus twelve! You say it like it's no big deal. An besides, your church has been doin this a long time."

Nora sulks glumly. "My two years have been rough." Nora sighs and shakes her head. "We should have just one year probation before ordination like your church does. They stretch ours out to two years. It makes life harder for all of us."

"You got to go with the flow."

"That's always your song. With that attitude, you'll have life much easier, but for me..." Nora trails off.

"Something you want to tell me?" Janet tries to read Nora's mind.

Nora looks to the ceiling and notices a round brown spot where it seems the roof leaks. She dismisses it and replaces it with the troubles of her mind. "You ever think about having a family?" She asks, as if addressing no one in particular.

"Family?" Janet grows thoughtful and hesitates. "Well, I guess like all women I would love to, but I don't let that bother me. I put my mind to other tings."

"Livin in Kingston is not so hard, but when you live in the bush where I live, way on top o the hill, all sort o thought come into your head," Nora chuckles at herself.

Janet shares the laugh and looks suspiciously at her friend.

Nora laughs at the look. "Don't worry, I don't do anyting... yet", she lets the last word linger before placing weight on it.

"You beginnin to scare me."

"Scare you? You don't hear nothin yet!"

"Tell me please, I'm in suspense," Janet mocks. "What, you 'burnin'?"

Nora laughs. "All that is part of it too."

"You miss Jason Peddy nuh true?"

Nora hugs the pillow. "Trus me, is nuff night I go to my bed wishin tings were different."

"It's normal to feel that way. But I tell myself this is something I knew could happen, so I prepare myself for it. I never chose this life for myself. God did. And I trus that God is doin what God knows best."

Nora hesitates a response. "It seems such an unfair burden though."

"It's not for me to question God. You beginnin to have doubts, the very night before your ordination?"

"Doubt? That's not it! I don't doubt this. I don't doubt my calling, if that is what you asking."

"So what is it?" Janet asks, clueless.

"I jus wish I was like any other normal woman an have a family."

"Nora, we all knew that when we went into this ting, we agree that some tings will have to be sacrificed."

"True, but…" Nora interrupts herself.

"Is having a man so important to you?"

"Man? The issue is not man. It's love, it's family, it's wholeness, it's… companionship. It's having someone to call your own. I don't want to grow old and be all alone."

"You still young."

"Girl, I'm thirty eight. How much chance you think I have to meet someone, especially way up in the bush on that mountaintop to the end of nowhere? People only go to Mason Hill because they have to go there. Those who are there it is because they have to be there or want to be there. It's not the place to plan or stake a future if your future is still far from being realized. What kind o life I goin have if I stay up in that place?"

"I thought things are going well."

"That's just it. Things are as good as they will ever get. There's nothing there, nothing. I like the scenery; I like the people, even though so many give me a hard time. But it's not the place to plan a future. And *I* want a future."

"You miss the excitement of your earlier life, nuh true?"

"I not sure if is excitement I miss. It's just that this is not what I had in mind for myself."

"May be it is what God has in mind for you," Janet retorts bitingly. "Tomorrow is ordination, and ordination is complete surrender to the church and to God. This kind of talk doesn't sound like someone just about to be ordained."

Nora falls silent. Janet feels guilty on being too hard and seeks to revive the conversation.

"So what is this talk about family?"

Nora sulks. "Nothing."

"So you vex with me now."

"Janet, You jus won't understan."

"Try me."

"So what have I been doin all this time?" She asks tartly.

"If I sounded insensitive, I'm sorry."

Nora still sulks.

"For what it is worth, I wished I had someone in my life. I would have loved to bear children of my own. But at 42, I don't hold out much hope of that happening."

"Suppose there was something you could do about it?"

"Do about it? How?"

"I'm just askin. Suppose there was something you could do about it?"

"Do about what?"

"Having children."

"Yes, *if* I was married."

"Who says that you have to get married?"

Janet flies off the bed and looks at Nora, mouth dropping open, eyes aghast, trying to speak but no words coming out. She is amazed that Nora is looking at her with the most serious of faces, fixing her with her gaze.

"Now, you're scaring me!"

Nora looks down glumly and idly at her hands, still hugging the pillow. She falls into long silence.

"Talk to me Nora, what goin on?"

"Nothin not goin on... yet," Again, she holds the last word before letting it fall like lead.

"So what goin happen that don't happen yet?"

Nora sinks a deep breath before bringing it back up. "I want to have a child," she says flatly.

"A child? You mean to adopt?"

"Adoption? Please!"

Janet, still standing, eases herself onto the edge of the bed as if afraid of sitting, but needing support.

Nora maintains a passive look on her face. "I've decided to have a child," she says with emphasis.

Janet finally collects herself. "And how're you going to have this done, may I ask?"

Nora maintains a vigilant silence that stretches an eternal minute.

"And when did you come up with this bright idea?" Janet coaxes.

"Six months ago."

"Six months! And how come I jus know this?"

"It was not something I felt I could share! And besides, it turns out I was right. Look at how you reactin?"

"Then how you expec me to respond? This is as way out and foolish as it can ever be."

"See, I knew it. You already jumping to conclusion and judging me."

"Judging you! Gosh Nora, you got to know that this is a silly idea. This whole thing sound like some fiction or something. I can't believe what I hearing. I know you have a radical bent but not this. Not this radical. Not this foolish!"

"So you callin me a fool."

"You're a fool if you go do something like this. What kind o friend would I be if I agree with someting like that?"

"So are you saying you could not be my friend if I were to do this?"

"Do you even hear yourself? Do you take what you're saying seriously? You have any idea what this is and what this could mean? How could you, Oh Nora how could you? First of all, it would mean that you would be in an illicit relationship. This is frowned on for even women who are not in the church, much less for us in the church, and we are pastors. Nora, we are pastors! Do you forget that? Have you forgotten what we are in the eyes of both God and man? Sheesh!"

Nora sits calmly and contemplates her hands, then returns her eyes to the small round brown spot in the ceiling.

"Who is it?" Janet coaxes once more. "Somebody I know?"

Nora looks bewildered, then smiles a smile that shows she finally gets the question. "There is no he."

"What do you mean there is no he? Is it some arbitrary person? I don't understan." Janet looks incomprehensibly at her friend.

"There is no he," Nora repeats with firmness.

Janet rolls an eye. "So what are we talking about here?"

"Artificial insemination."

"Pardon me?"

"Artificial insemination."

Janet goes into long silence as if allowing the latest piece of information to sink in.

"You're not serious."

"I am."

"You're not."

"I am."

Both drift into silence.

"If you're serious then you have an obligation not to go through with your ordination."

"Who's to stop me?"

"You're mad, you're stark raving mad."

"Perhaps I am, but I'm going through with it."

Janet is beside herself with puzzlement. "What, what would seize you to do something like this?

"How do you mean what would seize me? Am I not a woman like any other? And what rule would I be breaking, huh, what rule would I be breaking?"

"Jus about every rule in the book! Please tell me that you're only joking and are not serious."

"Do you see me laughing?"

"You know what you're doing? You're making life harder for every woman who considers ministry within the church. You're destroying everything that those before you have built, and you're destroying everything for those who're coming after."

"That's how you see it?"

"That is how I see it, and that is exactly what will happen."

"I don't agree."

"Well, you're fooling yourself."

"You're entitled to your own opinion."

"I guess I am," Janet answers hotly.

Nora sighs tiredly, as if a weight has been placed on her. "I did not come to this point lightly, so don't think I haven't thought about the possible consequences."

But Janet does not hear her. She slams the door as she storms out of the room.

Chapter eighteen

The ordination service is way into its second hour before the actual ordination takes place. All four ordinands – Nora, Basil Newton, Milton James, and Caswell Burton, sit on the platform, flanked by President Glenhope Peters and Vice President Oral Bailey, along with the preacher, James Andressen from Seattle in the United States.

All ministers within the Reformed Church and most leaders from other denominations are present. So are the Mayor of Kingston, the Chief Justice, and a cabinet member representing the Prime Minister, who tenders an apology for his absence. These take the prized seats at the historic national chapel, built in 1783, with its brick stone outer walls varying between dull red and dull burgundy, as weather and time take their toll.

The full throttle choir of singers from several congregations in Kingston gives a fulsome performance of Handel's *Messiah* and revels in Beethoven's *Ode to Joy*. The packed congregation buzzes.

The historic nature of this year's ordination is not lost on the organization. High anticipation awaits the first woman to be ordained to the Christian ministry and to be formally admitted to the office of pastor. Some media houses, grasping the significance of the occasion, send reporters. The National Religious Television and Radio Company provides live coverage.

Nora is relieved that her parents are present. Doubting their interest in the event, she made special arrangements for their transportation from Danvers, almost three hours away. They should not deny her this, she seethes privately. The driver, a past schoolmate of hers from high school, accepted Nora's plea to be her parents' chauffeur.

The act of ordination begins in earnest with the entire congregation repeating the Nicene Creed in unison:

"I believe in one God, the Father Almighty, Maker of heaven and earth, and of all things visible and invisible. And in one Lord Jesus Christ, the only begotten Son of God, begotten of the Father before all worlds; God of God, Light of Light, very God of very God; begotten, not made, being of one substance with the Father, by whom all things were made. Who, for us men and for our salvation, came down from heaven, and was incarnate by the Holy Spirit of the virgin Mary, and was made man; and was crucified also for us under Pontius Pilate; He suffered and was buried; and the third day He rose again, according to the Scriptures; and ascended into heaven, and sits on the right hand of the Father; and He shall come again, with glory, to judge the quick and the dead; whose kingdom shall have no end. And I believe in the Holy Ghost, the Lord and Giver of Life; who proceeds from the Father and the Son; who with the Father and the Son together is worshiped and glorified; who spoke by the prophets. And I believe one holy catholic and apostolic Church. I acknowledge one baptism for the remission of sins; and I look for the resurrection of the dead, and the life of the world to come. Amen. "

All four ordinands stand before Peters, clothed in his too loose black frock that cascades slightly backward. His too-thick glasses, glistening in the light, seem to send off a ray.

Peters addresses the congregation. "We are assembled in the Name of the Lord Jesus Christ in order that we may appoint Basil Newton, Milton James, Caswell Burton, and Nora Campbell to the office and work of the Christian Ministry.

"These four presented themselves to an Ordination Examining Committee who heard their statements of Christian experience, call to ministry, Christian doctrine and relationship to our denomination.

"After examination and deliberation the Committee affirmed their call of God to fulfill the duties of a minister of the gospel in accordance with New Testament practice.

We invite you to join with us in this Service of Ordination."

Turning sideways to the congregation to face the four, Peters issues the charge. "We exhort you to consider once more the sacredness of this office to which you are to be set apart, that with sincerity of purpose, integrity and holiness of life, and humble dependence upon God, you may fulfill the same, remembering that our Lord Jesus Christ said: 'If anyone would come after me, he must deny himself and take up his cross and follow me.'

"So also the Apostle Paul did say to young pastor Timothy: 'In the presence of God and of Christ Jesus... I give you this charge: Preach the Word; be prepared in season and out of season; correct, rebuke and encourage – with great patience and careful instruction. Do your best to present yourself to God as one approved, a workman who does not need to be ashamed and who correctly handles the word of truth.'

"And from the Apostle Peter we receive also this commission: 'Be shepherds of God's flock that is under your care, serving as overseers – not because you must, but because you are willing, as God wants you to be; not greedy for money, but eager to serve; not lording it over those entrusted to you, but being examples to the flock.'

"Do you believe that God is calling you to this ministry?"

"I do so believe," the four respond in unison.

"And now, in order that we may know your mind and purpose, you must make the declarations we put to you. Do you accept the Holy Scriptures as your authority for our faith?"

"I do so accept them."

"Will you be diligent in prayer and in reading the Holy Scripture?"

"Through God's help, I will."

"Will you proclaim the Gospel of Jesus Christ in season and out of season?"

"Through God's help, I will."

"Will you faithfully minister the sacraments of Christ?"

"Through God's help, I will."

"Will you, knowing yourself to be reconciled to God in Christ, strive to be an instrument of God's peace in the Church and in the world?"

"Through God's help, I will."

"Will you set a good example in your household, in the community, and among all people everywhere, following the way of Christ, so that you may be a pattern and example to Christ's people?"

"Through God's help, I will."

"Will you work with your fellow servants in the gospel for the sake of the kingdom of God?"

"Through God's help, I will."

"Will you depend on divine grace through the leading of the Holy Spirit, and to always stir up the gift of God that is in you?"

"Through God's help, I will."

While Nora, Basil Newton, Milton James, and Caswell Burton descend the steps from the platform to the front, all ministers within the Reformed Church surround them for the "laying on of hands." The congregation sings:

> Come, Holy Ghost, our hearts inspire,
> Let us Thine influence prove:
> Source of the old prophetic fire,
> Fountain of life and love.
>
> Come, Holy Ghost, for moved by Thee
> The prophets wrote and spoke;
> Unlock the truth, Thyself the key,
> Unseal the sacred book.
>
> Expand Thy wings, celestial Dove,
> Brood oer our nature's night;
> On our disordered spirits move,
> And let there now be light.

God, through Himself, we then shall know
If Thou within us shine,
And sound with all Thy saints below,
The depths of love divine.

The ordination prayer, led by Rev. John Chapman, is rendered with a practiced trembling voice, made solemn by years of experience. The old man stands as tall as his toes will take him, and pierces the large auditorium with a controlled shriek.

The robing is done with elaborate care and pomp, each having an invited family member or friend to assist. Milton James' aunt, with whom he grew up in the western end of the island, prissily walks up the center aisle and, with fastidious air, proceeds to robe the only one for whom she has ever truly cared. Caswell Burton, with strong middleclass roots and a deep history within the church, is assisted by both his lawyer mother and accountant father. Basil Newton's wife, both long married before he entered seminary, does the honors.

Nora wanted her father to do it, but thought better of it. She had hoped that one of her brothers would have attended, but neither could make it from Florida. She would never have considered her mother. A buzz goes up when Janet Ffrench rises from her seat and makes her way to the front, holding Nora's robe. The buzz develops into murmurs.

Janet is smarting from the quarrel the previous night and feels awkward and uncomfortable. This ordination ceremony is more elaborate than her church's and, despite herself, feels intimidated by the occasion. Her face stiffens when her eyes briefly meet Nora's and she averts her gaze. In stiff-jointed fashion, she proceeds to place the robe around Nora. Janet's unfriendly demeanor sodden the moment, but Nora immediately dismisses it and looks proudly at her colleagues and over at the mass of people staring back at them. Light bulbs flash in all directions.

Peters gathers himself in his frock and faces the four, giving each a Bible and in turn admonishing them, "Receive this book as a sign of the authority given you this day to speak God's word to his people. Build them up in his truth and serve them in his name."

Turning to the congregation, Peters announces in the strongest voice he can, "Ladies and gentlemen, I present to you your new pastors, the Rev. Basil Newton, the Rev. Caswell Burton, the Rev. Milton James," and with the slightest of pause, he ends, "And the Rev. Nora Campbell." The congregation bursts into applause, rising to its feet, shouts going up.

A little under an hour later Nora reaches across the aisle to her parents and invites them to join the procession as the service comes to a formal end. Shy, but with a slight hint of pride, both begin the walk beside their daughter.

By the time pictures and fellowship dinner are done it is near 8 p.m. Exhausted and relieved, Nora rides shotgun with Janet back to the United Evangelical manse. The silence thickens with the journey.

"Congratulations," Janet announces unexpectedly after a long ten minutes. Nora looks suspiciously across at her and decides to ignore the compliment. Her mind wanders to the ordination service and remembers warmly the smile offered by her father as he embraced her. She concludes that she has been wrong on how her parents feel about her being a pastor. She expected them to be lukewarm at best, and would have come only as a matter of courtesy.

She recalls with fondness the commendations of Mercel Pinto. "From one former high priest to another, congratulations." They reminisced briefly on her orientation week as a new student at the Jamaica School of Theology and laughed at the sermon she preached at the pigpen about "mad demoniacs gathering at the pigpens, hoping the hogs would relieve them of the devils within them."

"I was dying with laughter," he confessed. "If only you all could see me under that mask."

Pinto, who was in his final year and who was president of the student body when Nora entered JST, is one of the bright stars in the church and sits on the national council, one of the few pastors to do so within such a short time after leaving seminary. They developed a reasonably close friendship during the one year they had together as seminary students. It was he who initially convinced Nora that she had it in her to become president and high priest, a thought she initially dismissed but took up only after she and Jason Peddy broke off their relationship, two years after Pinto's advice. For her, it was a welcome distraction rather than a conviction to serve. The motivation to get over Peddy and move beyond her broken heart led to such passion for the student association that it threatened her own academic performance.

There was much confrontation. The student body boycotted meals for a week, forcing the college to renegotiate the contract it had with the concessionaires. There was marked improvement in meals after that. The students delivered an 80-page document proposing changes in curriculum, courses, and teaching methodology that resulted in the board forming a committee to review the academic program at the school. The academic dean resigned within six months and was replaced by a senior lecturer at the University of Jamaica who was seconded to the seminary. The work-study program, merely tokenism, was expanded. Nora was less successful in having electronic security surveillance on campus due to what the board said was inadequate funds, but extra patrols were done at night by a security company. For the first time, the students held Culturama, a week-long presentation of fashion, food, festival and music to celebrate the cultural diversity of students from the different Caribbean countries. At the end of her tenure, the students were in the process of putting together a proposal for the seminary to construct cottages to accommodate the families of married students.

A stifled cough brings Nora back to the present. Janet holds one hand to her mouth while negotiating a turn with the other. She makes the first turn that takes them off Spring Road, not far from Janet's home. Nora is unhappy with the poisoned atmosphere.

"It was good to see so many people we've not seen for such a long time," she tries to make conversation. Janet does not answer and makes as if she is concentrating on her driving.

"Thanks for the compliment."

"Pardon me?"

"You said 'congratulations' earlier."

"Oh," Janet answers distractedly.

"Unless it was not meant as a compliment," Nora notes, and immediately regrets not just the statement but the tone. Janet gives her a quizzical look.

"Take it as you see fit," she retorts.

"What does that mean?"

"Jus as I said. Take it as you see it."

"So you're being sarcastic then."

"Take it as you see fit."

"You know what, let me out right here!"

"Gladly!" and Janet screeches the car to a break-chugging stop.

Nora sits icily, and then whips around facing Janet. "What is it with you?"

"What is it with me? Me! Am I the one who has a problem here?"

"You sure behaving as if you have a big problem."

Janet's lips twist into an S and tremble to release pent up fury.

"That's the greatest display of hypocrisy I've seen in my entire life. You stood up there making vows you know in your heart you have no intention of keeping. And worse, you've included me in this entire charade!"

"You're speaking on things you know nothing about."

"And on top of that you're now calling me a fool! You're the most disgustingly selfish, narcissistic person –"

"There you go judging me again."

"You think only about yourself and what you want, and you absolutely do not care the effect or impact what you do have on others. It doesn't matter if the whole world comes tumbling down around you so long as you get your way."

"So now the truth is coming out! You obviously felt this way a long time but you just get the courage to say it now."

Janet is flabbergasted and looks at Nora with jaws set on loose springs. She restarts the car and looks ahead stiffly as she moves off jerkily. The car reaches an unnatural speed for the short, narrow driveways and, despite herself, Nora holds onto the inside door handle to brace herself. She is relieved when Janet reaches her gate safely, with a screech. Janet bounds out, opens the gate to the house, drives through, gets out, locks the gate, and then proceeds to open the grille that leads to the verandah. She leaves Nora sitting in the car, the grille ajar and the front door pushed up, but unlocked.

Nora remains seated in the car for a long fifteen minutes with churning thoughts. She is undecided as to what to do, thinking fleetingly of leaving to go to a hotel, but thinking better of it. It is too late into the night to experiment. She struggles out the door and makes sure all the car doors are locked, including her own car which is parked to the right of the house on the lawn, fastens the padlock on the grille, turns the knob on the front door and secures the deadbolt.

She hesitates, stopping herself after two attempts to knock on the door to Janet's room. She finally pushes the door open. Janet turns away upon seeing her. Nora walks up and sits on the bed.

"I need to explain everything to you."

Chapter nineteen

Nora sits in the car and wipes pouring sweat, the air condition not doing much good. A colleague walks by her car on his way into the headquarters building. She counts and tries to identify the cars and surmises that eight of the committee members are present. That means two are absent.

She pushes the door and steps out of the vehicle, her knees buckling. Nora puts it down to the weight of her bag with too many files forced into it. She wipes the sweat and steps toward the short flight of stairs. The buzzer rings as she stands at the door, cuing her to push the door and enter. A clerk gives her a reluctant nod as she passes. Another turns away to look at her blank computer screen. The secretary forces a half smile and asks her to sit in the waiting room. The committee will call her when it's ready, the secretary explains. She sits and nervously picks up a journal on the small table next to her chair and pretends to read.

Twenty minutes pass by and the secretary disturbs her troubling thoughts. "They're now ready for you Rev. Campbell."

Nora stands, tries to look determined, and heads for the conference room. The first time that she sat before a committee of the church flashes through her mind. That was eight years ago when she was interviewed upon her application to be trained for the Christian ministry. Two of the hostile faces in that meeting are present at this one. She suspects that neither wanted her accepted because of her gender and communist past, and imagines that none still wants her.

The all-male committee stands in mocked reverence as she enters the room. The president gestures to the chair at a separate table in the center facing the group.

"Rev. Campbell, we're happy that you've decided to meet us, especially at such short notice," the president intones.

"It's my pleasure to be here sir." Nora is just as mocking in her courtesy.

"We suspect you know why you're here."

"The purpose of our meeting has not been properly explained to me sir."

"We'll get right to it shortly. But first let me say that we're all here to learn from each other."

Nora looks at the bespectacled Rev. Glenhope Peters and decides that he is a kind and warm-hearted gentleman. He wears a permanent question mark across his forehead above his thick spectacles that gives him the look of a deep ponderer, perhaps much like a mythical Greek philosopher. He has never shown enthusiasm for female pastors, but she has never detected hostility either.

She weighs the committee members and concludes that at best she can count on the kind understanding of at most two. One is Rev. Mercel Pinto, her senior in college, one of the bright young minds in the church, who is also a friendly acquaintance.

Her other possible supporter is Rev. Jeffrey East. He is one of the more progressive thinkers in the church and has a mind and tongue feared by even the most senior clergy.

She glances at Rev. Harvey Johnson, hardnosed and uncompromising. He was a vice president of the church when her application for training was considered, and is a strong conservative voice. Pug-nosed, he suggests pit-bull fierceness and his opposition to granting clergy status to women is well known. It has been whispered he was religious advisor to the political Leader of the Opposition in the 1970s.

She does not know what to make of Rev. Neville Pusey, lecturer at Jamaica School of Theology. He wears a confident smile etched deep along his jaw lines. She remembers falling asleep a few times in his classes, and he seemed completely at sea as to what to make of the female presence on the mostly male campus of JST. He now seems over-prepared for retirement.

Rev. Samuel Henlon looks over his glasses at Nora with a half sneer. He grilled her hard in that committee meeting eight years earlier, suggesting that her political activism would be a constant distraction to her life as a pastor. He questioned whether her views and past actions were consistent with the teachings of Christ, and whether she had repented of such views and actions. She never felt she convinced him then, and shuffles uneasily in her chair at his stare now.

Rev. Noel Garrick is a firebrand. Highly popular, his rousing sermons make national headlines. It does not hurt that he pastors the Good Shepherd Church in the heart of inner city Kingston and lambasts all whom he believes have failed the poor. Nora admits to liking him too, and thinks he would have been an outstanding leader if only he were brighter.

Rev. John Chapman is the oldest person in the room. An elder statesman in the Church, she believes he has overstayed his time, but others value him for his wisdom. He served three separate terms as president and sits on most of the major committees of the denomination. His more prominent limp and deepened fissures in the face suggest ill health.

"By the way, Revs. Smith and Cole have apologized for their absence," President Peters says in a voice distracted by a paper he holds in his hand. Nora knows these two gentlemen well. Smith is all the way in Montego Bay and is seen as a maverick. He once urged the church in a sermon he preached during the national conference to accept those who live in common law unions and who are not legally married into its membership. Previously seen as having a bright future in the church, his star has dimmed considerably since that sermon a few years back. Cole is another of the younger ministers but straddles the fence on most issues. Nora feels he tries too hard to make an impression. She now wishes both men were here.

"Rev. Campbell, certain information have come to us that have created some level of disquiet. We want to know if there's any truth to it and get some clarification from you."

The eight men sit and stare at Nora, awaiting a response. She puzzles a look as if she is not fully aware of the subject.

"I'm sorry I did not get exactly what you were saying." A few shuffle uneasily in their chair while several clear their throat.

Jeffrey East decides to take the lead. "Miss Campbell, our information is that you're actively pursuing having a child. Is that correct?"

"What I'm most curious about gentlemen is how you came by this information, assuming it's correct." She decided before the meeting to play hardball. There are several more shuffles in the chairs.

"We understand this is a very sensitive subject and we do not presume to pass judgment. We just need clarification," East continues.

"Clarification on what, sir?"

"As to whether you, as one of our ordained ministers who remain unmarried, are pursuing the course of having a child," Henlon chimes in.

"But sir, whatever I'm doing, if I'm doing anything, is totally a private matter."

"How can this be a private matter when you were publicly ordained to the Christian ministry?" Chapman asks.

"I'm sure, sirs, that no other female has ever been brought before this committee, or any other committee of the Reformed Christian Church, for what they do with their own bodies or in private."

"You're missing the point," declares Pusey.

"Perhaps I'm missing it because there's no point." A few hostile glances are thrown Nora's way.

"Rev. Campbell, we did not call you here for a fist fight. We simply want clarification on a matter that has become a subject of concern," Peters tries to steady the conversation.

"Concern to who sir?"

"Mr. President, I see that this is turning out to be a waste of time," East declares. Nora does a rewind in her mind. She had not planned on isolating the little support she may have on the committee. She looks down on the table, takes a deep breath, and begins what she hopes to be the best diplomatic response.

"I've been exploring the subject of artificial insemination. It's been a matter of interest to me for some time. It's been so because our church, as most churches are, is filled with many single women, a number of whom have expressed to me a desire to have families. It's in an effort to help them to make choices that the subject has become an interest."

"So are you saying that this is mere research you're doing?" Peters asks.

"Not exactly. As a single woman myself, I find that I've been identifying with these other women in both their singleness and in their desire to be mothers. It's not an easy and simple subject as it may seem. A number of our women feel cheated. They're in the church, there are few eligible men in the church, yet they're told not to marry anyone outside the church. Their desire for families and especially for children is not any less than for other women. It's the same, sometimes it is stronger. They feel trapped, and I just think that, if there are alternatives, then such alternatives should be explored."

"So?" Chapman asks.

"So I believe it's a subject that somebody should look at, and that's what I've been doing."

A brief silence hovers in the room.

"So are you denying that you're trying to have a child?" Garrick asks.

Nora takes a deep breath. "No, I'm not denying it." Several quick glances are exchanged and Henlon and Johnson sit taller in their chairs. Chapman eases his frail frame a little higher. The lenses on Peters' glasses seem to grow wider with his eyes.

Peters butts in before Henlon could take his shot. "Don't you think it would've been wise to have sought counsel before you did this?"

"I did seek counsel, from friends, but I consider it to be essentially a private matter."

"Are any of these friends colleagues in the ministry?"

Nora looks at her hands resting on the table. She desperately wants to remove them and place them under the table but believes this would be a sign of weakness. "Yes they are. Some are of our church; others are not of our church." The committee exchanges furtive glances.

"What would ever possess you to do such a thing?" Chapman asks in dismay.

Nora smiles and tries to control the twitching of her nose. "Well, my exploration convinced me that, though some questions are yet to be answered, there's nothing essentially wrong with the procedure."

"You seem to misunderstand that the question or our concern is with the procedure. There are much broader issues at work here. Surely you must realize that," East says.

"I have thought about those, yes."

"You did? Then why in the name of God would you try to have a child if you thought through the implications?" Johnson interrupts.

"Because mostly I believe that the rules that are drawn up were made by men and are being enforced by men to the detriment of women."

"You do not possibly believe that do you?" queried Garrick.

"Yes I do."

"And in the case of the church disagreeing with a single person – man or woman – having a child, especially as a Christian, is a rule made up by men to enslave women?" Johnson shots back.

"Let us not get drawn into the wrong discussion here," Mercel Pinto speaks for the first time. He looks at her and she detects pain in his eyes. *This is not good*, she thinks to herself. "Miss Campbell, in your 'research,' you must have at least read some of the debate surrounding this very controversial matter of artificial insemination. And you must have considered that, for us as a church, this is a profoundly complex issue that cannot be dismissed as simply a private matter done by one who is a public figure in the church."

"Yes, I've read much of the debate."

"And you must be aware that there are very serious ethical questions involved."

"Yes, I've thought about those."

"And you must be aware that this is a matter that members of our own church will eventually expect us to take a stance on, whether we wish to do so yes or no."

"I'm aware that that is a possibility."

"So your argument that this is essentially a private matter is nonsense," Pinto closes with a daggered-tongue.

Nora sits quietly. There goes her one other possible support on the committee.

"Mr. President, may I lay out what I consider the issues involved here?"

"Go on, Brother Pinto."

"The first matter, Miss Campbell, is you getting pregnant, regardless of the method. You're a single woman who's a leader in the church, an *ordained* minister in the church. This poses possible severe and far reaching consequences. The matter of your singleness poses a problem if you were to become pregnant. Everything concerning our understanding of what family is comes into question.

"The second matter has to do with the child and the possible problems faced by the child in his or her upbringing. As this is largely an unknown experience in our society, it is difficult to calculate the possible risks involved in raring a child in such an environment."

"And if I may butt in here," East interrupts. "A question is who the father is and the role, if any, that the father plays in the life of the child."

All sixteen eyes focus on Nora, all seem to be getting bigger. She clears her throat and starts to stutter a response. Jeffrey East is anxious to make his point.

"Mr. President, since it appears that Miss Campbell is having trouble understanding the issues may I venture into the debate on the matter a bit further?"

"Yes Brother East."

"We in the church have taught for centuries that the place to raise a child is within a marital union. We who preside at wedding ceremonies, and I'm sure Miss Campbell does, often repeat the words that marriage is for the 'increase of humankind.' That's a simple statement that we believe marriage to be the best environment in which to have children. This is so despite the fact that the church has, in the past, been sensitive to cultural or social realities that dictate otherwise. But it is an ideal that we dare not lose. The statistics show, both here in Jamaica and other countries that children born and raised in marital unions are likely to have a more stable upbringing than children who are not raised in a family where the parents are married.

"Added to all this is the lack of commitment on the part of the sperm donor. We do not know what Miss Campbell's plans are, but in most instances, the sperm donor remains anonymous and never becomes part of the child's life. The question of the responsibility of the father remains unanswered. This person, this donor, is no more than a 'sperm salesman' who will have no responsibility for his own biological offspring. Sir, can you imagine us, the church, condoning that?"

"Mr. President," Nora interrupts, "I'm impressed by the knowledge of the committee on the subject, but all that have been said are mere presumptions. I know that I can raise a child; a wholesome, well adjusted child, even without a father. And why is it assumed that there won't be a father? Don't we all say that the church has many fathers?

"And this matter of family. Is not the church a family? I can assure you that this child of mine, if I were to have a child, would be a child of the church more than the children of some of my own male colleagues."

"Miss Campbell, your own assertions are bordering on rudeness," Henlon says, trying to hold back a shout.

"Mr. President, if my statements are construed as rude, I apologize. But you must understand that much of the debate on the issue is all based on unproven theories. Many of the fears expressed are unrealized fears. There's no evidence that children born of artificial insemination are less socially adjustable or less psychologically stable than other children. And it is not marriage itself that determines the emotional or psychological health of children. God knows that there are many dysfunctional homes where both parents are married and where the children are emotionally damaged and psychologically scarred. Most of my friends grew up in a single-parent household. Some of them do not know their father, or have no relationship with their father. Yet most are socially well adjusted, responsible men and women.

"What matters is whether children grow up in a loving home, whether they are nurtured in a loving environment. That, for me, is what makes the difference. It is not trying to attain some ideal that is impossible even for us in the church."

"So a loving home where both parents are married is an impossible ideal," Garrick huffs. "Have I been living a fantasy for the past twenty two years as a pastor?" he asks.

Chapman squints his eyes as he speaks. "Much of this is all new to me. Miss Campbell may very well be right. Growing up in a home where one's parents are unmarried or where even one is absent does not result in automatic dysfunctional behavior. I rather suspect that some of us who are pastors grew up with one parent or with neither as grandmothers have reared many of Jamaica's children.

"But Miss Campbell is asking us, the church, to give sanction to something that is still very much up in the air, where even the proponents, I gather from what I hear, cannot even agree with each other. And just because a thing is prevalent does not make it right. Because something is a problem for the church does not mean we should compromise on it. Adultery is widespread; at least, that is what is suspected. We would fool ourselves that it is not a problem, even for us. But does that mean we should accept adultery as normal behavior? Even those who have little regard for the ethics we teach and the morality we live by strive for fidelity in their marriage, or at least, view fidelity as an ideal. And adultery causes pain, even for those who reject the Christian faith.

"There's a problem of singleness in the church. We all know that. But is the solution Rev. Campbell's solution? Are we to tell our women that the answer to their singleness and childlessness is to go borrow some other man's sperm and have it inserted or whatever they do with it? The only difference I see here is the absence of physical contact between the man and the woman. What other name is there for it than what the church has called it all along? If we tell people that premarital and extramarital sex is wrong, what is essentially different about what Miss Campbell is doing?"

"What if it were the wife of a male colleague who does artificial insemination? Would it be an issue then?" Nora asks.

"That is a different situation. They're both married," says Garrick.

"Yes, but suppose the man is incapable of having a child and the couple seeks artificial insemination by a male donor?"

They all look at each other.

"That would not make the issue any less complicated. Artificial insemination itself is a thorny ethical issue, at least for us in the church," East declares.

"Miss Campbell, I do honestly believe that what you're doing could do severe, perhaps even irreparable damage to the church. That alone should make you think twice." Pusey's interjection catches her a bit by surprise, seeing he has played the role of bystander.

"Let's assume that all of us in this room were to agree with you. Let us also assume that we recommend to the national council that we give you our blessings. What then? I'm sure that other clergy, and our own members, the eighty thousand members we have in this country, would have their own say on it. Can't you see what that would cause?"

"Rev. Pusey, if we have the courage of our convictions, then nothing should stop us. When women were accepted for the ordained ministry, the support for such a move was not widespread. Remember that some congregations refused to have women as pastors, but persons and our churches are now beginning to come around."

"And your own actions would put that debate squarely on the table when we hoped we had moved on from there," Peters worries.

Nora shakes her head. She isn't going to budge anyone in this meeting, not even Pinto.

"I wonder, Mr. President, if there's an undeclared or unresolved issue that is not being discussed here," Samuel Henlon muses.

The committee members look at Henlon, hoping for some light. "It is about Miss Campbell herself. Perhaps Miss Campbell has unresolved issues in her own life and this is her own way of trying to resolve those issues."

Nora squints her eyes and looks angrily at Henlon. Pinto, East and Garrick hold their head down in disappointment.

"My suggestion is to recommend psychological evaluation for the sister," Henlon continues headlong with his theory. Pinto rolls his eyes. East looks to the window to his right. Peters clears his throat.

"Rev. Henlon, I'm sure we'll get there if we have to. But for now, I'm not sure if that is necessary. Rev. Campbell, is there anything else you would like to say to us?"

Nora starts to shake her head but then stops herself.

"Yes there's something I would like to say.

"I did not begin this journey in order to bring disgrace or dishonor to the church. It's certainly not my intention to cause embarrassment. But the church has had a long history of opposing new discoveries and inventions that the church itself embraced after they gained common currency. I need not rehearse the experience of Galileo.

"But you know what I've noticed? Most of the battles in the church for the last half a century have to do with women and their bodies; whether it is birth control or abortion or sex, or the matter of having children. It is always about us and our bodies, what we can do or cannot do. And it is always men who are telling us what is right from what is wrong as to what to do with our bodies, and our own sexuality.

"The church has been dictating to us for too long without exercising the patience of listening to us. We're treated as second class citizens by the church whose leaders have overwhelmingly been male. Even in this committee here today, there's not even one female to express a view as to whether what I'm doing is right or wrong, good or bad.

"What about choice? Isn't our faith about making choices? Choosing to believe in God or not to believe in God? You know one of the reasons why I became a Christian in the first place? It's the freedom that it promises. St. Paul says that 'It is for freedom that Christ has set you free.' That caught my attention. God led Israel out of slavery, into freedom. God did it even through seas and rivers and deserts and battles. But the aim was freedom. I came into the church at a time when I needed freedom in my life, freedom from the kind of life I knew. Freedom from the kind of life I lived. I'm happy for this freedom, and I'm not sure I'm that willing to surrender it."

"But it is this very freedom that you're now putting at risk," Pinto inserts.

Silence hangs in the air. Peters straightens himself. "Rev. Campbell, we ask you to wait in the general office as we consult among ourselves."

"Before I go, may I leave some handouts with you?" Caught slightly off guard, Peters nods. Nora reaches into her bulging bag and passes out brochures, pamphlets, and magazines.

"What're these?" Johnson asks curtly.

"Just some information on assisted reproductive technology."

Nora places the strap of the lightened bag on her shoulder as she steps out.

Chapter twenty

"Could someone please enlighten my darkness and explain what is happening here?" Chapman asks in bewilderment.

The eight men look around at each other. "What is happening is that we have an overzealous young woman who's about to bring disgrace on the church," Johnson remarks.

"And we may find we're powerless to stop her," Garrick expresses concern.

"God, why did we make them pastors in the first place?" Henlon asks.

"Gentlemen, let's not overreact. We need to get a proper handle of the issues ourselves if we are to do justice to the task assigned to us," East advises. "I think we first need to look at the procedure itself and move on from there. I know that most of us know something about the procedure, assuming we read the document that was circulated among members of this committee." He looks at the pile left by Nora, "We can also read these if we care to. The main thing is that we should not take anything for granted."

"Artificial insemination is one of the simpler forms of what is known as assisted reproductive technology. It is largely done by inserting semen into the womb by a syringe," Pusey declares, sounding as if he is giving one of his class lectures. "It is also one of the least controversial of the different methods developed but still finds disfavor with our Roman Catholic friends. But as you know, they oppose almost anything that interferes with the natural way of conceiving a child."

"The concerns of our Catholic friends should not be dismissed," advises Pinto. "Part of that concern is the possibility for genetic selection or the screening for gender."

"My concern is not with the method per se. I for one would not argue against its use in the case of a husband and wife who, for one reason or other, find it difficult to conceive the usual way. The problem for me is when it is by a donor." East looks around at his colleagues as he speaks.

"I take issue with the fact that women are using it to have children even though they're not in a committed relationship. In some societies it is also the preferred method used by lesbian couples to have children." Pinto's comments lead to a collective groan. He continues, "When it's by donor in some instances it is by an anonymous person, at other times it is someone chosen by the female. Whether anonymous or known, it poses theological and ethical problems. In either case, the father usually plays no role in the child's life, and, at least in North America, the identity of the father is usually kept hidden from the child."

"And this is what this young lady is asking us to accept?" Chapman responds with some feeling. "She is violating several ethical codes all at once, not least the deliberate bearing of a child that will grow up not knowing its father." A deep breath issues from Chapman as if he is having a slight seizure.

"We cannot tolerate this, we cannot!" Henlon says defiantly.

East frowns as he speaks, "We need also to remember there's a serious knowledge divide on this subject among our membership. Even if we were to be understanding, explaining it to them would be very difficult."

"What is there to be understanding about? This is a gross violation of almost everything ethical we stand for. It is irresponsible behavior of the highest order. We could never condone such high levels of irresponsibility," Johnson gives support to Henlon.

"Like the rest of us, Miss Campbell has been placed in a position of trust. We all have a collective responsibility to the Gospel of Christ. Despite the fact that we at times have our own views that may differ from the stated position of the church, none of us is expected to do or say anything that would cause harm to the body. Our own private notions cannot take precedence over the collective good of the church. I have no doubt that what our sister is doing will cause severe harm to the body," Pusey offers.

"Gentlemen, we need to make a decision," Peters chimes in. A collective silence descends.

Garrick is the first to speak. "We've had a long standing tradition of helping each other in moments like these. This is not the first time in our history when someone from among us holds a position that differs from the rest of us. We're always willing to tolerate different views and positions. That's why there's such great diversity among us."

"But this is very different from anything we've ever encountered before," Johnson butts in.

"Brother Johnson, allow me, please," Garrick sounds slightly irritated. He leans further forward. "The aim – our aim – should always be to offer help. I have several rules by which I operate in dealing with persons – grace over law, mercy over judgment. I believe in bending backwards, as far as is reasonable, to help persons who fail or fall into error.

"Unlike Brother Henlon, I'm not suggesting our sister has personal or psychological issues that are being played out in this way. I do believe however, that counseling is in order, and I suggest we go that route. I suggest we refer her for counseling."

Silence descends on the group once more. "I also suggest that we pray," Peters concludes.

Nora sits discontentedly before the eight clergymen. She detects uncertainty. A few refuse to look at her directly.

"Rev. Campbell," President Peters starts out. 'This has not been easy for us. We're mindful that we're to be sensitive to the needs and concerns of each other, but are also aware that the decisions we make often have implications far beyond us. It is true that we're private citizens with private lives, but we are also public figures as well, and this is something over which we have no choice or control.

"We're very unhappy with the course of action you've taken. We're even less happy with the way you've gone about it. What you plan on doing will have implications far beyond you or this committee, and that's something we cannot ignore. Besides, we believe there are other alternatives that you could have easily pursued, if indeed you wanted to have a child. The most obvious is adoption, an option we strongly urge that you consider.

"It is our view that you should desist from following through on what you're doing."

Peters pauses.

"We also recommend that you go through a period of counseling. This is not to suggest you have psychological issues. It's just that we believe it would not harm talking to someone who could help you clarify the issues involved. It would also help us in making a recommendation to the wider council of the church as to the best course of action to take."

Silence hovers in the room.

"Is there anything you'd like to say?" East asks.

"What is there to say? I already see where this is going. Whatever I say will make little or no difference."

Further silence.

Nora breaks the awkwardness.

"Is there a counselor that you're suggesting?"

"We have several from which you could make a choice," Peters answers.

Nora bristles at the list handed to her. "Can I go to someone of my own choosing?"

"You certainly can... if it's a reputable Christian professional. We would also prefer the person be of the Reformed persuasion," Peters offers. He immediately realizes the misinterpretation that could be placed on his last comment. "This is something we would rather keep within the family."

Chapter twenty one

The annual one-week conference of the Reformed Christian Church runs for two days without incident, until the youth representative from Hanover raises his hand to ask a question.

"Mr. President, some of us gather that there's an issue simmering for some time that has not been brought before this body, and a number of us are wondering why this is so. We're concerned that the leadership of the church has been less than forthcoming on the issue. Sir, I believe that it is in the best interest of the church to deal with it openly and directly, and we would like a direct response. Is it true that one of our female ministers, who is noticeably absent from these meetings, is pregnant?"

All eyes sweep in the direction of the young brother, then toward the president's chair. An expectant silence descends on the large group of delegates and pastors in the expansive sanctuary of the cathedral.

"The issue the young brother raised has had the attention of the leaders for some time. But it is our belief that the sensitive nature of the issue demands that we treat the matter with the greatest level of care. I'm afraid it would not be wise for me to say much more at this time," President Peters responds.

Several hands shot in the air. Rev. Ambrose Binns, one of the senior pastors in St. Elizabeth, gets up to speak. "With all due respect Mr. President, I believe we need a more definitive response than the one you just gave. Are you admitting that the sister alluded to is indeed pregnant, and if so, what are we as the body of Christ prepared to do about it?"

"Brother Binns, we appreciate the concern, but please be mindful that one of the mandates we have as leaders, as pastors, indeed as a church, is to deal with matters with the greatest level of care, lest we cause great harm. I'm appealing to this august body to put its usual trust in us to do the right thing in the right way and at the right time."

Binns persists, "Brother President. I perceive that you're skirting the issue and are avoiding answering the question. The question is simple and straight forward enough. Is or is not the sister with child, though she *is* a single woman?"

The vice president, Rev. Oral Bailey, sitting to the right of Peters, whispers in his ear.

Peters gets up, takes the microphone in his hands, and speaks in a slow deliberate voice. "The issue as raised before us came to our attention several months ago." Loud whispers immediately break out in the sanctuary and shouts of consternation erupt. Peters ignores the jibes and raises his voice above the din.

"We immediately set about clarifying the situation by calling in the sister for dialogue. We had a very fruitful meeting and the relevant committee that met with her made several proposals that are currently being pursued. Among the recommendations is that the sister go through a period of counseling. That, as far as we are aware, is still in progress, and we cannot at this time speak fully to the issue at hand until we meet again with the sister and get a report from the counselor. There's the matter of confidentiality to be respected."

Sophia Fray, a church delegate from Kingston, takes Binns' place at the audience's microphone. "Mr. President, I believe that the matter is not being addressed as it should. The issue is not so much one of personality but about church policy and practice. What is the policy of the church in the case of someone who gets pregnant though not married?"

"Believe it or not dear sister, there's no set policy across our denomination. Different congregations have adopted different postures. In some congregations, such a scenario results in immediate expulsion from the membership. Others take a more conciliatory approach and suspend the person while working for rehabilitation and reconciliation," Peters informs.

"Isn't that part of our problem? We have no set policy, no uniformity, so that when problems or issues like these arise we run around like chickens without heads," Mrs. Fray concludes with disdain.

"You may be partially right my dear sister, but you should remember that each of our congregations enjoys a level of autonomy, and matters of church discipline are one area where such autonomy resides."

"So what is the use of the national council or this conference, the highest decision making body of the church, if in matters such as church discipline you cannot provide guidance and counsel?"

"You have it all wrong. We always provide guidance and counsel, but it is within the ambit and context of the autonomy of the local church."

"Well if you ask me, some of us have way too much autonomy and this is one reason why we have it so difficult to get things done."

"I understand your sentiment, but that'd be turning back the clock on over two hundred years of our church's history," Peters informs with conviction.

A very impatient Rev. Samuel Murdock, recently retired after forty three years as pastor, speaks his annoyance. "I find this entire discussion rather disingenuous. We have for far too long and way too often hide behind the cloak of autonomy of the local church to avoid facing up to matters we should meet head-on. And in any case, the question raised is not a matter for the local churches to decide, but the national leadership, including we who meet in conference here this week. I'm amazed that those whom we elect to lead us are reluctant or afraid to provide leadership on a matter such as this. Even if it is true that each congregation has its own practice, that makes it even more incumbent and important for the national council to have a policy that can provide guidance to our membership. The question remains. What is the policy of the church with regards to persons who get pregnant and are not married? It's a simple question demanding a simple answer. And certainly in the case of a minister of the Gospel who gets pregnant outside of wedlock, the answer should be clear cut. I cannot see the need to pussyfoot around the issue."

"Yes, yes Rev. Murdock," Peters pleads with impatience. "But in all our dealings there are matters of procedure to follow, and all I'm saying is that we have set a procedure in place to deal with the question, and until that procedure is followed, or exhausted, I caution us to tread warily and carefully, lest what we do cause more harm than the good that was intended."

"But you've set a procedure in place where there seems to be no policy, or where you're most reluctant to state the policy. How can we agree with or support the procedure if we don't know what the policy is?" Murdock insists, a surprised and pleased look crossing his face as the meeting erupts in loud applause.

Vice president Bailey whispers another comment in the ear of Peters. Peters straightens himself to speak. "I ask the conference to allow the officers to confer and give a response later in the week. I promise that the matter will get the attention it deserves."

"At what point in our proceedings should we expect this response?" Murdock asks. A quick exchange of words between president and vice president has Peters announcing that it will be done during the last plenary session on Saturday morning.

"Well Mr. President, I will accept the proposal, but we expect no less than the resolve of this honorable house to handle the matter openly and honestly."

The muggy Saturday morning matches the mood of discontent and impatience among the conferees. A resolution from the floor is presented even before the leadership can state its decision to the conference and is read with deliberate care while the large group of delegates and pastors listens intently.

"Whereas the Christian Gospel dictates fidelity to the mission of Jesus Christ; and whereas such fidelity includes all matters of personal testimony and public witness; and whereas such testimony and witness includes family life; and whereas all ministers of the

Gospel are especially held to a high standard in upholding such personal testimony and public witness in their families so as not to bring dishonor to the church and to Christ; be it resolved that any minister of the Gospel who is found in breach will have his or her accreditation withdrawn and be immediately removed from the office of pastor."

Vice president Bailey is the first to respond. "Mr. President, this is precisely the kind of thing you've been cautioning us against. This resolution is so broad that it can be applied to almost any situation. This resolution could easily be used to remove a pastor if he's having marital problems. Or it could even be used to remove a minister if one of his children happens to fall into bad company and strays. This is a resolution that is ill-advised and ill-conceived. Rather than encouraging loving counsel, this measure is calling for draconian actions without the love and mercy that Christ taught."

Binns gets up to speak. "The point is well made that the resolution is too general, but it merely calls for a rewording to be more specific." He interrupts himself to peruse the paper in his hand before resuming. "I suggest that the resolution states:

"Whereas the Christian Gospel dictates fidelity to the mission of Jesus Christ; and whereas such fidelity includes all matters of personal testimony and public witness; and whereas such testimony and witness includes the matter of pregnancy and the rearing of children; and whereas all ministers of the Gospel are especially held to a high standard in having and rearing children so as not to bring dishonor to Christ and his church; be it resolved that any minister of the Gospel who bears or gets a child other than with a married spouse will have his or her accreditation withdrawn and be immediately removed from the office of pastor."

"Thank you Brother Binns, but even your own amendments are flawed," Peters counters. "For instance, the line that reads 'Be it resolved that any minister of the Gospel who bears or gets a child other than with a married spouse' is itself way too nebulous, because 'a married spouse' can easily be the married spouse of a third party."

"Mr. President, I'm surprised at you. We know the spirit within which the resolution is being framed, and we all know that that reference is to anyone other than the one to whom the minister is married," Binns rebuts.

"But my dear brother, what we do here is not only for us. It is for posterity as well. Ten, twenty or more years from now, those who come after us may not be privy to the context of our decision and may not be aware of the spirit in which we make such decisions. Hence the need to be careful. And I cannot see how this resolution addresses that which has been weighing on the minds and burdening the hearts of those who are here. This resolution is trying to deal with a profoundly personal matter in a way that does not respond to the human needs and concerns that are at the heart of what concerns us," Peters stridently asserts.

The delegate from the Mason Hill congregation, Deacon Henderson, is irate. The entire sanctuary goes still as he takes his place at the microphone. "I'm ashamed of what is goin on in my church. Why not let us call a spade a spade? Why are we goin on like this? I meet people on the street in our little community who askin me what kind o ting like that goin on in your church. I'm disgusted. This entire affair has shamed us and we in Mason Hill have not been able to live it down. We may never be able to live it down! An I come here an all I hear is big talk and big chat, an nobody seem to want to deal wit this disgustin disgrace that has been brought on all of us. Our shame is your shame. It shames all of us. An if you here can't deal wit it, what you expec us little folks up in Mason Hill to do?"

The applause rings for more than thirty seconds as he walks back to his seat.

Peters' eyes grow small and dark as he struggles with his confusion and anger. He looks over the sea of hands raised in the air and calls on the one hand he hopes can end the despair. "Rev. East, the floor is yours."

Rev. Jeffrey East stands and walks to the microphone in deliberation. His voice is barely audible as he begins speaking. A deeper hush descends on the group.

"It is obvious that we cannot rise from this conference without a resolution of this matter. For the entire week, it's been simmering and has been poisoning our meetings, even our worship. One way or the other, we need to come to a position that satisfies the majority of us, even if we cannot have full consensus.

"May I suggest that we deal with this the way we always deal with matters as a church? I think we should pray. Yes, pray, sincerely. Secondly, I suggest that we commission a study on the matter under discussion. Remember that what has happened has never happened before, certainly not in our circles. The sister has not, in the strictest sense of the word, committed adultery or fornication. She has reportedly used a scientific method to have a child. This, we are told, does not involve any kind of physical or sexual contact with any other person. And I do not think anyone of us in here can say with certainty that indeed she is pregnant because we have not been so officially informed, neither by her or by anyone whom she has designated to do so on her behalf.

"For the time being at least, the focus should not be on the person involved, but on the issue of someone using what some refer to as artificial methods for pregnancy. As a church, we have no policy on that, largely, I think, because we've been slow out of the blocks in putting such ethical issues and debates on our agenda. Other churches have, but we haven't. The fact is we are all speaking in the dark. The study should help us if we send it to our congregations for them to go through prayerfully and diligently. Everyone, including our auxiliaries – women's group, youth group, and all the others – should look at the matter critically and discuss it among themselves. Whatever we do and whatever decision we make should be done from an informed position, and with prayer.

"I beg that we put off making any kind of final decision in this conference. The sister is not even here to present her side of the matter, and I fear that if we proceed without allowing her full

152

hearing, then we can be charged with the same injustice we the church have often charged others with in other instances. I've sat on various reviewing committees of our church, and I've sat on the national council for a number of years – certainly for all the years the sister has served the church – and all reports on her and her ministry have so far been exemplary, up until now.

"Mr. President, this is painful and difficult. But it is not the first time we've dealt with matters that pain us and that were difficult for us, but here we are, still vibrant and strong. We, like in the past, will come away from this stronger and with a clearer understanding of the mind and the will of God. I have no doubt that this will be so."

Peters, grateful that the tone has suddenly changed, invites Rev. John Chapman to close the discussion with prayer.

Chapter twenty two

Nora tosses her mind as to whether she should attend the Sunday worship services at the National Conference Center, the final and largest day of the conference. She struggled with herself the entire week as to whether she should go to the meetings, but information out of the conference suggests she should stay away. She takes refuge at Janet Ffrench's house.

The Sunday morning newspaper decides her mind: "Church debates pregnant pastor." The last line reads, "Rev. Nora Campbell could not be reached for comment."

It is her worst fear. Rev. Basil Newton, one of only a few confidantes attending the conference, was almost breathless when he called her cell phone on Thursday. "This thing is getting stink," he warned her.

"How stink?" she remembers herself asking foolishly.

"Put it this way, everybody look like them know your business."

"That bad, huh?"

"Yeah, that bad."

The pause on the phone was awkward. She could tell he was torn between loyalties.

"Listen, Basil," she comforted him. "I'm the last person to ask you to put yourself in any difficult position for me."

"Why you say that?"

"Well, you know, this kind o ting puts a strain on friendships, and I don't want to place you in an unnecessarily difficult position."

He cut her off. "Look, our friendship has always been based on honesty. My support of you or friendship with you is not based on whether or not I agree with you."

"Thanks, I appreciate that."

"Okay, gotta go. Take care of yourself."

She rubs her hand over the now lukewarm cup of coffee before her thoughts are distracted by Janet's entry into the dining room. Janet hurries with bag and books and gobs down a mouthful of coffee from her unfinished cup. Nora needs to talk but decides she should not disturb her friend's mind on a Sunday morning. She remembers hating anyone annoying her or giving her bad news before a worship service. Besides, Janet is running late for the start of her own morning service.

"Nora dear, catch you later. I'll cook dinner when I get back."

"Sure you don't want me to cook?"

"With your state of mind? I don't want you to burn down the people them house."

"Might help to take my mind off tings."

"Anything you say, but make sure the house is here and in one piece when I get back."

"You go on."

"Later."

"Preach the Word for the both of us."

"I hear you." Janet blows a kiss, the sympathy and sadness in her eyes clearly visible.

Nora punches her cell phone.

"Basil, it's me." The voice on the other end sounds slightly irritated. "Call at a bad time?"

"I'm trying to park."

"You're early."

"You know how it go. Have to get here to get a seat. Can't take standing up the whole day. Place look like it full aready."

"You see the newspaper yet?"

"A buy it but I don't have time to check through it."

"Check page three."

"Hol on, I don't finish parking yet."

Nora holds for more than a minute before the voice returns.

"Remind me the page again."

"Page three."

She holds for what seems like forever until Basil's voice returns. She detects a slight tremble.

"Girl, I don' know what to say."

"How this ting reach paper Basil?"

"Trus me, anybody could pass on this information. A reporter could even have been there. After what happen earlier on Thursday, it not too hard to see that something like this can get passed around. Is like people came armed and prepared. Yesterday was no less."

"What I goin do Basil?"

Basil hesitates. "You want me to come check you later? Lunch time perhaps?"

"I don't want to put you out o your way."

"Look, prepare lunch for me. I don't have any special plan for lunch anyway."

At lunch time, Basil is not exactly sure how to greet Nora. One of the freer thinking pastors in the Reformed Church, he occasionally has strong reservations about Nora's actions. Though he has known her since they entered seminary, he is at times uncomfortable with her bullheadedness. He remembers her walking out of a lecturer's class because the lecturer suggested that Christian feminism overcompensated by making church practice unacceptable and in some instances unintelligible to the ordinary churchgoer. Her overreaction, he thought then, was an example of the point the lecturer was making. The walkout caused a minor stir as the matter came up for review with the Reformed Church warden and among the group of Reformed students on the ecumenical campus. The apology elicited from Nora was reluctant and was done only after other students pleaded with her in the face of a threat by the warden that the matter would be reported to church headquarters.

He pulls into the driveway and is confronted by someone who seems to have aged since he last saw her. The already small frame seems slightly shrunk but he tells himself it is the oversized housedress she wears. The dress seems a little too deliberate, he says to himself. While never a flashy dresser or one who has the greatest fashion style, Nora has always worn clothes that fits well. The unkempt hair throws streaks on her forehead with tufts jutting out at awkward angles. She seems unwell. He is now happy he has come alone as he thought fleetingly of asking Rev. Caswell Burton, another batch mate and friend, to tag along.

He walks inside the house behind her and sits on the well-used and over worn couch of the United Evangelical Church manse. Like so many other church manses, this one is in need of repair and a paint job, the furniture several decades old.

While he has never been shy in jesting with her, Basil does his best not to remark on her appearance. Out of place and poor in taste, he tells himself.

"Service went well today," Nora tries to get the conversation going, the statement more of a comment than a question.

"Nothing out of the ordinary."

"Listened to it on the radio. Couldn't help myself."

Basil scrutinizes her. She carries small bags under her eyes. He finally decides to be as he has always been with her.

"You look like you pass through storm."

Nora smiles sheepishly. She somehow never thought seriously of making herself presentable. This is Basil after all. She shrugs her shoulders, the right held up a little longer and higher than the left.

"More storm look like it comin," she says halfway under her breath.

"You consider your next move yet?"

"What next move? I'm here jus waitin for whatever happen to happen."

"The church is in turmoil, you know that."

"Well, so what must I do?"

"I can't tell you that. But doing something might make a difference."

Nora looks at Basil, her eyes widening, making the bags underneath shrink slightly. "I can't believe this. You of all people."

"What?" Basil feigns ignorance.

She looks incredulously at him and gets up to go to the kitchen. "Your lunch is ready. Let me put it on the table."

Basil hears a pot bang and he sits with a hand over his face. It is several minutes before she ushers him to sit at lunch.

"I thought you were going to eat with me."

"Not hungry. Besides, I waiting for Janet to get back before I eat."

She sits opposite him and leafs through a magazine.

"Nora, look, I jus feel that if you were to resign it might save you a lot of heartache."

"Save *me* a lot of heartache! You mean spare the church an all o you the embarrassment which I am. It means that I, the great embarrassment to all o you would go and hide quietly in my little corner where nobody will see or hear me."

"What you gettin so heated bout?"

"I expected better from you."

"Nora, this ting goin get much worse before it get better. Honestly, I don't see no better way out at this time."

Nora fumes. "Eat your lunch before it get col. An you running late for your afternoon session. Go an run to your other friends and colleagues and chat me and say all kind o tings you want bout me."

"You're being childish Nora."

"That's what you come here to do, to annoy me and disrup me peace o mind?"

"Remember is not only you alone involve in this ting you know. You should consider others as well."

"Those others who you refer to got involve even though they know what this whole ting is all about. It look like you lose your spine."

"An you are not prepared to consider their feelings and reputation?"

"Look, I never force anybody to do anyting. An all who are involve know exactly what them was getting into, so don't come to me with this nonsense. I have no respec for anybody who don't have the strengt o them conviction."

She looks intently at him. "What you worried bout, Mrs. Newton?"

"Look, I don't want to go into that."

"You is the one who raise it, now you don't want talk bout it."

A long pause follows as Basil forces himself to eat.

"May be you should tell her," Nora counsels.

"Listen, let me handle the ting my way and in my own time."

"And let me handle *my* problem in *my* own way and in *my* own time," Nora snaps.

Chapter twenty three

It is the first meeting of the national council of the Reformed Christian Church since annual conference four weeks earlier. The first item on the agenda deals with "ministry" and covers matters related to churches and pastors such as resignations, retirement, and ordination. "Rev. Nora Campbell" appears prominently with no written indication as to why her name is there. But all council members know why.

President Peters invites Rev. Jeffrey East to make the presentation on "Rev. Nora Campbell."

"Mr. President, the past weeks and months have been difficult for us as a church. We've faced what is perhaps our greatest crisis over the past sixty years. Not since the schism that split off the United Evangelical Church have we faced so divisive an issue. While I don't believe the impact on our church will be as far reaching as that sad episode, the repercussions may yet be widespread and long lasting. The issue has now become a matter of national discourse and the country itself is waiting to see what course of action we'll take.

"It is amazing the number of phone calls and emails that have come into our offices. Indications are that individual pastors are being bombarded not just by church members, but by others to state their own position. It is clear we cannot go on for much longer without, at minimum, stating a position to our congregations.

"The fact is we're being overtaken by circumstances. But we also need to be careful that our response is not dictated purely by public opinion. We're the church of Christ and we're therefore expected to respond theologically and ethically.

"Immediately after annual conference we had a bioethics specialist prepare a paper on artificial insemination. We also put forward both a theological and ethical position and sent these to the

160

churches, as was promised during the conference. The accreditation committee, the congregations and auxiliary groups studied the papers. In light of that, the accreditation committee invited the Rev. Nora Campbell to meet with us. We also asked for and got a written report from the psychologist who is counseling Rev. Campbell."

East pauses, perhaps to catch a breath, perhaps to steel himself. None of the thirty seven members of the council shifts gaze from his bespectacled square face.

"I'm sure council members understand it is inappropriate for details of the counselor's report to be divulged in this meeting. Suffice it to say that the report suggests Miss Campbell is very much of sound mind *but* is fully convinced of the rightness of her action. She reiterated as much in our meeting with her."

East takes a deep breath. "And in that meeting, the Rev. Campbell confirmed that she's indeed pregnant."

A weighty hush palls the meeting. East waits, as if hoping for the right words to come to him.

"The accreditation committee felt it in the best interest of all to suggest to Miss Campbell that she resigns. She categorically insists she has no plans or intention of doing so, that she is of the view she hasn't violated any policy of the church and is not in breach of church practice. It is her view that ethically, she hasn't crossed the line and is no different from other Christian women who have taken advantage of modern medicine and science to enhance personal health or well being and to enable them to have a family.

"We proposed a compromise that she takes a leave of absence of one year in the first instance. This, we believe, would've provided a graceful way both for her and the church to at least begin to make headway in coming to terms with this problem. We were most disheartened that she did not accept this offer.

"After prayer and much soul searching, we're now of the view that we have no choice but to part company with Miss Campbell. It is our recommendation to this council that we withdraw accreditation status from Rev. Campbell and have her removed from the pastorate of the Mason Hill Reformed Church."

East eases back in his chair as he fixes his gaze on the papers in front of him. The conference room remains quiet for an exhausting moment. The president of the National Reformed Women's League, Elaine Fisher, breaks the uncertain tension.

"The executive of the women's league met two weeks ago and the matter overtook our agenda. The majority of women were upset about the entire affair. They view the entire thing as scandalous and are of the view that we took too long to deal with it. But one question that kind of stumped the meeting was posed by one of the sisters. The question was if it would have made a difference if she was married and decided to use the same method to have a child. The ethical paper, it is felt, did not adequately answer that question. The sisters were not sure if the problem surrounds the issue of her using this method to have a child, or the fact of her singleness. We do not believe enough of a work went into the preparation of the ethical paper and that left us wondering."

Garrick speaks up. "The papers that were sent out cannot answer all the questions that will be asked. No paper can. The intention is to provide a framework for discussion and reflection."

"The question that most persons seem to find intriguing is who the supposed father of the child is, with all the rumors going around that she's pregnant, a fact that has now been confirmed," Rev. Sebastian Longmore chimes in. His comment elicits a few chuckles followed by an awkward silence.

"The lesson in all of this, if nothing else, is that we cannot continue to ignore developments in our society. We need to make ourselves ready to address and answer any kind of question that society throws at us," Garrick states.

"The recommendation has come from the accreditation committee that we part company with Rev. Campbell. What say us?" Peters interrupts.

The vote: thirty four for, three abstentions.

Chapter twenty four

Adam Goldstein sits lazily in the sunshine with a copy of "Veil" resting on his chest. He has long wanted to read the 1987 tome by Bob Woodward. Cathy shook her head when he took it out of his carry-on and wonders why would anyone read such a book on his vacation. She is more comfortable with what Adam disparagingly calls "trashy hotel novels." These are her two weeks to have wild abandoned fun with some trash, she told him.

Adam reads "Veil" partially out of respect for his more famous colleague. He became a fan of Woodward and Carl Bernstein after the Watergate Scandal broke while he was still a junior in high school. The great man inspired him to be an investigative reporter. He remembers his first scoop. He discovered there were plans afoot to scrap the women's swimming program at his college. Adam had a vested interest. His older sister had previously swum all the way to the state championships and her name was etched on the pool deck in the "wall of fame." His story in the school paper led to a protest by members of the women's swim and dive team, and a reconsideration by the school's administration.

Adam has never hit the really big times as a reporter. Moving from city to city, he never had the one big story he seeks. It was at his insistence that Cathy left her job as a partner in a small law firm in Kansas City from where they both moved to Los Angeles. He finally settled down as an Associated Press correspondent. Cathy likes the quieter, slower Middle American lifestyle. Adam wants to be where the big stories are – New York, LA, Washington, DC.

Now married for six years, he looks across at her with the same passion he did nine years earlier when they first met. Cathy desperately wants a child but Adam insists they wait a little longer, saying he needs to be settled in his career before they start having children. The real reason is that he wants to preserve her beauty as long as possible, fearing that child bearing would hasten the onset of gravity.

A waiter asks if they need a drink. He likes the rum punch and orders another. Cathy asks for a Jamaican beer. Adam shakes his head. He has never been able to equate her flawless beauty with the drinking of beer. But Cathy is a small town Midwestern girl who likes to hit it back whenever she can.

Adam puts the book aside and picks up the newspaper he had earlier taken from the lobby. He hadn't fully realized he did so until he sat down in the beach chair. Can't help myself, he says to himself.

Cathy looks over the rim of her dark shades at him. "Aren't you having a good time?"

"I'm having a swell of a time."

"You're having a great time reading the Jamaican news. What could possibly be in there to interest you?" Cathy asks mockingly.

"Just a bad habit, hard to break," he says, throwing the paper aside and leaning back on his chair in repose. Cathy turns over and playfully tickles the bottom of his foot. She gets up, grabs his hand, and chases in front of Adam into the water.

The ocean feels so good, Cathy muses to herself. I could stay here all day. She holds him captive in the water for more than an hour, playing with him, teasing him, at times goading him to follow her out to the ropes. Adam is the better swimmer but Cathy's frolic leads her to take more chances, splashing and bear hugging him with her legs before climbing up from around his back and jumping off his shoulders.

Taking a break from her water romp, she slams herself exhaustedly into the chair face down after pushing the backrest into its horizontal position, and playfully invites Adam to rub her back and shoulders. It feels so good, she says, so relaxing. Her eyes drift open when Adam's hands lose their rhythm before coming to a complete stop. She looks around to see him peering at the partially wet newspaper, which lies on the sand next to the chair.

"Oh Adam, can't you just take your mind off news for just one minute? We're on vacation dammit."

"Sorry honey. I thought I just saw something interesting."

"If you were really sorry you'd throw that paper in the trash."

Adam knows he cannot help himself. Even though Cathy begs him to join her in the bathtub, he makes the excuse that he needs to call to make the evening's reservation at the Italian restaurant, one of five restaurants at the hotel, and the only one requiring a reservation. That he does, but then he calls the office of the *Jamaica Independent* newspaper. He introduces himself as a college professor on vacation and was interested to know more about a story carried that day. Could they furnish him with the contact information for the Rev. Nora Campbell? The reporter on the other line claim not to know, but Adam suspects it is an unwillingness to give out information. The only numbers they would give him are those for the offices of the Jamaica Reformed Christian Church.

The female voice at the church office sounds reluctant when Adam asks to speak with the Rev. Nora Campbell. Rev. Campbell does not work in the office, she says. How may I contact her, Adam wants to know? She is no longer a pastor with us, he is informed. Does she know how to contact Rev. Campbell? No, she has no idea where Rev. Campbell is. Who would? Perhaps someone in Mason Hill where she was pastor, he is told. Do you have a number so that I may make contact? No I don't.

Adam hangs up the phone and tiptoes out of the room to the elevators, heads for a gift shop near to the lobby on the first floor, and quickly finds what he wants, a Jamaican road map. He asks the clerk to show him various points on the map to Mason Hill. Curious, the clerk does her best to help. She has never heard of Mason Hill, she says. After retracing the map several times, Adam finds what he assumes to be a small hamlet in the most rural part of Jamaica, a far distance from their hotel.

"What's the best way to get there?"

"I have no idea," the clerk says, growing more curious. "You know somebody there?"

"No. Just someone I'd love to talk to."

She looks at him with deepening suspicion. "You could hire a taxi or you could rent a car."

Back upstairs, Cathy is fuming as Adam tiptoes back into the room. "Adam Goldstein, you're up to something." She sits at the dressing table and looks at him with a question hovering on her opened mouth.

"You were in the bath for so long I decided to go get something from the gift shop."

"Really?"

"Yes really."

"So where's it?"

"Where's what?"

"Whatever it is you got at the gift shop."

Adam sighs, pulls out the map and plumps down on the bed.

"Well, a map makes sense on vacation in a strange country. But tell me Adam, what is it you really have in mind? What is going on in that head of yours? You're up to something, I know it."

Adam takes up the roughed up sheet of newspaper and points to the story on the Religion Page, "Pastor thrown out of church: determined to become single mom."

"Look at this story. It says that this woman, who is a pastor, is advocating her right to have a child even though she's not married. She's now pregnant and the church throws her out."

"That's an interesting story but not one that would set the world on fire," Cathy says, finding it hard to hold back her impatience. "It's not the first time someone in the church committed adultery or engaged in premarital sex."

"But you don't understand. She's having this child by artificial insemination." Cathy gathers her patience and sits beside her husband on the bed. She stares at the story in front of her.

"Where have you seen or heard of a story like that?"

"You're right Adam," Cathy says in resigned exasperation. "I can't say that I have."

"See? This is a wonderful story to take back home."

"Adam, please don't tell me you're going to ruin our vacation by pursuing one of your stories," she pleads.

"No my dear, far be it from me to ruin the wonderful time we've been having. See it as an adventure."

The drive to Mason Hill takes some three and one half hours. The last leg of the drive is the most horrendous they have ever taken, even counting their many camping trips in the US. The taxi driver curses every time he drops into a rut or pothole, until he finally gives up. "I not goin any further, you have to take it from here," he finally says.

"Will you wait for us?" Adam asks.

"I will wait. Jus don't take all day."

Residents throw curious eyes in their direction as Adam and Cathy walk toward the church a further mile up the road. Stopping to ask for direction, an over-willing young man offers to take them to their destination, perhaps out of inquisitiveness, wanting to ascertain the nature of their business with the church. Eventually, they struggle up the short, final incline. Adam takes several snapshots of the surrounding countryside. He especially likes the quaint small houses, some perched elegantly off the side of a hill. The church sits on top of the highest point in the village.

Adam was able to make contact with Nora in Kingston and made an appointment to meet with her, but wants to talk to the people in her former congregation and others from the village before that meeting. What do they think of their former pastor? Does she have their support? What effect does the controversy have on them and on the church? Where will this controversy lead? What do people in the community think?

He begins to ask some in the small crowd that has gathered out of curiosity at the presence of these strangers in their midst. At first, Adam cannot tell if they are reluctant or hostile, as most refuse to answer. Adam and Cathy walk over to a shop which has a bar to one side, and where some men had gathered. As it turns out, some of the men at the bar have a lot to say.

"What is dis worl comin to?" One bar patron says. "From I born, I never see or hear anyting like dis."

"It is a disgrace," another opines.

"Dis woman come ere an cause all kind o problem. It don't look good. I tell you, it don't look good. Dat is why I don't believe any woman should be pastor of no church," another aggressively asserts.

A wiser head declares, "Dis is a new and different generation from fi we own. The Bible done say dat in the las days dese tings will appen."

"Don't you think a woman has the right to do as she pleases with her body?" Cathy foolishly asks. All stare at her in dismay and turn away toward their domino game, bringing an abrupt end to the conversation.

Cathy and Adam walk toward the gate of Deacon Francis' house, which was pointed out by one of the schoolchildren who informed them that "He is the senior deacon in the church." Francis walks out to the gate with his slightly bent frame and ushers the two strangers onto his veranda. The modest home has bright red polished tiles, a type that Cathy never remembered seeing in her small rural town in Missouri. He is courteous, but noncommittal.

"Mr. Francis, we understand you're a leader in the church where Rev. Nora Campbell was pastor," Adam starts off by stating.

"Yes, I belongs to the church, but what business bring you up here?"

"Business?" Adam asks uncertainly.

"What you up here for?"

"I'm writing a story about the church."

"Story? For what?"

"A newspaper story."

Francis looks at Adam and Cathy with baleful eyes. "You not from Jamaica, you are foreigner."

"We're from the States."

"What interes you ave in what appen up in our little place ere?"

"We just think that this is an interesting story to tell, a pastor thrown out of the church for wanting to have a child."

The old man makes a little clucking sound with his tongue and shakes his head. "We making big foreign news now! So what you want to know?"

"Everything, about what happened."

"I'm not sure I can tell you anyting young man."

"But you know about all that happened," Cathy cannot contain her impatience.

"You talk to the lady yet?"

"What lady?"

Francis looks at them disdainfully and responds as if counting the syllables. "The pastor." He says the words as if they are improperly designated.

"We'll talk to her tomorrow."

"She's the right person to talk to, not me."

"You've been hurt by this haven't you?" Adam asks.

Francis looks straight ahead and edges to the margins of his seat. He reflects as if in deep thought.

"You know young man, I live on this earth a long, long time. I know dat tings an times change, but some o these changes not good. An some o we little folks up here not ready for dese changes." Then he speaks with feeling. "Dere is no way we could accep what dat woman was doin. What she was doin was an abomination. It is the kind o ting that would bring judgment down on we. Imagine, the woman not married an want to have a chil, an say she is pastor! You ever hear anyting like dat happening in the church amongst God's people?" His voice trembles with emotion.

"How do the other people in the church feel about it?" Adam is now happy he is getting some response.

"What you tink? You tink any reasonable, sensible somebody could agree wit dat?"

169

"So what effect has it had on the church?"

"You know the truth bout it! We shame. We in the church shame. We walk through the little community an hol down we head, cause we shame."

"So what happens from here?"

"What goin happn? We jus gots to move on, that's all, nothing more," he says in that definitive tone, marking the end of the conversation. But Cathy's curiosity gets the better of her.

"But would you agree, Mr. Francis, that the lady has some rights here."

"What kind o rights you talkin bout? I don't understan you! This is the church. People jus don't do as they like. Is God business you dealin with. Rights?!" he spits out the last word.

Adam presses on. "Would you ever have another woman as pastor?"

"We will answer dat question when the right time come." He takes a long pause and looks out the distance. "God is God. God know everyting bes, God know everyting bes."

The old man gets up and, without waiting for parting pleasantries, leaves them standing on the veranda.

Chapter twenty five

She seems way too frail to be carrying a baby but Nora walks with a determined stride. The couple awaiting her are already seated at a table and stand at her approach. She is easily recognizable. Nora has no doubt as to who they are, the only Caucasian couple in the Chinese restaurant. She sits with a little effort while Adam courteously offers assistance.

"We're happy you could make it at such short notice."

"I thought twice about coming. By the time I called to cancel you had already left your hotel," she confesses with a smile. "I trust you had a good drive into the city."

"It was very good. Your country is so beautiful," Cathy gushes too hard.

"Well, I say thanks on the behalf of all the Jamaican people," she says with a hint of mockery in her voice.

A waiter interrupts the conversation and takes their orders. Nora invites herself to a healthy meal of shrimp chow mein that surprises both Adam and Cathy. She notices the look on their faces and apologizes. "Well, you know the cliché. I have to eat for the two of us."

"How has the pregnancy been?" Cathy wants to know.

Nora pauses as if not sure of her feelings. "Different."

"Different?"

"Yes, different. Different from any other experience I've ever had, in more ways than one. Physically it's been stressful. I'm being constantly monitored because both my blood pressure and sugar count are up." She pauses as if realizing she is already giving away too much information.

"Well, I want to say congratulations. I'm sure all things will go well," Cathy tries hard to sympathize.

"Thank you. I can't wait for it to be over."

"How far along are you?"

"Six and a half months. I have a little ways to go."

"You'll get through it, I'm sure."

"Reverend Campbell –" Adam starts to say.

She interrupts him, smiling wistfully. "Nora will be fine. God knows, I may not be a Reverend ever again."

"Nora, I know this has been a most difficult time for you, but as I told you on the phone, I'm an Associated Press correspondent. We're actually here on vacation when Cathy and I came across your story. We believe it is a most fascinating story and would want to follow it up."

"I'm not too sure about this. As I said, I'm having second thoughts. I came here out of courtesy because I had earlier indicated a willingness to meet you. I honestly don't think it's such a good idea."

"This is not the kind of story that can be kept quiet. Sooner or later, some other reporter is going to pick it up and make it big news. As you know, it has already made local news here in Jamaica."

"Yes, but talking to the press is something different. I have so far not made any public comments on the entire thing. I think I should keep it that way."

"You can't keep quiet with this thing," Cathy advises. "This is too important an issue, not just for you, but for all women. Think of all the women who'll benefit from your act of bravery. What you've done takes courage, and other women need to know about such courage and strength."

Nora looks at Cathy out of the corner of her eye and makes a small chuckle. "Aw – I don't know. This has been a long, painful process for me. I wouldn't want anyone to exploit my pain. That'd just make it too much. Way too much. I have no intention of becoming the poster child for some cause."

"What led you to do this?" Adam tries to wrest the conversation.

Nora looks down at her stomach. "What? Get pregnant?"

"Yes."

Nora pauses and looks distantly at the wall ahead of her. "I just wanted to have a baby, plain and simple. I didn't do it to prove some point or to get on anybody's nerves or to challenge authority. I just wanted a baby."

"But you've rubbed some people hard along the way."

"I guess that's what happens when desires clash with rules. You either obey the rules and quell your desires, or toss the rules aside."

"There's a great deal of bitterness."

"You seem to know a lot," Nora responds with surprise.

"I've been talking with a few persons." Adam hesitates. "Including at your former church up in -" he tries to remember the name of the place. Nora helps him with the name.

She looks quizzically at him. "You do get around, don't you?

"The leadership of your church here in Kingston has refused to comment."

"You expected it to be otherwise?"

"You've been thrown out of the church."

"The national council took that decision, yes."

"What's next for you?"

"Honestly, I don't know, I'm still weighing my options. The priority at this point is to stay as healthy as possible and to have this baby. Nothing else really matters right now. I'm trying to stay as far away from the brouhaha as possible; which is why it's a mistake to be talking to you now."

"So far we've not detected any major support for you. How've you been coping?"

"I do have friends that support me. At least, I think I have their support, or sympathy. But you're right. Jamaicans are not that sympathetic to anyone that breaks long standing moral codes such as I have. Even if they're broken, the breach usually happens in secret. Truthfully, I had no intention that this should become a major issue. I knew it to be a stretch, but in my attempt to keep it as quiet as possible I argued that it is a matter of privacy. But as we say in Jamaica, pregnancy is not something that is going, it is something that is coming. People would've known about it eventually, no matter what I do."

"And the father, I'm curious about that."

Nora looks at Adam with the slightest hint of anger. "I've made a pledge that that'll remain confidential."

"So it's not a sperm bank donor."

"As I said, it's confidential."

"It is therefore somebody well known to you," Adam continues to press.

"Mr –"

"Adam."

"Adam. I've no intention of being rude. Let's not go there."

"Okay. Sorry."

The waiter delivers the orders, deftly places them on the table, inquires as to their satisfaction, and quickly takes his leave.

Adam searches for a question. "I understand that you have a political history."

"Is this really important?"

"Well, were you or weren't you?"

Nora looks away, and then answers. "You need to understand something of Jamaica's political history to appreciate my political past. Back in the seventies few people were neutral politically. It was the height of the Cold War. Emotions ran high. You were either on this side or that side. I chose the side I believed had Jamaica's interest at heart. It just happens that those who advocated socialism were the ones I believed to be truly interested in helping average, ordinary Jamaicans to advance themselves. Those who had the resources did nothing for the people. Those who advocated real change were the socialists. They wanted things to be different. They advocated a philosophy and shared a vision I could identify with."

"So you were part of a political program."

"I was what you may call a political activist, more a foot soldier than anything else."

"My information is that you were much more than that, actually a leader in the communist party whose activities were well known."

Nora remains silent.

"Do you now share those views?"

Nora responds slowly. "In some ways I do. In other ways I don't."

"Specifically? I mean, could you elaborate?"

Nora searches her mind. "Socialism is an excellent tool in assessing the ills of society. I know no other theory that can diagnose what's wrong with the social and economic spheres better than socialist theory. Where socialism fails is in correcting those ills. Socialism is like a doctor who brilliantly diagnoses what's wrong with the patient but lacks the skill or knowledge on how to cure the patient."

"So you're a reformed socialist."

"That's an interesting way of putting it." Her lighthearted chuckle lifts her mood slightly.

"Have all that have happened changed your mind about the church?"

"You know, I can't say for sure." Nora twirls a finger around her fork. "One of the first things I learned as a Christian is the value of faith. The ability to believe that, despite all that's happening, there's something good out there, or there's something higher and better. It's a belief that evil and ignorance do not have the final word. That somehow, that which is good and that which is right will rise to the top."

She looks at Adam then at Cathy and breathes a low, hollow sigh, as if the air is squeezing itself from deep in her womb. "Do you know the story of Job?"

An awkward silence follows the question before Adam answers uncertainly. "I'm Jewish so I know a little, but not much. I'm not a practicing Jew. Meaning, I 'm not an observant Jew."

"Well," she leans her head, "as you may know, Job is this biblical character who, though he was a good man, lost all he had –

his possessions, his family, his health. Three of his best friends came to sympathize with him but they only made him feel worse, for they blamed him for all the bad things that happened to him. Job, though he got irritated and lost his patience at times, never lost his faith. There was a happy ending to that story. Job was able to get back his health, have a new family, and acquire other possessions in life. Despite all the bad things that happened to him, Job still maintained his integrity and he was vindicated in the end."

"So you believe that vindication will come for you," Adam asks the obvious.

"I have to. I have no other choice."

Even though the tape recorder continues to run in his pocket out of sight, Adam Goldstein jots down all the major points that Nora, to his delight, is giving up so freely. He pinches himself under the table, hoping that this, indeed, will be his big story.

Chapter twenty six

Nora picks her way through the rubble, careful not to slide on the slippery stones. She looks with disdain on the light mud that sticks to her shoes. Persistent rains have been unkind to the unpaved road that leads from Orange Hill down to Danvers. It is more than two years since she made the journey, and the path is now worse than when she last traveled it.

The car could not make it all the way through, so they walk part of the way, about half a mile, down the hill. She struggles as her bulging stomach adds to the unease, and sighs wearily as she whispers quiet thanks that the walk is downhill, but worries what will happen when she has to make the walk back up.

Janet Ffrench looks around with awe as they walk gingerly through the rubble of loose stones. She has never been this deep down inside rural Jamaica, and it fascinates her. Though she traveled the countryside as a seminary student, and had been to a few deeply rural areas, she has never seen it this remote before. Danvers is a steep valley that goes down the bottom of a hole.

She stops, cocks an ear, and asks Nora what bird is that. Nora is embarrassed that she has to think about it, the swelter of the humid sun peering through an angry rain cloud causing her great discomfort. It's a Jabbering Crow, she says, relieved that she at last remembers.

They happen upon Mass John's little house two chains from off the road, to the left. All her life, Nora never knew his real name, just "Mass John." He cultivates his backyard garden, raises a few goats, and stays mostly by himself. She never knew him to be married or have children, and he is one of the few men in Danvers without a donkey, the necessary means of transporting persons and goods up and down the hill. He catches her gazing at him as they pass by and offers a curious look and disinterested wave, as if unsure whether to commit himself to a greeting. "Merry Christmas, Mass John" she calls out to him in the most polite voice she can muster. He nods, looks at them with awkward deference, and returns to the sharpening of his machete. She realizes he is bushing his yard and clearing an overgrown patch of weeds from in front of his house.

The guango trees lining part of the roadway spread their pods on the road and the adjoining properties. The pods ooze a slightly sweet smell and add to the mixture of the humid, heavy air, already pungent with the raw smell of the massive cotton tree they just passed. "It always seems to rain at this time of year," Nora says idly to herself, never really taking serious note of it before.

It is two days before Christmas and Nora is concerned that she is making too early a trip. She also worries that she is taking Janet from her relatives and church for the season, but Janet insists on accompanying her. Janet distrusts Nora, believing she will not take proper care of herself. Though never a mother herself, she spent time with a younger brother and sister and knows a little about caring for children. Besides, she regards Nora as her adopted sister, as someone who needs care and protection, who seems so abandoned and helpless.

Miss Nellie's shop has a few patrons hanging out at the front. On the right side of the building is the bar where mostly older men, but a few younger ones, congregate in the evenings and on the weekend to play dominoes and drink rum. On Saturdays Miss Nellie takes illegal bets on the horses as the brave ones gamble and listen to the hi-fi radio that she strings up to two large speakers. A crude poster on the wall advertises a post-Christmas grab bag and bingo party on Boxing Day. This is as good as it gets with entertainment in Danvers. On the left side of the building is the small grocery shop where one can get bread and bun and flour and sugar and cornmeal, as well as sanitary items. Nora made many trips as a child to this shop, and she sees some of the little faces she knew then now staring at her with growing curiosity.

Eldemire Biggs grins widely as he calls out, "Wha happn Miss Nora?" She tells him she is doing well and nods respectfully, greeting the others without breaking her stride. Strange and suspicious glances are cast at her stomach, several faces peering out the door. She sees Miss Nellie behind the counter inside the shop, even from the distance and angle where she is, stretching her neck to get a better look. A few whispers are exchanged and Nora reflexively quickens her strides as if to get as farther away as possible.

Nora's throat swells slightly as she stands at the intersection of the footpath that leads down to her house. The house is at the lowest level in the village, down at the very bottom, kissing the river's edge. She looks with a hint of trepidation at Janet who instinctively takes her arm. She feels a gentle warmth of reassurance.

How she appreciates Janet. They became firm, fast friends the very first week they entered seminary. They have had their moments, such as when Janet swore that Nora was responsible for the ritual ransacking of her room because she forgot to turn her lights off. It is one of the silly rituals performed by students as reprimand and punishment for those who go about their business without turning out the lights in their room. Janet accused Nora vehemently because she had easy access to her room. This happened in their second year, and it took Janet nearly a month to get over it. Her furniture were tossed and her clothes scattered and strewn about. Nothing was broken or taken. It was orchestrated disruption of her room, evidently done with care. She was livid, but the truth is she was more embarrassed than hurt, and she tried as hard as she could, against all the urgings in her heart, to be angry as long as she could with Nora.

Janet's kindness to Nora is not without mutual benefit. Having entered seminary financially broke, Nora took care of Janet's living expenses until her church came on board to offer help. That cemented the bond and made Janet to be in everlasting gratitude to Nora. Her life of pain was enriched by someone who seems to genuinely care. Nora was oblivious to the miracle she was to Janet while they were in seminary. This makes Janet ever more grateful.

Janet urges Nora to step down the rocky path, sensing, realizing, that this is the way down. The path is even more treacherous than the disheveled road. Sharp stones with knife edges rise up in the middle, held in check by the hard, red earth. It is with great care that Nora tries to avoid sliding, but, with the sensation that her stomach is pulling her faster than she dares to go, she slips with a stifled shriek, only to be caught by Janet, who grabs onto a nearby, sturdy brush. Nora stops, as much to catch her breath as to gather her nerves and to steady her feet. She waywardly wonders how she ran up and down the path as a child with little effort and no sense of danger. She queries her mind as to whether she ever fell, and with a sense of awe recalls that not once did she ever miss her step or lost her footing.

Her distraction is interrupted by Janet's urging. Janet is impatient. Though she is fearful of walking, (she tries to hide her fear from Nora), her anxiety to get off the path outpaces her fear. Besides, a wasp just flew across her face and she almost screamed for fright. Unsteadily, as if walking a tightrope, Nora inches down, and is relieved when at last the path levels off. She stops to take another breath. Here, the trees cast a covering, darkening the mid afternoon sun, which always seems to set far sooner down here than in the rest of Danvers. A low whistle comes up from further down the hill, and Nora recognizes it as the wind passing through the bamboo trees.

They resume their walk, more leisurely this time, and Janet even has enough confidence to survey her surroundings. As they turn the next corner, the sudden sound of trickling water greets them. It is the stream that runs by Nora's home. A smile of unexpected delight crosses Janet's face when she sees the bamboos, and, asking Nora what they are, the rose apple trees, swaying gently. It is as close to paradise as Janet has ever imagined.

The house emerges quickly and, with a sudden sinking feeling, Nora realizes for the first time just how small it is. It stays stuck in the middle of a fairly wide expanse of yard, but only about one hundred feet from the riverbank, not much above the level of the stream. Her embarrassment deepens the closer they get as she self-consciously examines Janet's face, who now walks beside her. The path gives way to a wider track. She idly muses that she does not recognize the donkey tied to a hog plum tree that, when in season, spreads its very sweet scent as far as up to the top of the path. That donkey does not look like the old Jennie that papa had, Nora says to herself.

The look on Janet's face cannot be interpreted. It is the first time Nora has ever brought anyone home, and she is beside herself with anticipation and anxiety. She dared not bring anyone while attending high school and, while in Kingston, she was relieved to be too far away to have anyone going with her on her trip "to the country." It is not that Nora is ashamed of her parents; it is that she feels the family can do better, far better. But papa is stubborn. He would not countenance the thought of leaving from down here. Even now, with both Jason and Paul living abroad, he refuses to go live with them, though the offer is made several times. Having traveled to and from the USA many times as a farm worker, he was never impressed enough by that country to want to live there, he would sometimes say.

Having now "retired" from traveling, he spends his days tending to his goats and pigs and chickens and to a small backyard garden. Some in the village regard Roy with disdain, muttering under their breaths that "Him can live better than that." They see him as mean and cheap. He does not gamble, drink, or bet the horses. Neither does he give much money away. Rumors are that he has more than one million dollars stashed away at a bank, waiting for it to do God knows what. The villagers' disdain for and envy of Roy Campbell deepened even more since they say that his children are in "big position" with the boys, Jason and Paul, living in prosperous "foreign."

Daisy Campbell, of course, refuses to leave her home and husband. Not that she feels she has a choice. She is too wedded to the man for whom she bore her first child when only sixteen years old. They have been together for a long time, and she is not shy

181

about telling anyone who cares to listen that "Roy is a good man." The villagers would grumble to themselves, "Good man but him mean."

Four years ago, she decided to travel abroad for the very first time, spending all of three months, first with Paul, then with Jason. She returned sprightly but relieved to be back, having missed the house, and declaring her dislike for "Having been cooped up like a mother hen." She did not relish not being able to go out as she liked, and was a recluse most of the time she was in Florida. But she is not above showing off to the villagers about her children, and often wears others out with stories about the boys and what they are doing.

But Roy and Daisy Campbell have never known what to make of Nora and her position as a pastor. Somewhat bemused, they greeted her announcement that she was going to become a pastor with mild shock. Being members of the Brethren church up in Orange Hill, where they are faithful members if not very active, they could not understand how their daughter could take on a role traditionally held by men. Roy's perplexed question to Daisy upon reading the letter was, "But how can a woman be an elder?" They were not happy that she got herself "mixed up" in a church that taught and practiced such "false doctrine." It was with grudging acceptance that they attended her graduation from the Jamaica School of Theology, and two years later, her ordination. They did not want it to appear as a slight to their only daughter after having attended all previous graduation ceremonies for their children, both high school and college.

But they have had to live down the shame in their church that their daughter has strayed and have brought disgrace on the family by being ordained. Roy felt obliged to step down from the one, albeit minor position he held in the church as a member of the choir. They still prefer to tell anyone who asks about her that she is a teacher, though they are aware that some know she is in fact a pastor. Without giving details, Roy and Daisy would tell inquisitive souls that Nora is a teacher in the church.

Nora stands as if unsure how to proceed, but another nudge from Janet prods her forward. As if walking on spikes shooting up from the ground, she steps forward, subconsciously straying from the front entrance toward the back. It was her habit as a child to enter the house through the backdoor, deviating onto a crook that forms in the path. A puzzled Janet takes her elbow and rights her way to the front door. No one seems to be at home, but Nora knows better. It is the day before Christmas Eve, and both mama and papa would be inside performing a family ritual – baking cakes and making sorrel drink. It is one of the few things Roy and Daisy do together; otherwise, like all other parents in Danvers, they keep a respectable distance from each other in public and in front of their children.

Now just about 80 feet from the house, Janet catches the whiff of baking, and states the obvious to Nora, who nods absentmindedly. Stones that surround the small flower garden gleam with whitewash, as well as the tops of the posts that frame the pretentious wire fence that keeps the animals from the river. It was the children's tasks, while growing up, to do the whitewashing. Nora idly concludes that papa did the painting as it is far neater and more expertly done than she has ever remembered.

Two strange dogs she does not recognize run from under the house, which rests on low stilts, yapping with annoyance and excitement at the approach of the two women. An older dog lazily pushes out its head, and, upon seeing Nora, bounds up with a frenzied wagging of its tail. It whines, rubs against her and hits her with its tail with full force. She bends down to rub its head. "Spider," she says to the aged beast. The dog gets more excited and attempts to jump on her, its paws resting on her stomach. Nora calms the mongrel with great effort. The other two younger canines follow the older dog's cue and begin sniffing around Nora's and Janet's feet.

The dogs have done a disservice to Nora. She wants to sneak up unawares, but when she looks up, she sees her mother standing at the door with a baffled expression. Daisy Campbell's features are

183

frozen with derision and unease. Nora finds the best smile she can. "Hi mama," she calls even from the distance she is, hoping the greeting would cut the tension that has already built up between them. Mama forces herself to smile and beckons an indefinite gesture. Nora takes the cue and with a surprising surge of boldness in her chest, steps forward assuredly. By now papa is peering over mama's shoulder and both watch the women get closer, the three dogs now dancing in between and around them.

Nora's legs grow stronger under her stride while Janet, unnerved by the new spirit that suddenly engulfs her friend, struggles to keep pace with her. Within a few moments she covers the wide yardage and stands at the foot of the low steps, looking up into her mother's twisting features. Nora stretches out her right hand, "Mama, how you do?" Looking around her mother she announces cheerily with a hint of defiance in her voice, "Good afternoon papa." Both parents, taken aback by her unexpected arrival, greet her with grudging notes of respect. They step backward and away, allowing her, followed by Janet, to take the three steps into the room that doubles as living and dining area. The room is darker than it should be, and Nora and Janet squint to adjust their eyes to the gloom. The aromatic smell of Christmas cake fills the house mingled with the faint smell of rum.

Nora introduces Janet as a friend and colleague, with Roy visibly flinching when she elaborates that "Rev. Ffrench is pastor in the United Evangelical Church in Kingston." Trying to escape the awkward silence, she steers Janet to the dining table where they both sit. Roy and Daisy follow them with their gaze, as if uncertain what to do. Nora surveys the small room that threatens to close itself around her. It seems so eerily sinister, yet it is no different from how she knew it as a child. Tucked away in one corner is the very old stereo, long out of use, but which her parents devotedly keep. It stands regally, strangely, with its four, short, stubby legs set at an angle, just the way they were made. Even in the gloom there is a dull, delicate sheen on its laminated, wood-colored surface, no doubt a result from much polishing.

The cabinet is clean, even with pealing varnish. The best of the household's silverware, glass sets and chinaware, sit inside, mostly unused, much of it older than Nora and her brothers. These are normally taken out at Christmas, washed and used carefully, just about the only time of year when these precious treasures are used. Other times the family makes do with ordinary knives and forks and plates and plastic cups for drinking.

The sofa and matching chairs are surprisingly in good condition, though they show slight wear. These were bought when Nora was about nine years old. The newest item in the room is the refrigerator, the second one the family ever owns as the first had its boiler broken. Attempts to have it repaired were fruitless. The new fridge is only about ten years old. The dining table and chairs are nearly twenty years old, of the old Formica type, and stand resolute despite the poor quality. Nora guesses that much of the rest of the house is the same, with the same spring beds from the 1950s. She surmises that the old kerosene oil stove is still tucked into a corner in the kitchen, despite being replaced by the gas range many years ago.

Nora tries to rid herself of the suffocating familiarity and asks her parents if the sorrel is ready, trying to minimize the dismay welling up in her chest. She now concludes it is a mistake to have come. She immediately dismisses the thought, telling herself she needs to see her family before the birth of her child.

"I would love for Janet to taste the wonderful sorrel and the cake you bake every year," she says with much sincerity, desperately hoping mama and papa would ease the burden in the room.

"Cake not ready yet," Daisy says abruptly.

Silence.

"You mus be hungry," Roy says at last, and moves to the table, summoning warmth and friendliness. "How you all make it in this rain?"

"It rained part of the way from Kingston," Nora answers, slightly relieved at the livelier conversation. "It was particularly bad through the Bog Walk Gorge. Janet was afraid to cross Flat Bridge."

"You a brave woman to drive through Flat Bridge," Roy offers respect to Janet. "With all this rain we been having."

"It wasn't that bad after all, though I was a little scared," Janet joins in.

"Two cars plunged in two weeks ago," Nora informs, and causes a chill to enter the room. She immediately regrets turning the conversation toward such morbid detail, but Roy picks up on it.

"I ear that some even want to overtake on Flat Bridge. Dese people mad. Dem no have no sense. Dem drive too crazy on dese roads. Christmas time now everybody get madder and lose them ead."

A slightly less awkward pause follows.

"So oonu ungry?" Roy asks.

"We could do with something to eat, but don't bother yourself too much," Nora says while glancing at Janet.

Roy ignores Nora's attempt at self-deprecation and hastens to the kitchen. They watch shadows of Roy milling about, taking down bowls, gathering cutlery, and pouring contents. Janet and Nora are fixated on Roy, as if trying to escape the burning tension smoldering from Daisy. Nora can take it no longer and turns to her mother. "Mama you looking well. Papa taking good care of you." Daisy offers a grudging grunt, as if to say, so what, that is none of your business.

"How long you goin stay?" Daisy finally offers. Nora glances at Janet.

"I'm here for Christmas mama. Is a long time we don't spend Christmas together. You wouldn't want everybody to be here except me. Paul and Jason comin to spend time, taking their families with them. I should be here too."

"At leas they have a family."

Roy interrupts the words on Nora's lips as he enters with two bowls of soup, and she breathes relief, feeling he saved the moment. "I hope it not too hot. It finish cook not too long."

Nora, Janet and Roy join in animated discussion while Daisy escapes to the kitchen.

Chapter twenty seven

The group saunters into the yard, the children chattering excitedly. One little boy chases the dogs that, disturbed by the invasion, come out barking at the top of their lungs. Jason and Paul walk proudly with their wives and five children, Jason's two and Paul's three.

Nora and Janet are by the riverbank, sitting under the shade of a tree, talking. Roy is at the back of the house, Daisy inside. All four converge to greet the happy group of nine even before they reach the house.

Nora is unsure and nervous as she walks toward them and plasters a resolute smile on her face. She suddenly feels self-conscious among the glamorized looking women at her brothers' side. She detects surprise in the eyes of the two men as they hug her, the wives dutifully following the routine.

Roy and Daisy are happy and sheepish to see their sons' families. Daisy gives off that silly giggle whenever she feels she is in the presence of someone important as the women first greet her, then Roy. Jason and Paul give their mother that respectful hug, and heartily shake the hand of their father. Janet stands to the side and waits to be introduced.

It is mid-afternoon, and Christmas dinner is ready and waiting.

"The place looking good Dad," Paul states.

"Well, you know, I have to try to do me bes," the grey-haired man says with the broadest smile. He says it as if talking to a superior.

"You having a baby?" The little boy who had chased the dogs asks.

Everyone goes quiet.

Nora stoops and plays with his nose. "Yes, your aunt is having a baby."

"Is the daddy here?" An embarrassed Roy clears his throat. Her two brothers look away. Their wives look on inquisitively. Daisy's face twists in anger. Janet's heart sinks.

Nora does her best to keep her breath from stifling. "No, the father is not here," Nora says with the plastered smile.

"So he's not having Christmas dinner with us?"

"And what's your name, you who are so bright?"

"My name's Kamal!" he says with practiced precision.

"And Kamal, how old are you?"

The boy holds up three fingers. "I'm three."

"Good! You're a big boy," Nora says extravagantly. She grabs his hand and leads him as they walk to the house.

Mannish water, curried goat, oxtail, fried chicken, rice and peas with vegetable, followed by cake and ice cream with sorrel – the Jamaican entrée is shared around the table made to seat six. Pride of place is given to Jason and wife Veronica, Paul and wife Sharon, and Janet as special guest. Roy sits at his usual place and delights at the stories shared by his sons.

The children sit at the "side table" where Nora and Daisy busy themselves sharing their meals. It is the first time mother and daughter have had any direct interaction since Nora and Janet arrived two days earlier.

Nora tries to ease the tension by deliberately getting physically close to her mother and exchanging chitchats. Daisy is not in the mood and responds only in monosyllables.

Nora mentally recalls the conversation she and Janet had the previous morning, on Christmas Eve. Sleep was difficult the night before. The buoyancy of the spring frame, the unevenness of the mattress, her bulging stomach, and Janet beside her in the bed had Nora looking at the dark ply board ceiling for hours. She was relieved when day broke.

Daisy was annoyed that Nora had volunteered to prepare breakfast, but grudgingly gave her space in the small kitchen. Janet later stumbled out of the room, rubbing her eyes.

"Wow, you up pretty early."

"Couldn't sleep."

"I caused it?"

"Not really. I guess I was too tense."

"What you cooking?"

"Callaloo with salt fish, dumplings and boiled banana. I brew some nice black coffee too."

"Smells good. It's the smell of the food wake me. Long time I don't eat that." Janet looks around. "Where're your parents?"

"Papa gone to tie out the goats and feed the pigs. Mama gone to deliver a cake to a neighbor up the hill."

"So we alone?"

"For now, yes."

Janet looked around once more as if to make sure. "Your mother not very happy."

"Understatement of the year."

"I don't feel very comfortable with your mother so vex."

"Cho, don't worry yourself. That is mama all over. It don't mean nothin."

"But you mus care how she feel."

"Yea, I guess. But at the end o the day, mama is jus mama. She not goin change no matter what."

"Mama not goin change," Nora now whispers to herself as she steps back to give her mother space as she passes with a glum stare, but smiling with the children as she places plates piled high with food before them.

Janet, feeling awkward sitting in the midst of an unfamiliar family during their most important gathering, volunteers to help clear the tables and wash the dishes after dinner. She insists that Nora takes her place at the table. "You mus be tired. You on your feet the whole time."

The children take the clearing of their plates as a cue to go outside and play.

"Be careful, stay away from the water!" Veronica shouts, immediately showing embarrassment as to how loud she spoke.

Silence hovers as all eyes train on Nora while she sits.

Jason breaks the silence. "So Nora, tell me about... this," gesturing in the direction of her stomach."

"Cho, Jason, there isn't much to tell. You don't want to talk bout that now."

He fixes her with his gaze and a raised eyebrow. "I hear that nuff bangarang goin on."

"You sure you hear right?" Nora tries to make light of the comment.

"You tell me," Jason pushes. All at the table, except for Roy, grow curious.

"It's simple really. I jus decided it's time to have a child."

"But you're a pastor."

Nora does not answer.

"And you're not married."

Nora stays silent.

"How's that supposed to work?"

"You may be happy to know that I'm not currently in the service of the church."

"Because they threw you out."

"I guess you could say that," Nora answers matter-of-factly.

Veronica nudges Jason to get him to stop but he is determined.

"Did you think about your family before you did this?"

"What that have to do with anything?"

"It has everything to do with everything."

Veronica whispers to Jason, "Now's not the time or place." Jason looks at her sternly and she shuts up.

"If you really care to know, it was precisely because of family why I did this."

"Huh?" Both Jason and Paul ask in unison?

"I don't get it," Paul interjects.

Nora sulks and hesitates before saying under her breath. "Junior."

"What was that?" Jason asks.

"I did it because of Junior!" and Nora covers her face in tears.

The entire family goes stony silent.

Daisy, overhearing the conversation from the kitchen, walks into the dining room and stands at the door. Janet pauses her washing to listen.

Sharon looks around puzzled at everyone. "Junior, what does she mean?" Everyone remains stony-faced until Paul, with quivering lips, explains.

"Junior was our little brother who died in an accident."

"Gosh, I didn't know. You never told me."

"Now you know," Paul says with clenched lips.

"So how – what does her pregnancy have to do with that?"

"Because they all blame me for his death and I can never get it out of my mind!"

Nora erupts.

She looks at her mother and father with eyes wild with tears. "Mama, papa all I wanted to do was to try and replace Junior. I know it sounds silly and all that, but I felt that in some way I have to give him back to you. That is all I wanted. That is all I wanted to do," her voice trails off.

Nora's body shakes violently as she sobs. She turns and rests her head on her father's shoulder, who sits next to her. Roy places an uncertain arm around his daughter.

Chapter twenty eight

The ballroom waits expectantly. The high powered women view the very pregnant woman in their midst with quaint fascination. It is the annual banquet of the Business Women and Professional Club, a group of mainly upper class business and professional women and wives of the rich and powerful. "The idle rich," Nora used to call them. She feels strange among them and regards herself as an irony. These are women she vilified and ridiculed for much of her life.

Adam Goldstein's article turned her plight into an international drawing card. Women's groups in Europe, the United States, Canada, and the Caribbean contacted Nora, and she has since received invitations to be interviewed by local media and to speak at various functions, but this is her first public event. Other than the Associated Press interview, she has not commented publicly.

Too many of the guests want her to talk about herself during the pre-banquet reception. Nora deftly deflects the questions and seats herself, focusing on the uninteresting program in her hand. She tries little chitchat with those seated with her at the head table and forces herself to smile. The meal is totally tasteless, though she guesses it is some high society fare. She now desperately wants the evening to be over. Nora smiles across at Janet who sits at another table.

The time finally comes for her to speak. The emcee's introduction is superfluous but Nora accepts it graciously and lumbers up to the podium. A hush descends on the room and the clatter of silverware on plates subsides. She looks over the room of mainly females with a few husbands and boyfriends towed along. Cameras flash, reporters place tape recorders on the podium and four television cameras train focus on her. The nervousness runs down her spine to her toes.

"Ladies, gentlemen, it takes some bravery on your part to have me in your midst this evening." The audience gives an uncertain chuckle. "Courage is a most uncommon virtue these days, so I do not take your invitation lightly," Nora smiles, deliberately flattering the crowd. "I dare say it takes some courage for me to be here, being in the condition I am. I hope there's a doctor in the house cause you could be called to attend to an emergency any minute." The audience laughs, reading well the tone of her voice even as she glances down on her protruding stomach.

"I'm sure some of you are most curious to hear juicy details about my pregnancy and conflict with the church. I can't say I blame you. It does read like a good story. But for me, this is not a media event to celebrate. It's a most personal struggle that has taken on gargantuan proportions. I feel that I'm being drawn into a most public debate and battle when I'd rather stay in my little corner.

"I'm the first to admit that what I've done is most unusual, perhaps unique. I've dared to challenge long held traditions and beliefs. What makes it especially difficult is that I'm female. A female rebel is itself an oddity in our country. But there're some battles that only a woman can fight. Men cannot fight them for us, nor should we expect that they should." Several handclaps sound round the auditorium.

"As you may have learned by now, based on a published article that has gained widespread attention, I did not engage on this quest to strike a blow for women's liberty or women's rights. I did what I did because the same blood that runs through all other women's veins runs through mine, and the same desires and aspirations that other women have I too have. I'm a woman like any other woman. And one of the aspirations of many of us is that of having a family, or more specifically, the desire for children. Mine has not been any less.

"We're told that children should only be had within the traditional confines of a family where both parents are married.

Again, I do not take issue with that. That is an ideal I support. But that ideal is promulgated within a context where women are deprived, where there is the remotest chance that we can have a family with children.

"A number of you may be part of the church, and I understand if you disagree with what I'm doing. But it seems unfair, doesn't it, that the church is filled with mainly women – very few men are in the church – and yet we're told not to marry men who are *not* part of the church, or worse, we should not marry any man who is not part of *our* church because that would make us 'unequally yoked.' So you have a situation that a woman who desires children either does not have any, or she must leave the church if she is to have children. A number of women have done that. They leave the church, have their children, and then return. The church then receives them *and* their children with open arms. Some of these children eventually become leaders or prominent members within the church. Where does the hypocrisy stop?"

The crowd mutters and several heads nod in agreement, scattered handclaps rounding the room.

"One of the things said to me is that having a child is not a right. Well, we do lots of things that are not ours by right. Men arrogate to themselves an authority over us women that are not theirs by right. Men withhold from us our rightful place in business, in the professions, in the church, in the home. We have a right as equal participants with men in all spheres of society. Yet men assign to us the place we should be while they keep for themselves the positions of influence and power and wealth. We're placed in positions of dependency where we have no choice but to be dependent on men.

"So the church tells me I don't have a right to a child, a church whose leadership is overwhelmingly male, and most of whom have had their own children. Can you imagine if your boss were to say that to you, that you don't have a right to a family, or to have children, and fires you if you do? Can you imagine if the government was to say that to us, that if we were to have children we would lose certain benefits, because we've exercised an option that is not ours by right? What word is there for that other than tyranny that I, or any one of us women in here, are told that we do not have a right to have children?

"I made the decision to have a child because I believe it is *my* right to do so. And I made the decision that I would not leave the church to have that child and then return, as other women have.

"The church, of course, would have none of it. They threw me out. I determined not to leave voluntarily, so I was booted out. Well, I guess one could say they exercised their right to oppose my rights as a woman."

She pauses for the irony to sink in.

"Part of the smokescreen put before us is the legitimacy of the method I've chosen to have my child. But let's not be fooled. The method doesn't make a difference as to how the church would've reacted. But let's think about the method for a moment.

"The church has always been the last institution to embrace change, whatever the change is. The church is by nature suspicious of anything new or different. Most religions are. There were instances when the church rejected a new method or invention or discovery or thinking but has since embraced these. When the pill came into common use, one of the strongest opponents to the use of the pill was the church. Today, most major Protestant churches embrace the pill and other forms of birth control, or at least, they do not oppose its use. When reggae music became popular, the church was at best lukewarm toward this form of music. Now, the most popular gospel artistes in this country have embraced both reggae and dancehall music.

"Artificial insemination and other forms of assisted reproductive technology are relatively new. These are options available to women to have children, and because the church has not grounded its feet where such technology is concerned, it stands opposed to it. But I dare tell you that by the time my child becomes an adult, such technology will be embraced by the very church that now stands opposed to it.

"I've thought about this long and hard. Several choices are left open to me – either accept the church's ruling and walk away, or challenge the church's ruling. Neither is a palatable choice. None is painless. To accept the ruling would be to agree that what I've done is illegitimate and wrong. I honestly do not believe so. To challenge the ruling is to challenge that which is dearest and closest to my heart, because I still feel a strong bond with the church. I have therefore thought long and hard in contemplating my next move, and it is in that vein that I conferred with my attorney."

Nora pauses for dramatic effect. Low mutterings sweep through the room followed by a further and deeper hush.

"The advice given to me is that I do have just and reasonable cause to take action against the church."

Again, Nora pauses for dramatic effect. She shuffles her papers, then looks at the audience with a steely gaze.

"A motion has therefore been filed in the Supreme Court that my constitutional rights as a woman and as a professional have been violated by the action of the church."

A buzzing sound bursts through the ballroom as awe wends its way through the audience. Nora lifts her voice as she speaks.

"I can assure you that this action gives me no pleasure. I feel compelled to do it out of sheer necessity, both to clear my name and, even though this was not my original intent, to safeguard the rights of women, especially my sisters within the church.

"Some people will find it strange that I would take such action against the church. I know some will view this as blasphemy of the worst sort."

Then Nora begins to look pointedly into the faces of some of the ladies as she speaks in a stronger and firmer voice.

"Tell me, if you were working in a law firm, and you were fired for getting pregnant, what action would you have taken? If you work in the offices of any of our financial institutions and you were dismissed for having a baby, what is the most reasonable course of action that you could think of? If as a woman you were deprived of your livelihood and from practicing your profession simply because you desire the most precious gift in the world, the gift of a child, what would be the most natural course of action?

"I'm a professional, a trained professional within the church, and I've been denied my rights to practice my profession simply because of my pregnancy, not because of any other action on my part. I've been deprived of my livelihood as a minister of the gospel because I dare to have a child. Which other profession, which other sphere in society would tolerate such illegal and oppressive action?"

Nora's voice rings even louder as the audience listens in awestruck silence.

"And I dare anyone to get biblical with me! Mary the mother of Jesus got pregnant before her marriage to her husband, yet it is he that we serve and it is she that we revere. Rahab is listed as a female heroine in the scriptures and she was a prostitute – a prostitute who is an ancestor to Jesus! Tamar tricked her father in law into sleeping with her so that she could have a child – this Tamar too is an ancestor of Jesus!

"As far as morality goes, these women ought to be disgraced rather than lauded. Have I tricked anyone? Am I a prostitute? I have neither tricked anyone nor am I a prostitute, yet I'm treated as if I'm worse!

"If the way the church has treated me is reasonable, then we need to root the stories of these women out of the very Bible we revere."

The stunned audience, after a split-second silence, thunders into applause. The roar of hands runs for more than half a minute. Nora calms herself and speaks in a lower, more modulated tone.

"Frankly, I have no idea what will come of this action. I'm sure that a long road lies ahead. It's never easy to oppose or confront a bastion of power. It's never easy to stand up to those who feel that their rules operate outside of the ambit of the laws of society. That's the situation with the church. Its rules are supposedly beyond the pale of the general system of justice. It sets its own rules and it enforces those rules. In terms of its internal operations, it scoffs at the idea that others should tell it how it should manage its own affairs, or challenge its own laws.

"But the church cannot operate as if it's an independent state within a state. When it comes to trampling the rights of others, the church should be made to give an account in the same way any of the other institutions you represent here tonight are expected to. If the church is obligated to give heed to the laws having to do with taxes and finance, it should not be exempt from those having to do with the rights of persons. Discrimination on the basis of gender has for too long been a feature of the life of the church and it is time that it stops."

Nora surveys the room in the middle of her final pause.

"I hope some of you here will stand with me. But I intend to fight this to the very end, even if it means going alone."

A standing ovation continues until Nora is fully seated at her table.

Chapter twenty nine

The courthouse steams. In the corridors police officers, led by a muscular and heavily built sergeant with a mouth to match, urge onlookers out onto the streets. Several "coaster" buses park across the road as persons, in different forms of dress, some as if headed for Sunday morning worship, merge in the direction of the judicial halls. Several news vans place themselves strategically on the streets. Bystanders press against windowsills, hoping for a glimpse of the defrocked Nora Campbell.

Nora, clothed in an exaggeratedly loose maternity dress, sits next to her counsel in the swelter of the courtroom. The ten o clock sunshine spikes its way through the dirty glass windows and casts a hazy glow through the room. The gallery, jammed from as early as 8:30 a.m., is listless, as loud murmurs waft along the rows and columns.

Nora is annoyed. She sits as if trying to prevent the hard board of her chair from causing a chafe. The ferment and intensity of her discomfort cause her to second guess herself for being there. She wants to be there, she told her lawyers, despite the judge's earlier ruling that she need not be present for all court sessions. She wants to be there on this final day, she said, because she wants to be part of it to the very end.

At the start of the second week of the case, a fainting spell led to the adjournment of the court sitting for the day, amid widespread speculation and rumor that she suffered a miscarriage. The rumor mill swirled even more when she failed to turn up when the case resumed the following day. It's been an incredibly difficult two weeks.

Nora hates the speculation that attaches itself to her. A frenzied interest is the identity of the sperm donor. News reports suggested she visited a sperm bank in Miami. One other source suggested the local University Hospital as the source. One curious suggestion, and the one Nora is most uncomfortable with, is that the sperm came from someone she knows very well.

The talk shows have been relentless. Repeatedly, Nora and her lawyers have had to decline invitations to appear on radio and television, and these invitations subsided only after the case began. The church has not been spared. Leaders of the Reformed Christian Church refuse to comment publicly, except to issue a written release through the church's lawyers stating the reasons for the decision to defrock Nora. But leaders from other denominations are not shy to weigh in on the issue. Most vehemently support the stance of the Reformed Church and suggest that their actions would have been harsher and swifter. Two ministers, one an ethicist and both of whom lecture at the Jamaica School of Theology, beg to differ. The position of each makes them a favorite on the media circuit.

Women's groups have had a field day, using the case to champion women's rights. The head of the Women's Bureau indicates the case as a watershed in the country's history as it affects women in their personal and professional rights. Nora is now the poster child for feminist and other women's groups in Jamaica.

The unsettling murmur in the court subsides. Her honor, Geneve Richards, enters the chambers as a police corporal bellows for all in the court to rise and be orderly. Appearing to enjoy his role a little too much, he, with much fanfare and flourish, introduces the judge to the court.

Richards is a surprising choice as presiding judge, and one greeted with relief by women's groups. They feared having a male judge, whom they felt would be insensitive to the cause. Richards has gained a reputation for toughness, repeatedly handing out maximum sentences to offenders in criminal cases. In civil matters, she is known to heavily disfavor persons and groups who fail to fulfill their fiduciary and other responsibilities. A year earlier, she slapped a ten million dollar fine on the power company for failing to adequately compensate customers whose household appliances were damaged by power surges.

Richards is a young 46 year old who grew up middle class poor. Pugnacious, she is hard-bitten and hardboiled, traits developed while she rose through the ranks of the judiciary. She became tough and callous by virtue of her experiences in the male-dominated profession. The soft, baby face belies the steely backbone she carries, her features softened even more by the fashionable tested glasses she wears.

Judge Richards is as much disturbed by the atmosphere as Nora is. She squints with annoyance in the direction of the gallery and looks with disdain at the crowd gathered outside the windows.

"Why is not my court cleared of all these people?" She bellows, more in exasperation than as a command. The police officers do not move. They understand the judge by now. Her contempt is more an act of frustration than disrespect for the people.

"Counselors, I'm sure you're ready to bring all this to an end?"

"We're your honor," Bill Marks, Nora's lead counsel responds.

"Good. I'm as anxious as anyone else to get this –" she stops herself. "Well counsel, you aren't ready?" She points her face in the direction of the defense.

"We're anxiously waiting, your honor," Jeff Miles quickly reassures.

"Then let's get this thing going. Closing arguments will now begin. Mr. Marks, please."

Bill Marks' grey hair glistens, the thinning wavy strands pasted down on his scalp with too much goo. He gets up with an air that suggests he knows more than the presiding judge. There are just a few judges he respects, and Judge Richards, he believes, has been elevated beyond her competence. He wishes he had Judge Lucius Grandison to argue before. He reveled in the idea of arguing this groundbreaking case before an intellectual equal. But that was not to be. He has to make do with an underling and inferior kind.

He snorts as he opens his folder at the podium and stands in Mark Antony fashion to face the judge, swiveling himself first to the left then to the right in acknowledgement of the gallery. He always likes to put on a show.

"A fundamental right of every citizen in Jamaica is the right to employment, this without discrimination on the basis of race or gender. Jamaican laws make it clear that women should not be discriminated against because of their desire to have children. The Maternity Leave Act number 44 of 1979 states very clearly that women are entitled to maternity leave for twelve weeks with full pay for eight weeks, and they should not lose their jobs just because of a pregnancy. It is these laws that the Jamaica Reformed Christian Church is attempting to turn on its head. The church has violated every law in the books that protects workers' rights from discriminatory practices."

Marks pauses as if wanting the point to sink into the judge's head. He is unsure as to whether she grasps the complexity of the case.

"That would be bad enough your honor, but the right of privacy is also at issue here. My client has had her privacy rights violated in a way that few other women in Jamaica have. Her private life is being played out in the public sphere and her right to have a child of her own, to bear a family of her own, is being questioned. Which other woman in her professional capacity would be removed from her position and have her livelihood undermined on the basis that she decides to bear children? The organization that does that would be roundly condemned by all and sundry.

"But the church is asking to be exempt. Why should the church be given the freedom to violate the rights of one of Jamaica's citizens in a way that no other organization, private or public, would be allowed to? Why should this institution, which is bound by the laws of the country as any other, be allowed to indiscriminately dismiss an employee without the consideration of the rights of that person?"

Then, as if in acknowledgment of the intellectual inferiority of everyone else in the court, he counts the words. "The issue is pretty simple your honor. What we have is the private decision of a private citizen to do one of the most private things that many women want – to have and bear a child. What is so wrong with that?"

Several handclaps ring through the gallery. Fire flashes in Richards's eyes as she fixes on the group of women neatly dressed in their upper middleclass garb, looking out of place in the sweltry of the courtroom. The handclaps quickly die. Feeling that he has somehow got through, Marks lifts the tone and tempo of his voice.

"It is claimed that my client broke the rules of the church in doing so. What rule? The Reformed Church developed a policy on artificial insemination only after the fact. Only after the fact of her pregnancy! It is clear what this is. A rule was created, specially targeted at my client, to have her removed. At the very least, that is immoral. You want to get rid of someone, so you create a rule or a law with the specific intent of doing so!

"How can the church have the nerve to accuse my client of acting immorally, or of breaking its moral codes, when the church itself acted immorally? And what are the moral codes that my client is accused of violating? Mention has been made of fornication and adultery. They even quoted a Jewish Rabbi Waldenberg's belief that the injection of sperm is itself a prohibited form of adultery. But for fornication or adultery to take place, there has to be physical contact. My client did not have physical contact with a person. All she did was utilize a simple technology through artificial insemination to have a child. She, like other women in their 30s and 40s and who, not having a life partner, became concerned as to whether she will be able to have children. We're fortunate to live in an age when women have more choices than their forebears, where women no longer need to rely on the presence of a male partner in order to have children. It is this choice that Rev. Nora Campbell took advantage of."

Marks mops a brow, as much from theatrics as is to remove sweat.

"It was argued by the defense, and they had their experts on the stand, claiming that children born of single parents have a higher incidence of delinquency, emotional trauma, and psychological problems than those who have both parents within the home. But the studies they cited were largely done on children who suffered trauma in their lives, who suffered the loss of a parent through divorce or death. Such studies do not represent the children of those women who became single mothers by choice. We have ample evidence of well adjusted children who grow up to be outstanding citizens in this society who were born to, and who were reared by a single parent. I am one of them.

"Much has been made about creating an ideal family atmosphere for the rearing of children. What is an ideal family atmosphere? That question has not been adequately answered by the defense even though it raised the issue. There are other factors that go into creating an ideal family than the mere presence of two parents. What of love for the children? What of the presence of an extended family to love and nurture? What of the economic means to provide for the child? What of the maturity of the parent to properly guide and grow a child? All these and more go into making an ideal family atmosphere and my client is more than willing and capable of making up for any so-called deficiency of not having a male partner around."

After surveying the gallery once more, Marks pointedly fixes his gaze on Richards, who looks at him with the same level of contempt in which he holds her. The old coot should have taken his leave of these chambers long ago, she squeals to herself. His irascibility is more a deterrent than a help to his clients. She stopped short of citing him for contempt three cases back when he refused her order to discontinue a particular line of questioning. Earlier in this case, he snapped at a defense witness after the witness dared question Marks' ability to grasp a minute point of Christian ethics.

"In considering the matter, the court needs to be absolutely careful that it does not interfere with the right to human reproduction. The court would be siding with the church in stating that women should be restricted in their reproductive rights. What difference would there be between this stance and that of the horrendous practices done in some unenlightened countries to have

205

compulsory sterilization, compulsory abortion, or restricting parents or families to a specific number of children? All these have been roundly condemned by modern, civilized societies. There would be no difference between those actions and a decision for the defense if my client, and by implication all women, were restricted from having children by artificial insemination or any other means. Or that the threat of loss of job and income were to hang over their heads if they were ever to choose a particular reproductive technique."

He turns to look at the discomfiting figure to his left who sheepishly lowers her eyes at his gaze. His look pulls all other eyes in the court toward Nora.

"Has the Rev. Campbell failed in her role as pastor? Even the records of the Reformed Church show that she is an outstanding pastor to her parishioners. She has exceeded every expectation of her. When the decision came for her ordination after having served a two-year probationary period, an internal report on her says, and I quote, 'We believe that the Rev. Nora Campbell is an outstanding example of what a pastor should be. She is a credit to the Jamaica Reformed Christian Church, and we unreservedly recommend her for full ordination to the Christian ministry.'

"This is the woman – it is this outstanding professional which the same Reformed Church now seeks to victimize in its discriminatory and immoral act of having her removed and revoking her accreditation as a minister of the church."

The old attorney, refocusing his attention on the judge, and tipping to his toes as if to make one hard, final push, ends with his usual ostentatious flourish.

"We ask that your honor rule in favor of my client who, in her years as pastor, has done nothing wrong, except to want to have a child. For this she should not be punished. We ask that her rights, which were violated, her integrity, which has been impugned, and her dignity, of which she has been robbed, be returned to her, that she be reinstated as a pastor within the Reformed Church. We also ask that she be duly compensated for the loss of income and damage to her reputation."

Chatter breaks out as Marks struts to his chair, looking around the gallery as if acknowledging the silent applause of the crowd. Richards sounds the gavel once and the crowd stammers into silence.

Jeff Miles sits up in his chair in anticipation.

"Mr. Miles, we're ready for you. I trust you won't keep us beyond lunch."

Miles teases a wry smile. "Definitely not my intention your honor."

Miles knows he has the full support of the gallery. The atmosphere has sometimes taken on the air of an evangelism service where persons nodded and gave affirmations to testimonies of defense witnesses. He plays that support to the hilt, often sounding like an evangelist in a tent meeting. Not that Miles cares much for the teaching of the church. But he knows the church, having grown up in Sunday school and is now an occasional visitor. He remembers the old time evangelists of his childhood and uses their oratorical devises to the max.

Richards is not impressed with Miles' showboating and finds him to be way over the top. It is very difficult to be patient with him. She rolls her eyes as he steps up with that arrogant superiority not dissimilar to Marks'. Why do these lawyers consider themselves gods? She muses to herself.

"Your honor, the past two weeks have served to throw much light on the issue at hand, making this case one of precedent in this country. Several experts on both sides testified and the defense acknowledges that the issues raised are both complex and discomfiting. The plaintiff's case revolves around what she claims to be the violation of her rights in the termination of her employment as a pastor.

"The first thing to note, your honor, is that historically, the courts in this country have been loathed to get involved in the internal affairs of churches. These institutions have traditionally been governed by church law, so long as such laws do not violate civil law. Our contention is that no civil laws were violated in this instance as the church acted within its rights and prerogative to decide whom it sees fit to serve as ordained clergy. I repeat. It must be the right of the Jamaica Reformed Christian Church, as indeed it is the right of any church, to decide on its own qualifications as to who should serve in its ranks."

Miles learns much of his showmanship from Marks, whom he quietly regards as a mentor. He looks at the old man with mild admiration but with a stare that suggests a younger bull intending to displace an older bull that has lost much of its manly vigor.

"If you were to rule in favor of the plaintiff, then a most dangerous precedent would be set. The judiciary, which is an arm of the government, would be setting itself up as a regulatory body that decides the qualification for a minister of religion. That, in the very extreme, is unconscionable, and we would be placing a burden on the state that it is not competent to fulfill. It is also contrary to any understanding of natural justice. Indeed your honor, we do not even tell private businesses the criteria they should use to hire, or fire, their employees. Why should we ask the courts to tell churches what criteria to use to determine who should or should not be an ordained minister?"

Miles straightens his back and smiles, unsurprised at the 'Amen' that erupts from the mostly female gallery. Richards, wearied at this unseemly display in her court, sounds a tired gavel.

"The plaintiff has argued that the removal from her office as pastor is gender discrimination, and that it is because she is female why she was removed from her post. Nothing is farther from the truth. The Reformed Church still has in its employ two other women who, in a matter of a year or two, will be ordained as pastors, and three more are currently in training. None of these women feel threatened because of their gender. None of these women believe their future in the church is threatened simply because of their gender. There's no case of gender bias or discrimination here.

"Your honor, it is a simple case that the plaintiff has violated one of the most basic and ancient tenets of the Christian Church, a teaching that did not originate with the Reformed Church, but that have existed from the very dawn of Christianity. The bearing of a child outside of wedlock is a serious moral breach. This has been the case for centuries for ordinary church members, it has been more so for ordained clergy. It matters not whether you or I agree with that position. That has been the traditional stance of the church through the centuries, and it is a stance that should be respected."

The loud applause runs simultaneously with "halleluiahs." One lady in an oversized hat stands, and in spasms as if caught by seizure, makes two turns on the spot and rings out, "Yes, Lord, bless your church Lord," then sits trembling on the hard, uninviting bench.

"Any other outbursts like that and I'll clear all o you out o my court!" Richards yells.

Miles mocks annoyance at the gallery, lifting his hands in a questioning gesture.

"I apologize for that interruption. You may continue Mr. Miles," Richards shrugs a frustrated shoulder. Miles pauses, as if willing the court to continue hearing him.

"It is the contention of the defense that the church has the right to rule on such matters, and not the courts of this land. For the courts to so rule would constitute interference in the operation and the internal affairs of churches. This is a precedent that this honorable court should not be too anxious to set."

Miles shuffles his notes and makes as if he misplaces something, then shows satisfaction as he apparently finds what he searches for. He turns his attention to the group of women sitting uncomfortably in the mix of the crowded gallery in their upper class attire.

"Your honor, the church took the decision to have the plaintiff removed from office on the grounds that artificial insemination by donor is not recognized by the church as an effective substitute for having a family. This method was created to assist infertile couples to have children, not as a license for single women to have children without reference to what the church considers to be the ideal family."

His face shows disdain as he returns attention to the bench.

"The church also regards this method as having myriad problems, ethical and otherwise. Not least of these ethical problems is the fact that the procedure can be used for gender selection. It is something that even the medical community agonizes over, is generally rejected as unethical, and in most if not all countries is illegal. There is tremendous unease that the procedure could be used to select the sex of a child and this is rejected not just by the church, but also by professionals in the legal, medical and other fields.

"There are serious social problems associated with the procedure. There is the question of what it means to be a parent, a question that is not moot to the church but is of real significance and consequence. A drawing of lines as to what it means to be a father as against a parent is most unfortunate, particularly in a society such as ours where there is a rallying cry for fathers to display greater responsibility as parents to their children. The instant case before us flies in the face of all that concern. A concern to the church is who the father of the child is. The concern is not over the personality of the father, i.e., the person to whom the sperm that impregnated the plaintiff belong, but the concern is the message it sends that men can merely father children without performing their obligation as parents. Will this child have a father to call a parent? The plaintiff is most unmindful and insensitive to the church and the wider society about the role that men should play in the life of their offspring."

Miles makes a quick survey of the gallery, holding the gaze of two young women for a split second before homing in on the judge, whom he knows to be a divorced mother of two.

"I'm the first to admit we have some outstanding single mothers in Jamaica. These are women who've made tremendous sacrifices on the behalf of their children. But the average woman is not single by choice, but by circumstance. What the plaintiff has done however, is to present single-motherhood, indeed, single-parenthood, as an ideal, something that our own experts contend cannot, and should not be an ideal, not when the evidence clearly shows children of single parents have higher adjustment problems than those reared by two parents. What message is being sent to the young girls in this country about having and rearing children?

"We heard testimony that one concern of ethicists is that children who are born of this procedure often do not know who their father is. The possibility exists that such children may end up marrying their brother or sister as they would not have a clue who their siblings are.

"And what of the possible discrimination and slander this child may face? The church is duly concerned that this child, growing up in this conservative society, may suffer taunts and discrimination from others. It is the contention of the defense that enough consideration has not been given to the effects all this will have on the child. Certainly no responsible person, least of all a pastor, should do anything to increase the likelihood of discrimination against anyone, particularly children.

"Artificial insemination is just one of the several methods of artificial reproductive technologies that the church has serious ethical concerns about. It falls in the same category as surrogate motherhood, embryo transfer, and in vitro fertilization. These and other procedures pose serious ethical and moral questions because of the aforementioned gender selection or screening, possible commercialization of wombs 'for hire' by women, and perhaps most important of all, the destruction of embryos, which the church claims is the destruction of life. The church believes life begins when a female egg is fertilized by a male sperm. In order for success to be gained from most forms of artificial reproductive technology, an excess of fertilized eggs or embryos are created as the failure rates are extremely high. There is hyperfertilization, an excessive production of embryos. In the case of artificial insemination, the success rate is as low as fifteen percent. Several of these procedures result in a high loss of fetal life.

"We're being told her privacy rights have been violated. There's no law to suggest there's such a thing as a right to have a child. Neither our society nor the church recognizes such a right. Indeed, the privacy of parents may be restricted for the protection of health or morals as is provided for under international law, to which Jamaica is a signatory. There's the matter of legitimate public interests which must be of consideration. There are other persons involved that are affected, not just the plaintiff. The Human Rights Committee of the United Nations says that it may be 'necessary in a democratic society in the interests of national security, public safety or the economic wellbeing of the country, for the prevention of disorder or crime, for the protection of health or morals, or for the protection of the rights and freedoms of others' to restrict some personal rights. I remind the court that Jamaica has adopted these laws that are enshrined in our statutes.

"The action to remove Ms. Campbell as a pastor within the Jamaica Reformed Christian Church was taken to protect the morals of the church as well as the public interests of its members, as stated in international and Jamaican law."

Miles, for the first time, looks at the group of ordained clergy seated in the front row of the gallery, and offers an affirmative nod to Rev. Peters. The gallery is brought to full attention with the brief silence and Miles, winding up as for a kill, trains his voice to sound like an evangelist about to make his final appeal.

"The eighty thousand members of the Jamaica Reformed Christian Church have been profoundly affected by her actions. The action of the plaintiff has been scandalous and has caused severe embarrassment to the Reformed Church. The reputation of the church has suffered severe damage as a result of what she has done. Prior to all this, the Reformed Church has had an outstanding record of service to the citizens of this country. Its pastors and leaders have been looked upon as men and women of integrity. It has an enviable reputation in the establishment of schools and colleges in this country for nearly two centuries, in helping the poor and downtrodden, in the provision of shelter for the homeless, and generally in meeting the needs of thousands of Jamaicans. The church could not be expected to sit idly by and do nothing to protect its reputation.

"The plaintiff, being unmindful and insensitive to these concerns of the church is deemed unfit to hold the office of pastor, and was duly removed from her post. It is the church's right and prerogative to do so, not the legislative body of this country, and certainly not the judiciary.

"What this honorable court is being asked to do is to legislate, something it has neither the power, nor, I am sure, the willingness to do. The case of the plaintiff is without merit, and we ask your honor to rule in favor of the defense."

Resounding shouts of 'halleluiah' and 'amen' echo off the walls of the courthouse as Richards, with futile effort, sounds the gavel, only to be drowned out by ecstatic shouts from the gallery.

Chapter thirty

The vigil is in its sixth hour. Two security guards twirl their batons, daring anyone to step past the threshold at the hospital's entrance. A cacophony of voices and murmurings express displeasure at the constraints. One of five reporters among the crowd dares the guards' composed seriousness and asks to speak with "Someone in authority." The two men snicker simultaneously and turn disdainfully away. The young man, with camera in hand and a bag over the shoulder, peers through the door and steps back immediately when the two men converge on him.

Inside, Janet pats Nora's hand reassuringly as she is prepped. The labor pains have been constant the past eleven hours, and the midwife looks with disinterested professionalism at the fussiness displayed by the expectant mother and her friend.

It is a long day, and Nora is praying that it ends quickly. At 2 a.m. she awoke with a strong urge to use the bathroom. These visits, fifteen minutes apart at first, grew more frequent and intense. It was only at the start of a dull pain low down in her tummy that it hit her – she was in labor. The room swirled for long seconds as comprehension deserted her. Nora, standing in the bedroom with knees buckling, reached for the phone before reminding herself she is at Janet's house.

Janet tried to appear composed, but the urgent insistent clamor of Nora as she barged into Janet's room startled her, matching Janet's confusion with Nora's. Both women got hold of themselves and, with sheets and towels strewn on the car seat, Janet eased Nora into the back.

The thin early morning traffic enabled Janet to make good time, but the minutes stretched into mental hours as Nora felt pain bearing down on her insides. The deep pain deepened as needles forced their way into her most inward parts. Janet flitted eyes between Nora in the back and the road ahead of her, praying deep in her heart that the baby does not come before they arrive at the hospital. Nora's deep moans intensified into mournful cries. Pains that previously lasted seconds grew to almost a minute. Intervals that were several minutes became only seconds. Pains that were small needles became daggers.

Janet's anxiety caused her to jerk the car to a halt at the hospital's entrance, causing Nora to squeal in agony. Janet's apologetic shushing only led to more baneful wailing, and the confused pastor rushed into the hospital, panicky calling on a bleary-eyed porter, the first person she saw, for assistance. The reluctant gentleman took many moments to rouse himself, and with bitterness and boredom etched in his face, fetched a haggard stretcher before pushing it lazily outside. The porter stood disinterestedly as Nora struggled onto the stretcher with assistance from Janet, then wheeled her sullenly inside.

It is now past 1 p.m. and Nora looks pleadingly at Janet, hoping her friend can do something to ease the pain. "Can't I have a painkiller?" she asks the midwife. The woman, who by now knows who Nora is, having herself read and watched the national headlines with interest, shakes a derisive head."

"What's taking so long?" she wails.

"You're not yet fully dilated," she is brusquely informed.

"Can't you dilate me some more?" The nurse laughs and, satisfied that the infusion is properly set, leaves the room.

"Pray for mi please, pray for mi please," Nora begs Janet, her eyes widening with fear. Janet looks on helplessly.

"You not praying! Why you not praying?"

Janet holds down her head and rests it on the stretcher while clasping Nora's hand. Janet flinches under Nora's vice-like grip.

"You praying? That is good. Good that you praying. Ah-h-h! Lawd it hot. Lawd it hot. Lawd it hot."

Janet lifts her head to stare at fright in Nora's eyes.

"Please, do. Help me. I can't bear it. I can't bear it. I can't bear it. Help me Pleeease!!"

Janet bounds up and runs out into the hallway. "Hello! Hello!!" She calls to no one in particular, and dozens of curious eyes meet hers. A nurse looks up and Janet seizes on her disjointed gaze. "I think she's ready." The nurse pauses with a sniff and Janet looks her squarely in the face and, in her preacher's voice yells, "Do something!"

The midwife emerges, and Janet shakes her head as she watches the woman saunters her way to the prep room.

Sweat streams down Nora's face as she looks wildly at the midwife and Janet when they enter. The nurse takes one look and makes the page for Dr. Henley and starts fussing with the preparations for delivery. Nora is quickly whisked out as they head for the delivery room.

Outside the hospital a hum rises after a hospital attendant casually passes by and whispers to a bystander in the crowd. The whispers go around until it becomes a buzz. The group, steadily increasing until it is now close to one hundred, converges closer to the entrance, hoping to gain closer access. "She ready to have baby!" one person shouts out.

The frenzy subsides into scurried calmness in the delivery room. Dr. Henley looks with concern on Nora and asks if "You want me to apply the epidural." She looks at Janet who is bedecked in hospital garb and who shrugs a shoulder.

"I've been bearing this thing the whole day, I'll bear it out."

Nora surveys herself and the room. The stirrups are a little too tight and the lights harsh, but the gasping pain distracts her. She feels exposed, much too open for the world to see. That world is the four persons milling around the small room, Dr. Henley, Janet, the midwife, and an attendant.

She detects a smile in the eyes of Henley. A pat on the hand assures her that things are going well. That reassurance leads to a sharp piercing pain. Her insides churn. A quick glance and a nod of heads send the attendant scurrying to get some implement. It matters not to her that what the attendant holds in her hand seems a little too sharp. The menacing implement is placed between her legs and she wonders if the sensation she feels is labor, or a different kind of pain.

"It's coming," a voice mutters, much too sanguine for the occasion, she thinks.

"Push."

The pressure is deep, the pain intense. Her mind swings.

What the hell am I doing? Her entire body throbs.

"Give it to me." Brief confusion etches all eyebrows.

"Give me the epidural, dammit!"

"Too late," the doctor says.

"No."

"Just push," the impatient midwife says to her, and the doctor gives her a reproving look. The nurse softens her tone and face.

"You may want to hold her hand," Dr. Henley instructs Janet.

"O my God."

"Push."

"No!" Nora gives out a bloodcurdling wail.

"Wait. Stop pushing," Henley commands. He checks his screen and mutters to the nurse, "Blood pressure is high." He makes a quick decision. "You have to listen to me carefully, we can do this but you have to follow my instructions carefully. We're almost there. You've been doing well so far but you need to do a bit more. You're not pushing hard enough."

Nora nods her head. "Yes, yes, yes."

"Push."

"Urgggh!"

"Doing good. One more time, we're almost there."

"Urgggghh!"

The pain vanishes, and the room is interrupted by a piercing cry.

"Congratulations. It's a boy," the doctor announces.

Nora looks up and the midwife places the tiny infant on her chest. Nora amazes at the little thing and rubs her hand gently over its back.

The weight of motherhood descends on her, and her tears ease its pain.

Chapter thirty one

Judge Geneve Richards shuffles her books and papers, deliberately keeping the courthouse waiting before taking her seat. She squints in the direction of a window where a sharp sunray lights the room. Finally, she sits, allowing all to do the same, and the courtroom takes a collective deep breath.

She looks with a mixture of pity and outrage at the new mother. Nora sits beside her counsel, a baby carriage blocking half the passageway beside her. Richards thinks better of giving an order to have the infant removed. Locking eyes with the frail figure, she communicates her disgust and displeasure.

The judge takes her time to write notes in a book, as if, for those moments, she was alone in her private chambers. Shuffling feet and clearing throats break the silence, and she looks up suspiciously, as if annoyed at being disturbed. She returns attention to her note taking and suddenly, as if stung, she lifts her head and closes the book with an audible 'flap.'

"This case had me revisiting the Bible." She pauses as if unsure of her next statement. Lifting her voice as if gathering a lost thought, she continues in a high pitched tone. "God knows I need to read it more often, if only to know how some people think or why they think the way they do."

Then a smile breaks across the slightly textured lips, her voice dipping to a slightly lower tone.

"I returned to the Bible because I remember how confused I used to be as a child as to why some women grieved about not being able to have children. It was a problem for Sarah, Abraham's wife. It was a problem for Jacob's wives, two sisters who were jealous of each other over their ability to bear children. And I read the horrible story of two other sisters who made their father drunk in order to sleep with him just so that they may have children. One other woman gave up her child to the priest just because God answered her prayer by giving her a son."

Richards raises hands as if challenging an audience. "The Bible does have some rather nasty details about women and children and families, of how some women hated other women because of their children, or women throwing out other women and their children due to jealousy. Such barbarity, unfortunately, still exists."

The smile disappears and a shadowy look crosses her eyes.

"The defense bases much of its case on what the Bible says. I'm no expert in theology, but I find the Bible to be a very poor defense in matters of morality, at least in a case such as this. And I cannot help but wonder that, if many of those women in the Bible who yearned to have children, women such as Sarah and Elizabeth and Hannah, if they were alive today and wanted children as they did then, if they would not have taken advantage of the opportunities modern medicine provides. If nothing else, these biblical stories show that women from the dawn of time have always wanted children, and some would stoop to any level, including getting their father drunk and committing incest, in order to bear a child of their own."

She looks at Nora, trying not to let her annoyance at having an infant in her courtroom show. "I guess Ms. Campbell is no different from these women in the Bible. She wants to have a child, and she, like those women in the Bible, is determined to have a child. And so she has. Congratulations to her."

The mockery is difficult to hide. "The difference between her and those women is the technology. Rather than wait on some angel to visit her, if we were to believe such stories, or doing what some of those women did, she utilized modern technology."

Richards looks at the group of clergymen seated near the front row of the gallery. "I therefore wonder about the defense's use of the Bible to claim that Ms. Campbell has acted contrary to Christian ethics. But then, I'm no Bible expert. I leave that to you gentlemen of the cloth."

Richards opens a file and flits several sheets before settling on the fourth sheet from the top. She dons her glasses and softens her look.

"This case has proven difficult because there are tremendous shortcomings in our laws, both criminal and civil, with regard to modern techniques of human reproduction. It is also difficult because it touches labor law, family law, privacy law, and the relationship between church and state. Not least is the fact there are thorny ethical issues involved. Adding to the complexity is the fact that the medical community, the legal fraternity, the church, and of course, politicians, all feel they have a say on the matter, as well they might.

"But perhaps what makes it all the more difficult is the controversy surrounding the issues raised. Such controversy raises emotions to very high levels, which makes it difficult for even rational persons to see through the maze."

Looking at both plaintiff and defense, Richards feigns modesty. "For good or ill, it has fallen to my lot to not only hear the case, but to make a ruling. The problem is that there's an absence of any generally accepted standards by which to make such a ruling. There's no generally accepted moral standard; and from what I can gather no generally accepted religious standard; and sadly, there is an absence of any legal standard, at least in our jurisdiction."

Richards stops briefly while finding another page. Her gaze fixes on Nora for the third time, then the carriage beside her. "One standard I can use to measure this case are those having to do with human rights. I agree with the plaintiff. Her rights to having a career were seriously violated in this instance. Not only her own rights as a person. It can also be argued that the human rights of her child have also been compromised. It appears to me that in all of this, the rights of the child have largely been ignored, which I find amazing coming from the legal luminaries that participated in this case.

"A key question is, should the status of the child be affected in any way by the methods of his conception and birth? The obvious answer is that it should not. It is true that in monarchies one's lineage may determine if one should rule as king or queen. But even if we were to grant that, it is more the exception than the rule. It is a philosophy generally to be rejected. Hitler tried it by indicating that one's birth should determine one's status, whether one was inferior or superior. Racists both past and present have tried it.

"The fact is, punishment of Ms. Campbell is at the same time punishment of her child, and that is a serious human rights violation. The child is without doubt the innocent party and the real victim in this matter. It seems gross to suggest that because this child was conceived through artificial insemination, then this child's rights to a life where he can be brought up in a secure environment should be taken away. To separate his mother from her means of livelihood simply on the basis on how the child was conceived and the circumstances of his birth appears to support the violation of the child's human rights.

"It is a throwback to the pre-1979 era in Jamaica when children born outside of a marital union were not entitled to the same rights of inheritance as those born within a marital union. Our politicians, for once at least, saw through the gross violation of the rights of such children and passed the Status of Children Act. Also, up to the seventies, women, such as female teachers, lost their jobs if they were single and pregnant, and their children were often discriminated against. Again, thankfully, the law was changed to not only prevent women losing their jobs, but to allow them to get maternity leave with pay. And this was done over the objection of the teachers union itself, the very body that was to protect the rights of these women. The society was up in arms against the law at the time, but the country now accepts the legislation as enlightened."

Richards shuffles more pages before continuing.

"International law is perhaps our best guide here. United Nations resolution 2263 on the Elimination of Discrimination Against Women reads in part, 'In order to prevent discrimination against women on account of marriage or maternity and to ensure their effective right to work, measures shall be taken to prevent their dismissal in the event of marriage or maternity and to provide paid maternity leave, with the guarantee of returning to former employment, and to provide the necessary social services, including child care facilities.'

The judge looks up from her notes and points her nose at the defense. Her voice goes slightly shrill.

"It is patently clear that the church has violated this provision, which has been adopted by our own country. Ms. Campbell has been discriminated against both on the basis of her singleness and her pregnancy. The UN makes it plain that neither should be used against women, particularly in respect to their employment, neither 'on account of marriage or maternity.' Rather than giving Ms. Campbell leave with pay, and ensuring that she returns to her job, the church dismissed her, effectively ending her career as a pastor."

The judge pauses and then takes a deep breath.

"That being said, there's good reason why the state has been reluctant in the past to get engaged in the internal affairs of the church, and to maintain a level of separation between both. Our government is not allowed to direct persons in their religious observances. We in the courts nor the executive nor the legislature are not allowed to tell persons how, where, or when they should worship. We are not in a position to tell persons *who* to worship. So Christians worship Jesus and Rastafarians worship Haile Selassie while Hindus have their gods.

"When it comes to religious matters, we have very limited authority. To ask us to reinstate a clergy member to his or her position can be construed as interference in the internal affairs of the church. Not least because the church appoints persons on the basis of a special divine call, or so it is claimed."

Richards puts on her most commanding voice. "For the most part, our jurisdiction resides in the area of religious liberty. We are to see that people's religious liberties are protected. I cannot see where the religious liberty of Ms. Campbell was violated. Her removal had to do with her substantive post as pastor, not her status as a member within the Jamaica Reformed Christian Church.

She is not prevented from worshipping in any of the congregations of the Reformed Church, and she is not prevented from worshipping the same God or any other god that she so chooses. She can, if she chooses, start a church of her own, or even a rival religious movement of her own. The actions of the Reformed Church do not seem to put any such restrictions on her."

For the fourth time, Richards picks out Nora. "Ms. Campbell, you're a brave woman. It takes guts to take the action you did, and you have served to exercise the mind of the country in a way few have. This is why it gives me no pleasure to make the ruling I'm about to give."

Richards sweeps her eyes across the courtroom and levels a gaze at every row in the gallery while she speaks in rapid tones. "While it is clear your rights were violated, there's a preponderance of the separation of church and state where, if I were to order your reinstatement, it would open the door for the state to so interfere in the future, in other, more mundane instances. That is a chance I'm not prepared to take. The use of a human rights standard in this case is less weighty. Human rights violations focus on 'some protection, status, benefit or freedom that has been robbed or undermined.' But it is shaky to suggest that rights are absolute or can never be overridden by other considerations.

"A decision for the plaintiff would violate one of the basic principles enshrined in the Jamaican constitution. The overriding matter is that of freedom of conscience, a guaranteed protection under constitutional law."

With a swift glance on the file in front of her, Richards lifts her pitch even higher. "Of particular relevance is chapter three section 21 and subsection 3 of the Jamaican constitution which states, 'The constitution of a religious body or denomination shall not be altered except with the consent of the governing authority of that body or denomination.'

"Having read the constitution of the Reformed Church, I'm satisfied that if the court were to reinstate you to your previous position as pastor it would be tantamount to rewriting the constitution of that body without the due authorization of the designated authority of the church. Article II of their constitution reads in part, 'The Reformed Church shall consist of such ministers and other persons as are in agreement with the Articles of Association.' The regulations of the church further state, 'Any minister who violates any of the fundamental principles of the Church shall be removed from his/her position and shall cease to be recognized as a Minister of the Jamaica Reformed Christian Church... Any minister wishing to be readmitted into the Church shall apply to the President in writing, in accordance with the regulations. The President shall refer the matter to the appropriate committee for consideration.'"

Then, as if giving final acknowledgment to Nora, Richards looks her in the eyes as she throws the dagger. "It appears that in order to be reinstated, you will have to reapply to the church through the designated authority. I therefore have no choice but to find in favor of the defense. The suit of the plaintiff is hereby dismissed and I further order that legal costs for the defense be borne by the plaintiff."

The court erupts.

Twenty minutes later, outside, on the steps, Nora stands in a daze. She swirls as the streets separate then converge, the dizzying spell creating monsters of the large crowd that stands in rapturous amusement. Janet Ffrench stands to her left, Bill Marks to her right. Both rest a hand on a shoulder. Janet gently releases the overly tight grip that Nora has on her sleeping son, fearing the child will suffocate against her bosom. He makes a sleepy fuss as she takes the child and places him against her own virgin chest.

A jeer breaks out. Marks prods Nora forward and she makes the first, then the second heavy step. They descend with Marks and Janet casting wary glances at the high fists, the wide-mouthed grins, and the mocking voices. Nora moves at the will and impulse of Marks who urges her impatiently down the flight of steps.

The Rev. Basil Newton steps out of the crowd, climbs a few steps, and extends a hand to Nora. She takes it, unsure of the gesture, but grateful for it. Marks releases her to his advance and he walks her, holding her close, to the car. "Come with me," Newton whispers in her ear.

At the car, Newton allows Nora, then Janet, still holding the baby, into the back. He quickly pushes himself into the driver's seat. Crowded hands bang the hood as the car reluctantly makes a path through the thronged streets. The baby wakes up with a desperate, ear-piercing wail.

Nora's mind wanders back into reality as the crowd eases behind them. The baby finally calms as she places a breast in its mouth. "You didn't have to do this," she says with gratitude. Newton glances in the rearview and says nothing. They drive along in elaborate silence. "Are we stopping anywhere other than your place?" He finally asks, looking in the mirror at Janet.

Janet glances at Nora and shakes a weary head.

Chapter thirty two

Rev. Basil Newton sits before the committee, his right fingers playing a silent rhythm on the slightly scratched cedar table. The lump refuses to dislodge itself from his throat despite deep and persistent swallowing. Rev. Glenhope Peters, Rev. Mercel Pinto, Rev. Jeffrey East, Rev. Harvey Johnson, Rev. Neville Pusey, Rev. Samuel Henlon, Rev. Noel Garrick, Rev. John Chapman, and Rev. Junior Cole regard him with pitiful suspicion. Rev. Patrick Smith offers a knowing nod, perceptible only to Newton. Nine sit in confused bewilderment, while the other, Smith, shares a smile. Finally, East takes a two-week old edition of the evening paper and throws it in front of Newton.

Newton stares blankly at the headline and photographs on the front page tabloid and averts his eyes. He is too familiar with the story by now.

It was the second biggest story to hit the nation since the verdict sixteen days ago. The biggest story was the verdict itself. "Father Newton?" the headline reads, with a photograph of an infant boy and that of Newton.

Peters brings himself to speak. "Brother Newton, is there any truth to that story?"

Newton surveys the paper, allowing his eyes to wander over the words.

"Speculation is rife that the father of Baby Rico is none other than a man of the cloth. Information reaching the *Evening Standard* is that the sperm that impregnated the Rev. Nora Campbell came from a former male colleague, the Rev. Basil Newton. The striking resemblances between both child and pastor have set tongues wagging that the pastor lent his sperm to his female church colleague in one of the most sensational and bizarre stories to have broken in this country in recent times. Rev. Newton, who is married to a schoolteacher with no children in the marriage, declined to comment."

Newton scrutinizes his colleagues without looking them in the eye and dithers the direction of his thoughts. The lump grows larger as he futilely clears his throat.

"Mr. President, I'm now giving notice of my intention to resign as pastor of the Shiloh congregation and as a minister of the Reformed Church."

All ten members of the panel exchange furtive glances as each reaches to catch his breath. Pinto speaks up. "You will at least share with us the reason for this sudden decision?"

Newton regards Pinto and the others with distrust. "My reasons are personal and I'm not at liberty to share them at this time."

Realizing that the initiative has been taken from the committee, Johnson tries to wrest control. "My brother, I'm afraid it's not as simple as that. Your resignation, if and when it does come, does not in itself address the dilemma we're now in as a church. Our church has been wounded beyond anything we've experienced in the past, and we hoped that the healing would've begun soon enough. But this new..." Johnson trails off. He recomposes his voice. "This new development has only served to deepen our pain even more."

"My brother Basil, I notice you've not denied the report, which leads to speculation as to its truthfulness. Frankness on your part would greatly aid us in moving forward," Garrick urges.

"Under the circumstances, I believe my resignation will best help the church move forward and avoid any undue embarrassment or pain."

The room dissolves into dumbness.

East is the first to gain the courage to state the obvious, "Is that an admission the story is indeed true?"

Other members of the committee clear their throat in anticipation of a response.

Newton weighs his mind further. "For personal reasons, I believe it best I do not answer any questions directly related to the issue at hand."

Peters offers a heavy sigh. He surveys the faces of the committee, whose members throw quick glances at each other. "How soon will we have your resignation?"

"In the coming week."

Chapter thirty three

Nora surveys the congregation, inhales deeply, and begins speaking.

"Many societies show general disregard for persons in pain. We're taught to be brave and strong in the face of danger and hardships. We live in an increasingly competitive environment where feelings and emotions are neglected and ignored.

"Due to lack of concern; because the pain and feelings of persons are ignored; because we're taught to be brave and strong; and because we live in an increasingly competitive environment, we're not expected to do that one thing all of us feel like doing at some point in our lives – cry.

"Crying is out of fashion. Crying is out of step with what society expects. The person who cries is seen as weak, pitiful, and helpless.

"No one, of course, should live in constant mourning. No one should feel as if she is carrying the weight of the world on her shoulders. It is not good to live with a gloomy countenance and a heavy heart. Such constant stress and distress is not healthy. That life is hopelessly unhappy and burdensome.

"But there come those times when you feel like crying; those moments when weeping is necessary; those periods when crying is the only thing you can do.

"It is okay to cry. You should cry when you feel like crying, because crying is therapeutic. Crying can heal the soul.

"The Bible has many examples of persons who cry because of the agony in their lives, and the Bible shows that whenever the cry is directed to God, God answers.

"Beginning with the Exodus, we see God responding to the cry of the people who were under bondage in Egypt, while they were under the yoke of pharaoh. The peoples' groans went up to God. 'The Israelites groaned in their slavery and cried out, and their cry for help because of their slavery went up to God. God heard their groaning... and was concerned about them.'

"As a result of their cry, God called Moses. 'I have indeed seen the misery of my people in Egypt. I have heard them crying out because of their slave drivers, and I am concerned about their suffering. So I have come down to rescue them.'

"And even after the Israelites became a complaining, mumbling, grumbling bunch in the desert, whenever they cried out and called to God, God answered. Listen to their complaint: 'The rabble with them began to crave other food, and again the Israelites started wailing and said, If only we had meat to eat! We remember the fish we ate in Egypt at no cost... But now we have lost our appetite, we never see anything but this manna.'

"Moses cried out to God in his own distress. 'Why have you brought this trouble on your servant? What have I done to displease you that you put the burden of all these people on me? Did I conceive all these people? Did I give them birth? Why do you tell me to carry them in my arms as a nurse carries an infant?'

"Moses grew weary with the burden of leadership, and he felt inadequate. What occasioned this particular cry was the peoples' complaint about the desert diet, what they had to eat in the desert. They had grown tired of manna and wanted variety in the menu. Moses was at his wits end. Where, in the middle of nowhere, could he find a varied diet for these many thousands? Yet, we read that, in response to Moses' cry of frustration, God brought quails into the camp, offering the Israelites a healthy protein diet.

"During the period of the judges, again and again the people cried and called out to God, and God delivered them. The refrain was always the same, 'But when they cried out to the Lord, he raised up for them a deliverer.'

"The prophets also cried out to God. It is Isaiah who said, 'Seek the Lord while he may be found, call on him while he is near.'

"Jeremiah cried, 'Alas, my mother, that you gave me birth, a man with whom the whole land strives and contends. I have neither lent nor borrowed, yet everyone curses me.' But then God answered Jeremiah, 'Surely I will deliver you for a good purpose.'

"When the Israelites were threatened with genocide, Mordecai's wailing petition and Esther's three-day fast saved the people from extinction. When Nehemiah heard the state Jerusalem was in, how the walls were broken down and the gates burned, he wrote, 'When I heard these things, I sat down and wept. For some days I mourned and fasted and prayed before the God of heaven.' As a result of his lament, God opened the way for Nehemiah to go to Jerusalem to rebuild the city.

"The Psalms in particular are filled with instances where God answered the cry of the people. In Psalm 22 the poet wailed, 'My God, my God, why have you forsaken me? Why are you so far from saving me, so far from the words of my groaning? Oh my God, I cry out by day, but you do not answer, by night, and am not silent.' Yet, by the time we get to verse 23 we hear joy in the Psalmist's voice, 'You who fear the Lord, praise him! All you descendants of Jacob honor him! Revere him all descendants of Israel! For he has not despised or disdained the suffering of the afflicted one; he has not hidden his face from him, but has listened to his cry for help.'

"Psalm 34 is the same. 'I sought the Lord, and he answered me; he delivered me from all my fears... This poor man called, and the Lord heard him; he saved him out of all his troubles.'

"Right throughout the Old Testament, we see God delivering people after they cried and wept and pleaded their cause to God.

"It is the same in the New Testament. We see in the Gospels that Jesus responded again and again to the cries of those who needed him. A Roman centurion came to Jesus and petitioned Jesus to heal his servant and Jesus responded to his plea for help. When Jesus heard the cry of a widow whose son had died, he had compassion on her and raised her son to life. When, after the mad demoniac, filled with legion, went and knelt at Jesus' feet, Jesus healed him and set him in his right mind. When Jairus pleaded to Jesus for his dying daughter, Jesus turned tears of sorrow into tears of joy. When Jesus saw the desperation and the need of the woman who was crippled for eighteen years, he reached out and healed her. Jesus, while on the way to Jerusalem, met ten lepers who were outcasts of Jewish society, and when they called out to him, 'Jesus, master, have pity on us,' he healed them of their dreaded and dreadful disease.

"When blind Bartemaeus heard Jesus passing by as he went through Jericho, Bartemaeus called out desperately, yet hopefully, 'Jesus, Son of David, have mercy on me.' Even though others tried to silence him, he cried out even louder, 'Son of David, have mercy on me.' After learning that the man desired a return of his sight, Jesus declared, 'Receive your sight; your faith has healed you.'

"When Zacchaeus the chief tax collector wanted to see Jesus but could not because of a hostile crowd, Jesus invited himself to Zacchaeus' house and changed this man's life. When Mary and Martha lost Lazarus, their breadwinner, protector and brother, Jesus, seeing their pain and hearing their cry, brought their brother back to life.

"Jesus always responds to the cry of those who call to him.

"We see from scripture, both Old and New Testament, that whenever a cry is directed to God, God responds. Whether because of slavery or torment or suffering or pain, God heard and answered.

"There may be situations in our own lives that might lead us to cry out to God. We find ourselves in desperate situations. We feel the same agony and pain biblical Israel felt. We experience anguish, heartache, emptiness and fear that persons in scripture felt.

There is good reason to weep and mourn in the presence of God. When we see, hear, read, and experience people killing people, we often have the overwhelming urge to cry to God. When we become aware of corruption in high and low places; when we hear of them, read of them, when we witness them, there is indeed cause to cry out to God.

"When we feel the pressure of high bills and mounting debt; when money problems plague us; when we cannot make ends meet; when we can't buy the food or pay the rent or the mortgage; when we can't meet the monthly deadlines, then it is time to cry out to God.

"When husband and wife are at loggerheads; when brother and sister can't agree; when parents and children are falling out; when family problems persist, it is time to call out to God.

"When pain wracks your body; when you suffer day in and day out; when the doctor cannot help and the price of the medicine is too high; when there seems to be no end to the suffering, then it is alright if you feel like crying out to God.

"When in our distress and in our pain; when in our terror or in our fear; when in our agony and in our torment; when in our need; when we feel we have failed; when we know we've fallen; when we know that times are too hard and things are much too rough; then we may, we can, we ought, we should, cry out to God.

"When life gets to be too much; when too many problems push us and pull at us, then perhaps the only thing we may do, perhaps the only thing we can do is to cry. Cry to God for help. Cry to God for deliverance.

"Yes, it is okay to cry. Cry if you want, cry if you will. Cry out to God, for God will help you; cry out to God, for God will answer you; cry out to God, for God will deliver you.

"If you feel you have done your all and there's nothing else that can be done, then cry. Cry to God who can save you; cry to God who can help you; cry to God who can rescue you; cry to God who can deliver you; cry to God who can restore you; cry to God who can hold you up.

"The politician may not hear us when we cry; the doctor may not be able to help us no matter how much we plead; the lawyer may not fix our problem no matter how much we pay.

"But the one who helped Bartemeus in his blindness; the one who helped the demoniac in his madness; the one who restored Lazarus from death; he can save you, he can help you, he can release you.

"All it may take is for you to cry."

Nora's eyes fill with tears as she stands at the podium, handclaps sounding throughout the sanctuary, the congregation on its feet. A slight bubble of tears purses from her lips as she offers a broad smile, acknowledging the acclamation. She moves from behind the pulpit and walks down the steps into the center aisle as the congregation breaks out singing.

Here my cry oh God attend unto to my prayer
From the ends of the earth will I cry unto thee
When my heart is overwhelmed
Lead me to the Rock that is higher than I
That is higher than I

For thou hast been a shelter for me
And a strong tower from the enemy
When my heart is overwhelmed
Lead me to the Rock that is higher than
That is higher than I

Her cheeks grow damper as her tears mingle with those whom she embraces. At the end of the five-minute walk, she stops and widens her smile.

Little Rico gives a delighted yell upon seeing his mother passing his pew. Nora grabs her son and walks slowly through the door, holding hands with his father, the congregation following close behind.

Deacon Jim Sheppard interrupts. "Excuse me pastor, but this is the report you requested for our meeting on Tuesday."

Nora dries a tear and takes the file from Sheppard. "Right. Thank you."

Fifteen minutes later Basil Newton settles behind the wheel of the car and waits patiently for the traffic to ease before turning north onto Broad Street. The Philadelphia traffic slows in front as the cars negotiate the melting snow.

At the traffic light, three year old Rico asks, as he usually does. "Daddy, when are you going to teach me to drive?" Nora, as she always does, looks at Basil slyly and offers a chuckle.

www.ingramcontent.com/pod-product-compliance
Lightning Source LLC
Chambersburg PA
CBHW032040240626
47154CB00003B/1010